Maxwell's Academy

ALSO BY M.J. TROW

SCHOOLMASTER MYSTERIES

Book 1: Maxwell's House
Book 2: Maxwell's Flame
Book 3: Maxwell's Movie
Book 4: Maxwell's War
Book 5: Maxwell's Ride
Book 6: Maxwell's Curse
Book 7: Maxwell's Reunion
Book 8: Maxwell's Match
Book 9: Maxwell's Inspection
Book 10: Maxwell's Grave
Book 11: Maxwell's Mask
Book 12: Maxwell's Point
Book 13: Maxwell's Chain
Book 14: Maxwell's Revenge
Book 15: Maxwell's Retirement
Book 16: Maxwell's Island
Book 17: Maxwell's Christmas
Book 18: Maxwell's Return
Book 19: Maxwell's Academy

MAXWELL'S ACADEMY

M.J. TROW

A Schoolmaster Murder Mystery Book 19

JOFFE BOOKS

Revised edition 2025
Joffe Books, London
www.joffebooks.com

First published by Thistle Publishing in
Great Britain in 2015

This paperback edition was first published in
Great Britain in 2025

Cover art by Imogen Buchanan

ISBN: 978-1-83526-918-3

A NOTE TO THE READER

Please note these books were published in the 2000s, when social attitudes were different.

Not many ordinary people ever get the opportunity to watch frost creep its way across the land, but stalkers are not ordinary people. They have an almost infinite capacity for stillness and patience and so, by default, they get to see things most people don't — and on this December night, that happened to be the advance of a hard frost. He had started out in a doorway, eyes peeled through the slits in his balaclava for movement beyond the blinds, but the cold had eventually defeated even his deep-seated hatred, love, resentment, jealousy, paranoia; call it what you will, it just wasn't enough to keep him warm.

He had retreated to his car, almost as cold as the outside now and because by the very nature of his task he couldn't run the engine, he was getting colder by the minute. He became transfixed by the advance of the ice crystals marching infinitely slowly across the windscreen, on the outside fuelled by the chill, damp air, on the inside by his own breath as it cooled on contact with the glass. It was soporific and mesmerising, as unpredictable and hypnotic as watching raindrops trickling down a pane and his eyelids began to droop.

His head nodded forward with a jerk and he sat up straight, wriggled his shoulders, adjusted his scarf and reached for the flask of coffee on the passenger seat. The caffeine hit would keep him awake for what was left of the night and the sugar would give him a temporary rush. He took a long swig and focussed through the filigree of frost on the window again. It was dark now and he felt his heart and stomach clench in an agony of envy and loss. Who did she have in there? What were they doing?

Then, he was peering into the dark. Was that a light, coming on downstairs? He looked at the figures on the dash; five o'clock. What was she doing up and about at five o'clock? This wasn't her style at all. Perhaps she was ill. He squared his shoulders again; this might be his chance to play the knight errant, to save her from whatever ailed her. He it would be who would call 999, who would be found administering CPR, who would save her life . . . but no, that didn't seem to be the case. A sliver of light showed around the edge of the front door and a figure, swathed in scarves against the cold, slipped out and started off down the quiet lane at a brisk walk, watching his step on the icy patches.

A gleam came into the watcher's eye and he turned the ignition key. The engine gave a cough, then caught. The man hurrying down the lane looked back over his shoulder and then hurried on. No need for headlights. The glow from the main road was enough to silhouette his prey. Easing through the gears, he drove as smoothly, as silently as he knew how.

The man, *the* man, the one he had always known existed but until now had been invisible, was just yards away now, looking over his shoulder as he broke into a run. His haste was his undoing as he slipped on a puddle and went down hard onto his hands and knees. It could be taken as a sign, almost; no, it *was* a sign. With a smile, the watcher gunned his engine and grunted with an almost orgasmic pleasure as he felt the big car roll over ribs, spine, head. He opened the window and peered out, just in time to see the last convulsive kick of the only unbroken limb the man still possessed. He watched until the cold started to bother him and then he rolled up his window and drove away without a backward glance.

CHAPTER ONE

Friday afternoon. Peter Maxwell happily hummed his own version of the Mamas and Papas song as he strolled along his empty mezzanine corridor to his office. Life was good, generally speaking and not just because Leighford High School had become that most perfect of educational premises; one empty of squalling, squawking, whingeing kids, although that was indeed a bonus. No. It was a Friday and not just any Friday. It was the Friday before half term and his Jacquie, his lovely wife, was due a long weekend. His equally lovely but in a very different way son Nolan was on a playdate with his bestest friend in the whole world, Plocker, and even Metternich the cat had moderated his vole-innard leavings in recent days. Mrs Troubridge of the next-door persuasion had settled down into her usual winter torpor some months before and, lizard-like, only looked out occasionally to test the temperature which was happily not yet to her liking. So, generally, life was good.

Before he pushed open the door of his office, Maxwell paused, holding his breath. Silence. Perfect. He listened closer and he could, in fact, just discern the tiny sounds in the office next door, mouse-like scrabblings made by that quintessentially unmouse-like woman, his trusty assistant,

Helen Maitland. For someone who would never see fourteen stone again, Helen was a very quiet mover and it was only someone with Maxwell's honed faculties who would know she was there at all. But that she was was a constant comfort. Smiling to himself and almost smelling the coffee which was their end of week ritual, he turned the handle and pushed on the door.

* * *

Friday afternoon. Helen Maitland smiled to herself and reached into her bag for the special beans, ground only that morning, which she brought in every Friday. Maxwell loved the blend and it was not for her to tell him that their special piquancy came from having passed through a civet cat before they passed through her grinder. He was a gentleman as well as a scholar, so she didn't fear spitting or anything of that nature, but even so; Friday afternoons were their special time and if it meant not mentioning civet innards, then it was a price she was prepared to pay. As it was half term, there would also be biscuits.

Perfect.

* * *

Maxwell didn't turn on the light, although by now it was very much of the crepuscular persuasion in his office. The posters glowed softly from the walls, where Jean Harlow, the 'w' forever silent, looked anything but reckless in the film of the same name. Below her and slightly to the left (her favourite position, the more risqué of the bios contended) Gary Cooper looked ridiculous in a solar topee, for all he was supposed to be a Bengal Lancer; and Fred Astaire and Ginger Rogers were tripping the light fandango in *Top Hat*. Maxwell smiled; he never tired of telling Helen, and others of the female gender, to remember that whatever Ginger did, poor old Fred had to do it forwards and without high heels.

He rummaged in his briefcase and brought out a box of biscuits, Helen's favourite chocolate gingers, quite literally, if the label were to be believed, the very finest that Messrs Tesco could provide. He wrestled briefly with the packaging but that was all part of the ritual. He even put them on a plate, in a rather pleasing half-moon shape and looked at his handiwork proudly. Eat your heart out, Tracy Emin.

Cocking a practiced ear, he could just hear the kettle coming to the not-quite-boil through the wall. Helen was a stickler for water temperature when it came to their Friday coffee. He sat idly on the back of his row of chairs which faced the window and the pearl of the late February afternoon, holding as it did the promise of spring. In his younger days, he had had a habit much criticised by Sylvia Matthews, school nurse and guardian of his back, of letting himself roll back onto the seats and lie prone, considering life and its ups and downs. He smiled again to himself.

Why not? After all, you're only a mad old buffer once.

* * *

Helen poured a drop of hot water onto the perfectly ground coffee, to moisten it and let it breathe. She didn't care how much she was laughed at for her care over her brew. She was a Geisha manqué, in need of the little rules and regulations that governed her life. She made coffee every day of the week, but none with the care she lavished on this. She pictured Maxwell next door wrestling with the glue on the flap of the box that held her ginger biscuits. She knew he was more of a Hob Nob man himself, but rules were rules. And where would we be without them? Maxwell always answered that question with one word. 'France.' But even that was part of what hedged her world. She didn't like surprises, although having worked with Maxwell for so long, she should certainly be inured to them by now.

* * *

Closing his eyes and with a little chuckle, Maxwell let go of the back of the chairs and let himself roll back.

* * *

As she heard the scream, Helen Maitland let the coffee pot crash into the sink. She had never heard anything so blood-curdling in all her life, and that was saying something. She had worked at Leighford for long enough to have heard it all. Her heart in her mouth, she dashed next door, afraid of what she might find. Maxwell was at such a funny age.

It was hard at first to make out what was happening. There was no light, except for the orange sodium glow that was joining the dusk through the window. Against the wide, uncurtained pane the silhouettes of two men showed, black against the sky. One had wild hair, the other was hunched, at bay.

'For all that's holy, Headmaster,' the wild-haired one was saying in trembling tones. 'I could have crushed you. What on earth were you doing lying down in my office?'

It was clearly English and yet Helen Maitland was having difficulty grasping the meaning.

'You've dislocated my elbow, Max, I swear.' The mild and flat tones of Legs Diamond seemed out of place here. He didn't come to you. You went to him. It was the way of the world, if the world was Leighford High.

'Rubbish!' The Head of Sixth Form was brooking no hypochondria. He needed to know what the hell was going on. 'I ask again, what were you doing?'

The Head didn't answer, but carried on rubbing his elbow, in what Maxwell considered to be a rather threatening and theatrical manner.

Maxwell saw Helen for the first time and decided that explanations were in order. 'I jumped on the Headmaster, Helen,' he said, with an airy wave of his hand. 'I think you should perhaps bring another cup.' If truth were told, Peter Maxwell had been getting the jump on Legs Diamond for years, but this was somehow different.

James Diamond turned hollow eyes on the Assistant Head of Sixth Form. 'Coffee?' he asked quietly.

'Kopi luwak,' Helen said; she didn't know why.

The head teacher was surprised. He somehow didn't have Maxwell down for someone who would like something crapped out by a cat; Metternich could have borne that out, had he been asked. 'Lovely,' he said. 'I need something, that's for sure.'

Maxwell relented. 'You seem somewhat distrait, Headmaster,' he said and ushered him back to the chairs they had so inelegantly vacated moments before.

With only a small flinch, the man sat down. 'I am,' he said. 'I have just had a meeting with the Chairman of the Governors.'

Calling the weaselly little git to mind, Maxwell could see that it probably had not been marvellous, but Diamond had never resorted to lying in the dark in his office following such meetings before. There seemed no coherent answer to give, so he just cocked his head and gave Diamond an encouraging smile, rather wasted in the by now almost completely dark room.

'You don't understand, Max,' the head said. 'It was the news I had been dreading.'

'Don't tell me we are being Ofsteded again!' Helen was aghast.

'Worse.'

Maxwell and his assistant thought for a moment. What could be worse?

'We're going to be an Academy!' The head shut his mouth with a snap and let his head fall forward on his chest.

Maxwell and Maitland exchanged glances.

Oh.

That.

CHAPTER TWO

'So, remind me again why that would be a bad thing.' DI Jacquie Carpenter-Maxwell spoke from behind the fridge door as she rummaged for something to nibble.

'Sorry?' Her husband raised an eyebrow.

'Academy status. Why is it such a bad thing?' She emerged brandishing a cold sausage. 'I though there were all kinds of financial inducements involved.'

'I think that's what a lot of people think,' Maxwell said, taking the sausage out of her hand and biting it in half. 'But that isn't actually the case. They still get funding from the government, just not filtered through the local authority. The pots of money legend is just a misunderstanding about the sponsorship thing — that won't be happening to Leighford anyway, because the school has chosen to become an Academy rather than have it forced upon them, so it won't need a sponsor. So at least we won't be known as . . . oh, I don't know . . . the Furniture Village Academy of Leighford or the Marks and Spencer Academy.'

Jacquie snatched back her half-sausage and ate it in two quick bites. 'So, what's the problem?' she asked, somewhat indistinctly.

'There may not be one,' he conceded, 'although on the current showing I can't see it ending well. For a start, everything was done rather under the table, with a few governors whispering in corners and then coming out with pretty much a fait accompli, excuse my French.'

Jacquie nodded her acceptance of his lapse into the dreaded language and shrugged a shoulder. 'It might all work out, then.'

'Legs is in a bit of a state,' Maxwell remarked.

'You did jump on him,' Jacquie pointed out, quite reasonably.

Maxwell flapped a dismissive hand. 'I mean, he was in a state well before I jumped on him, though I grant you that probably didn't help. The trouble is, the man is an idiot. He's always been the same, he bottles things up until they are much worse than they need be. The Chair of Governors had been to see him weeks before. He could have put it to the staff then and that would have given him some ammunition.'

'They'll be against it, you think?'

'It's always hard to tell which way the combined staff cat will jump; beg pardon, Count.' The enormous black and white beast was curled up on a chair which was pushed under the table, but somehow his presence still filled the room, along with his rumbling snore. 'Legs has the half term to stew over it, which means that when we go in afterwards, he will be all up in the air, all squawk and ruffled feathers so by the end of the meeting nobody will be happy.'

Jacquie sat down at the table, carefully avoiding using the cat's chair. She still had the scars to show for the last time she had made that mistake and usually Metternich avoided causing damage to the woman who bought his favourite food. 'The trouble with you, Max,' she said, fondly, levering a piece of left over sausage out of a back tooth with her tongue, 'is that you know that place far too well. It makes you meet trouble halfway.'

'Cowards die many times before their deaths. The valiant never taste of death but once. Weasel words, madam — look what happened to poor old Julius, after all.' He lapsed into an impeccable Kenneth Williams, 'Infamy, infamy, they've all got it in for me.'

'I still think it will all be fine. Different name, same school building, same pupils, same staff . . .'

'But not the same head, probably.' Maxwell looked solemn. 'I've almost finished training Legs — it seems a shame to close the experiment before it's complete.'

'I had no idea.' Jacquie was surprised — the senior management team at Leighford had had its ups and downs, its arrests, suspensions, its deaths even, but she had never considered a world without Legs.

'Well, it's not certain, of course. Some Academies do go forward with the same head. That one, Thing, you know . . .'

Jacquie shook her head. Thing could mean so much.

'*Thing*! That school in . . .' Maxwell gave up. 'There, anyway, they kept the head for one term and then turfed him out. Replaced him with some so-called Super-Head who didn't really manage to do anything except alienate the staff, piss off the parents and generally lay waste. I don't think poor old Legs stands a cat in hell's chance.'

Jacquie laughed. 'Again, the cat metaphor. You really are dicing with death today.'

'That's true,' Maxwell agreed, pushing back his chair. 'Come on, let's go and watch some totally rubbish television, light the fire, pour out something alcoholic and forget about Leighford High School until week Monday.'

Jacquie stood up and came round the table to give him a hug. 'Really? Is that actually possible?'

He chuckled and kissed the top of her head. 'No,' he said, 'but we can put it in the box, like good old Schrodinger and see how it likes them apples.'

'If it's anything like the Count,' Jacquie said, 'it would prefer fish fillets in gravy, hold the mayo.'

Under his table, curled on his throne, the cat agreed with a throaty rumble and settled back into his dreams of vole au vent as far as the eye could see.

* * *

The television was, as predicted, rubbish. For some reason that Maxwell had never managed to fathom, early evening viewing — and, had he but known it, morning and afternoon as well — consisted of semi-famous people doing things for which they had no talent. Why anyone would want to watch a dancer making a cake, or a chef dancing for that matter, was just something that made the Head of Sixth Form's head whirl. And yet, here they sprawled, watching anyway. Maxwell gestured with a languid hand.

'Tell me who he is, again?'

Jacquie looked up. She had given up and was reading the paper. 'Who?'

'Him. The one with the shaved head.'

She peered, watching the glacier-slow action on the screen. 'There are three with shaved heads,' she pointed out, reasonably enough.

Maxwell looked dubious. 'Really? I thought it was all the same person. They certainly seem very alike. Are you sure?'

Jacquie folded the paper and pointed. 'Yes, look, he . . .' and she waited until her quarry's face filled the screen. 'He's that footballer, you know the one, he was married to that singer. That singer you like.'

'I don't like any singers, do I?'

She smiled at him. 'No, not really. Not since Gene Pitney.'

Maxwell nodded. 'Lovely girl,' he muttered, reminiscently.

Jacquie ignored him. 'But you don't *mind* her. And the other one, the one with the tattoos, he is . . . do you know, I don't know quite who he is, but he's on the telly a lot. And the other is the presenter.'

Maxwell blinked slowly once or twice, like something that had just unaccountably found itself on a primeval beach instead of in the soup of the same name. Without another word, he extended his remote arm and clicked, decisively.

Jacquie smiled again and, shaking out the paper, continued to read.

'It's odd that no one has been in touch,' Maxwell said, a tad plaintively.

'About what?' Jacquie didn't put the paper down this time. She couldn't claim to be fascinated by the article she was reading, but she could see that this evening was going to be a long one and she was holding out as long as she could. There was a silence, which dragged on for what seemed like hours. She slowly lowered the paper to find, as expected, her husband's face only inches from hers.

'You know what,' he said, in sepulchral tones.

She poked him on the end of the nose and he stood up. 'I can see you won't be happy until we have picked this thing to bits,' she said. 'I'm just amazed you have taken this long to come out with it.' She looked around him to the clock on the mantelpiece. 'Never mind, not long to go now.'

'Until what?' he asked, perplexed.

'Until Sylv gets here with the chips, Helen with the wine.'

Maxwell looked at her, amazed, proud and in love in equal measure. 'You are amazing,' he said. Then his brow creased. People had homes to go to, after all. Husbands. Stuff like that. 'What about . . . ?'

'Don't you worry about them,' she said, slipping her feet into her shoes. 'We're all going out for a drink while you three put the world to rights.' She stood up just as the bell pealed below. She kissed him on the forehead. 'I'll let them in on my way out. If work rings, tell them to try me on my mobile. If mother rings . . .' she flapped a hand, '. . . tell her I'm at work, or dead or something.'

'Any preference?' Maxwell stuffed the paper behind a cushion, his one concession towards tidying up.

'Um . . .' Jacquie puffed out her cheeks. 'Let's go for dead.'

The bell pealed again.

'Must go. Your chips will be getting cold.'

'Or the wine warm. Off you go. Don't drink out of any damp glasses.'

The clatter of her feet on the stairs was soon replaced by the chatter of voices, saying hello, saying goodbye. The waft of fish and chips came up the stairwell and Maxwell went into the kitchen to sort out some plates. Suddenly, the room was full of women, or so it seemed. Helen could fill a room very well on her own; it wasn't a size thing, Maxwell decided, it was just something about how she wore her personality. Sylvia Matthews, the school nurse, was altogether more all together, but she and he went back so far that he could almost read her mind. And her mind was full of worry, which wasn't nice to see.

'I'll get the glasses,' Maxwell said, edging out of the room as the portions were divided up and the women tried to work out how they had ended up with a pickled egg no one wanted.

Eventually, everyone was settled around the table, cod and chips in front of them, mushy peas in a bowl in the centre and the pickled egg eying them malignly from the worktop behind Maxwell.

'This was a good idea,' Helen said, cracking her batter with a decisive stab of her fork.

Sylvia sighed. 'I think the whole thing is going to be an unmitigated disaster,' she said. 'In other schools I have heard about, the ancillary staff are the first to go.'

Maxwell and Helen dropped their forks with a clatter. 'But . . . but, you're not *ancillary*!' Helen spoke for them both. 'The whole school depends on you.'

Sylvia smiled, but sadly. 'That's very sweet of you, Helen, but there is a problem. What I do is covered already by agencies which won't need to be paid for by whoever runs the Academy. A&E for accidents. Counselling services through the various arms of the local NHS or council for talking things through. Science staff for those little talks about the birds and the bees; although that won't matter soon. They're already giving out condoms to Year 8 in some places and goodness only knows what the Nursery class will need to know about bodily functions before they are allowed to graduate to Reception. Believe me, I know I've come close to feeling the axe on my neck before. But this time, I'll feel more than the draught as it misses me by a whisker, begging your pardon, Count. No, I'm for the chop, no mistake.' And she filled her fork with fish and shovelled it into her mouth.

Maxwell was aghast on so many levels. Firstly, he had had no idea that Sylv had ever faced redundancy and was saddened that she hadn't told him. But mainly, he was forced to face the seriousness of the situation; Sylvia was never poetic. She was sensible. She was reliable. Goddammit, she was *Sylv*. So all this talk of draughts and axes was hiding something. What? He turned a piece of fish over and picked off the soggy batter. His appetite had suddenly gone west. 'Sylv?'

'Mmhmm?' Sylvia was struggling with a recalcitrant bone.

'This is all just theoretical, isn't it? All this talk of redundancy?' Maxwell could feel a cold front creeping up his back and suddenly he didn't fancy fish and chips. Helen was sitting frozen, a forkful of peas halfway to her mouth.

Sylvia smiled brightly at them, then looked away. 'Theoretical? I'm not sure what you mean.' And she took another mouthful of fish. 'Nice, this, isn't it?' she asked, gesturing at her plate.

'Lovely,' Maxwell agreed, in a flat voice. 'I'm sure someone with a scientific bent such as yourself, Nursie, knows what theoretical means. But I will rephrase it if I have to.'

The table was silent. Maxwell had ended a sentence with a preposition. The two women waited for the crack of thunder, the whiff of sulphur but the heavens didn't open; Hell's gate did not yawn this time.

Maxwell looked at Sylvia, not blinking.

'So?'

She shrugged. 'So, no, perhaps not theoretical.'

Helen Maitland was a stalwart woman in any crisis, but she looked up startled, her eyes already filling with tears. Like all people who took the world on her shoulders, she needed someone to dump the load onto sometimes and when she needed to, Sylvia was where she went to do it. Leighford High without Sylvia would be . . . well, it would be Leighford Academy.

The school nurse leaned over and patted her hand. 'Helen,' she said, 'I don't mind. Guy got that promotion, don't forget. We can move nearer his work, cut his commute. The house is worth . . . well, it's not on the market yet but the next door one just sold for stupid money. We won't exactly starve. Don't worry about me.'

It took Maxwell to get to the point. 'It's not you we are worrying about, Sylv,' he said, and though the words were harsh, the voice was gentle. 'It's us. How is Leighford High School going to manage without you?'

'It will have to manage,' she said. 'It's a done deal. I won't be back after the half term.'

'That seems a bit silly,' Helen said. 'Leaving with just five weeks to go to the end of the year.' Her voice was shaky, but she had resolved, in true Maitland style, to make the best of it.

'No,' Sylvia shook her head and managed to smile, just a little, though one corner was a little wobbly. 'Not next term. This.'

The meal was now officially forgotten. It was like dust in their mouths and with a splendid show of synchronised table manners, they all pushed their plates away and got up from the table. They headed for the sitting room and, the next obvious step, Maxwell headed for the cupboard where the drink was kept. Sylvia and Helen waited until he had handed them their glasses and then all three sipped in silence. The unthinkable had happened. Like the ravens leaving the Tower, surely Leighford High would crumble without Sylvia holding it together.

It was Helen who cracked first. 'But what are they *thinking*?' she spluttered, gesturing with her glass, Southern Comfort sloshing perilously near its edge. 'Why you, Sylv? Why not one of those idiots from IT?' Maxwell raised his glass in salute. 'They've got more caretakers than you can shake a stick at. And science technicians — there's hardly room for them in that back room of theirs.'

Sylvia looked at her glass, cradled in her hands, resting in her lap. 'Not any more,' she muttered.

'What?' Helen's ire had begun to lose its momentum but this brought her up short.

'It's not just me. The IT department is cut by one, the science techs have all had their marching orders — like me, they have all been sworn to secrecy, but it will all be out in the open soon. Apparently, the argument is if you can teach it, you can prep it. The caretakers are down to two, with one as back-up on some kind of retainer.'

'Well,' Maxwell tried to look on the bright side, 'at least we won't have to run the gauntlet of that megalomaniac lollipop woman in the morning. I nearly had her the other day . . .' he paused, feeling some explanation was in order . . . 'although not, clearly in anything approaching the biblical sense. She stepped out to see some oik over the road so he could get to the Jobcentre. She sees anything over the road, child, man, woman or hedgehog. She's a menace. So there is a tiny silver lining in this cloud.'

'You would like to think so,' Sylvia said, looking up at last.

'What!' Maxwell roared. 'They've got rid of you and kept that . . . that . . .'

'Essential tool for health and safety?' Sylvia filled in the blanks, although not with any words that Maxwell would ever utter. 'Indeed. But,' and she spread her hands, seeing the other's point of view in true Sylvia Matthews style, 'I suppose she is cheaper than me. Ten hours a week instead of what sometimes feels like millions. And then there's the visibility. If you don't need me, you might not even know I work there. You see Mavis every day, Hi-Vis and all.'

Maxwell clicked his fingers. Mavis — that was it. Although it wasn't what you heard motorists call her as she stepped out as if she were immortal, with only her lollipop for protection.

Helen had been thinking. 'But, surely, Sylv . . . people can't just be got rid of like that. Unions — surely the unions will have something to say?'

'They have chosen well,' Sylvia said, 'and they are following the law on redundancy which I admit I knew nothing about until a week or so ago. It is the post which is made redundant, not the person. So as long as they don't replace any of us, they haven't done anything wrong.'

'There's a nice package, though?' Maxwell hoped it was a statement but made it a question.

'That would be lovely, yes,' Sylvia said. 'But, in a nutshell . . . no. I'm not too badly off because of how these things work; I'll get the maximum allowed, twenty weeks. Some of the kids from IT and the labs will not do so well — some of them will come away with less than a month's money, although if they take pay in lieu of notice, they won't do quite so badly. But then they won't be able to sign on . . .' Finally, the tears that had been threatening began to fall and Maxwell and Helen were simultaneously on their knees in front of her, patting, kissing and stroking according to their fashion.

Helen was the first to really lose her temper. 'This is all wrong, Max!' she shouted. 'If you hadn't jumped on Legs . . .'

'Pardon?' Sylvia smiled at them through her tears.

Maxwell waved it away as a bagatelle. 'As one does,' he said. 'Long story short, it's how we found out about all this. I can't believe everyone has kept so schtum.'

'Part of the deal,' Sylvia said. 'An extra week's pay as a gag. It means a lot to some of them. They've got families, bills to pay. At least Guy and I are better off than them. But I kept quiet for their sakes.'

With a final pat, Maxwell sat back in his seat. Helen was not quite so limber, despite being the younger of the two, but soon everyone was nursing their drink again and plotting their revenge.

Sylvia held up a hand. 'Children, children,' she said, although Maxwell could give her a good five years and rising. 'Please don't make a fuss. It may not happen. I mean, it may not go any further. This was just the SLT showing their muscle. They needed to sort the budget out and they did it in their usual ham-fisted style.'

'Really?' Maxwell asked. 'Really, do you think it was them? Legs? Bernard? They're not perfect, but they're not like this. I thought they had, if not integrity, at least a touch of loyalty. Legs seems a broken man. And,' he added before either of the women could, 'not just because I jumped on him.'

Sylvia considered and then nodded. 'It wasn't one of them who saw me, as it happens,' she said. 'It was that Chair of Governors, a piece of work if ever there was one. He was polite, but definite. I could go with a package, money in lieu, keep quiet or I could stay until the Academy was formed and end up doing the shredding for everyone else, mopping the toilets in a restructured role until my self-respect gave out. Not a choice as such, as you can see.'

Helen was still simmering, the steam all but visible around her ears and Maxwell patted her knee. 'There's nothing to be done now, Helen,' he said, soothingly. 'We'll have to wait until we get back before we can get at all the facts. Legs said he would be telling the staff next week and so that's all we can do. Wait.'

'But . . .'

Maxwell smiled and raised an eyebrow.

'Well, all right, but . . . where will it all end?'

Sylvia spoke for them all. 'In tears.'

CHAPTER THREE

The Maxwell family sat at breakfast on the first day of the second half of the Spring term and scarcely a word was spoken. Nolan had the look of a boy who would have to recite some times tables before the day was out and even he would admit that it wasn't his strongest suit. Snatches of *Lepanto* or *Charge of the Light Brigade* and he was definitely your man. Nine sevens . . . not so much. Mrs Whatmough was a bit of s stickler for old-fashioned values and no child left her hallowed portals without a grounding in mental arithmetic and eye before e except after sea — as far as she was concerned, if a teaching method wasn't broken, don't try to mend it. She was vaguely aware that the common phrase was rather more colloquial, but she had no truck with ain't.

Jacquie watched her son fondly. He got more like his father every day, which was delightful, of course. But sometimes she worried about him, about that little crease that was appearing between his brows. He was a baby, still, and shouldn't have the cares of the world on his shoulders, as he seemed to have this morning. It was probably the class gerbil that was bothering him. All over Christmas, he had worried that it would be lonely. This had turned out to be a baseless worry — Gerry had turned out to be Gemma and had a litter of babies to keep her company as the new year had turned. Bless him. She stroked his hair. She could read him like a book.

Metternich, licking his bum in a desultory fashion on his chair under the table looked as though he hadn't a care in the world. But there had recently been a rather attractive 3-for-2 offer on luxury cat food and Mrs B, the woman who does, had bought some for him in a mad excess of friendliness. The two existed in a state of armed neutrality — he didn't wee on the stairs, she warned him before she switched the hoover on — and he had shown his appreciation by shedding only the black hairs on dark surfaces for as long as he could. But now he was back on the cheap stuff and he was working out how, short of physical violence, to show his people that he didn't approve.

Maxwell's thoughts were more complex, batting as they did around in his head, randomly striking sparks off each other. They ranged from thinking how lovely his wife was looking, suited and booted for another day of Detective Inspectordom; how quickly Nolan was growing and what were the odds that he might turn into something awful like a rugger hearty or — worse — a scientist; how the cat was off his food and could he be finally showing his age? But, over and above all of these, like a thunderhead on a summer day, was Leighford High School and what the morning meeting would have in store. He recalled Sylvia's words of just over a week ago and feared there would be at least tears. And sweat. But hopefully, no blood.

* * *

Jacquie dropped Nolan off at school, smoothing his hair back from his brow and planting a kiss on the end of his nose. She was grateful that he had either not reached or — better — had avoided the male child antipathy for any public signs of parental affection and this moment was still one of the best in the day. 'Anything bothering you, darling?' She couldn't help it. She was a mother and also a policeperson — asking questions came with both territories.

Nolan was on the horns of a dilemma. He knew how she worried about him and did his best to shield her from his little ups and downs. And anyway, she had never struck him as a woman with times tables at her fingertips. So he smiled at her and shook his head. 'Nothing, Mums, thanks. Better go — mustn't be late.' And he shouldered his satchel, which seemed far too big for his little body and clambered out of the car. He skipped off towards the gate, muttering 'Nine sixes are fifty-something, nine sevens are sixty-three . . .' He felt better. If he could remember some of the dratted thing, perhaps the rest would just come to him. Who knew?

Jacquie watched him go and then turned the key in the ignition. Time to stop being a mother and start being a policeperson. It was mercifully quiet at the Nick at the moment but on the downside that did mean there was more paperwork than she had ever dreamed possible. Six months into her new role and she was beginning to understand why Henry Hall sometimes had a faraway look in his bland eyes. He was dreaming of a world without paper, the one they'd all been promised thirty years ago, when PC still meant a copper, not a personal computer and still less political correctness. Negotiating the one way system that was Leighford with hardly a hiccup, she was soon pulling into her designated parking space, something which still made her smile. Detective Inspector Carpenter-Maxwell. Like Wile E. Coyote, she liked the way that rolled out. No traffic jam. No one in her space. Today was going to be a *good* day.

* * *

'Nolan Maxwell.'

He put up his hand and pinned on his best smile. 'Yes, Miss.'

'Let's have the nine times, shall we?'

‘Once nine is nine.’ Going well. ‘Twice nine is eighteen. Three nines are twenty-seven . . .’ He smiled at the teacher, relief written all over his face. Today was going to be a *good* day.

* * *

Metternich lay in the warm patch in front of the radiator on the first landing at 38 Columbine. It had all the advantages, as far as he could see. Not only did it keep the cold out in these last days of winter, but it also gave him a bird’s eye view of anyone coming up the stairs. Escape to the country? What would be the point? His grasp of days of the week was tenuous at best, but some memory lingering at the back of his cat-sized brain told him that when he had been surrounded by people for a couple of days and then they were gone, what usually happened next was that strange old woman who smelled of all kinds of foreign odours he couldn’t quite place would come and start pushing a big noisy thing around the house. But sometimes — and he could count the occasions on the claws of one paw — she brought lovely treats. And he wanted to be in a position to avail himself, should today be one of those days. Ah, there was that scritching sound outside. That usually meant that . . . yes; it was her. But did she have anything with her, that was the question.

Mrs B clambered up the stairs, hauling herself along using the banister. It seemed to her the climb was getting steeper every week, but nothing would stop her coming to do for Mr and Mrs M; death itself would be the only barrier. She paused halfway up to catch her breath and give vent to a smoker’s cough that shook the house from rafters to foundations. Next door, Mrs Troubridge twittered in distress and started cleaning up. Mrs B did her after the Maxwells and it would never do for the cleaner to find anything dirty or untidy; whatever would she think?

Metternich, stretched out in his warm place, cursed the woman up in a heap and down again. Did she think he was made of stone? A cat had to keep body and soul together and all fifteen pounds of him tensed with the pressure. Did she? Didn't she? The suspense was killing him. To show how excited he was, he flexed one paw.

The woman looked up and narrowed her eyes. She loved the cat as she loved the humans in this house, but it would be a cold day in Hell before she let any of them know it. 'I know what you're after, you great thing,' she said. 'You think I've bought you summat nice.'

The cat cocked an eyebrow. It didn't do to show too much enthusiasm.

'Well, as it happens, I have,' she said. 'But like as not it'll be the last. That wet nit Diamond will be tellin' 'em about now about what's going on at Leighford. And it won't be pretty. People getting sacked off left and right. The nurse. Them snooty lot in the labs. Them computer kids.' She reached into her bag and extracted a box of something gorgeous, should you be of the feline persuasion. 'And me.' She bent to stroke the behemoth along his rippling back. 'Time I went, you might say, but nobody knows your . . .' she was momentarily stuck for words. Maxwell could hardly be described as Metternich's master, after all. 'Mr M like what I do. But who knows? He might be next for the chop. C'mon, Count. Waddya want?' She turned the box to the light and squinted at it. 'I got duck 'n' beef; lamb 'n' chicken; liver and rabbit . . . I dunno, cat. There's people don't eat as well as this.' And, grumbling to herself, she went into the kitchen and broke open the box.

Metternich, in his quiet way, was a bit of a student of human nature and he had detected that the woman wasn't happy. But, then again, there was liver and rabbit. So, despite it all, it was a *good* day.

* * *

Mavis the lollipop lady was by nature a curmudgeonly soul but was universally described as a 'lovely woman'. She ascribed this misapprehension to the fact that she led children and indeed anyone else who presented themselves at the kerb across the road rather than hurling them into the traffic, which was in fact what she would have very much preferred. She hated Mondays. She hated all days except the holidays, when she didn't have to stand at the side of the road, unable to have a fag, wearing a stupid hi-vis coat that didn't keep her warm in winter and sweated pounds a day off her in summer. She hated the hat. She hated the lollipop. But most of all, she hated Peter Maxwell, who, even as the thought entered her head was bearing down at her out of the early morning sun, like the Red Baron in his Fokker. She didn't have much grasp of history as a rule, but she had seen the film only the night before. Look at him, she thought to herself. Smug git. He could easily afford a car and at his age should certainly not be riding that ramshackle old bike. It was a good thing you could hear it coming, what with the skirling brakes and rattling chain, because he never seemed to make much effort to miss her, whether she was in the middle of the road or on the pavement. Yes, yes, look at him; straight at her, as though she wasn't the most high visibility thing for miles. She stepped out, although there wasn't a child to be seen. Yes, that had given him something to think about, mad old sod. Never mind. An evil smile crept across Mavis's wind-tanned features. With all this academy nonsense, he was probably for the high jump anyway. He must be a hundred years old.

'Morning, Mavis,' the Head of Sixth Form yelled as he missed her by the customary whisker.

'Morning, Mr Maxwell,' she shouted back as he took the turn into the school drive, leaning over to make the angle and not crash into the gate. One of these days it wouldn't work and he would either hurtle over the handlebars or turn himself into chips through the bars of the gate.

Now that really would be a *very* good day.

* * *

Maxwell chained White Surrey to the bike rack and bent down to undo his cycle clips, not something he always remembered to do until later in the day, but he had a sneaky feeling that today was going to be difficult enough, without loss of blood flow to his feet. Why he chained the bike up he would never know. The chances of it being stolen were slim and anyway, anyone who tried to ride it away would soon find that it was almost impossible to steer without several decades of practice. Even he had only just managed to miss Mavis this morning, although why the woman always chose to stand in his path was a mystery he thought he would probably never solve. He shrugged his shapeless tweed jacket straight, shoved his shapeless tweed hat more firmly on his barbed wire hair, slung his Jesus scarf more nonchalantly around his neck and marched resolutely into the school building, ready for the fray.

He hadn't got far before he heard it.

'Psst.'

He looked round for the source of the noise, but there didn't seem to be anyone there, so he took another step.

'Psst. Mr Maxwell.'

It was midway between a whisper and a cough and it was coming from his left. He went over to the Reception desk and leaned over. 'Thingee?'

'Mr Maxwell,' the girl said, looking furtively left and right. 'I've been looking for you. The ladies of the office would like a word.'

'Why? What have I done?' Maxwell was used to people wanting a word. It was usually due to some minor infringement such as they couldn't read his writing on UCAS references, crumbs in the keyboard of his hated laptop, things of that nature. But they didn't usually 'psst' at him. In fact, it was usually a case of a face off across a desk, with tight smiles and tighter voices.

'Nothing, Mr Maxwell,' Thingee One said. 'It's . . . well, we've heard. About, you know . . .'

He pinned on a friendly if bemused smile. 'Sorry, Thingee old thing. You're going to have to spell it out. Monday morning, first day back, not at my best.'

It fooled no one, but Thingee gave it a shot. She leaned forward and mouthed, 'The Academy.' The effect was something like reverse ventriloquism, but Maxwell got the gist.

'Sorry, Thingee. I don't know much more than you do. There is bound to be something in the meeting this morning, but other than that, I don't see how I can help.'

The girl raised her voice a little. 'There's a rumour they are sacking all the staff and starting again,' she said, her eyes wide.

'I don't think it will come to that,' Maxwell said. 'There may be a paper exercise, applying again for your job, leaving and being reinstated on the same day, that kind of thing.' Despite his promises, Maxwell had done a little reading around the subject over half term and it seemed that gaining academy status was something of a curate's egg as far as staff were concerned. As long as you got a good bit, you were happy. If you got a bad bit, you were left with a nasty sulphurous taste in your mouth and a whole lot of time for doing the garden. The girl looked stricken and he hurriedly added a rider. 'There isn't likely to be so much as a ripple, Thingee, really. I shouldn't worry about it — look, I'll pop in after the meeting, would that be helpful?'

She nodded, her eyes still wide with worry. 'Thank you, Mr Maxwell,' she said out loud and made him jump.

'That's no trouble at all, Thingee,' he said, feeling the hot breath of Bernard Ryan on his neck. 'Just try not to drop them again where people might trip over them.' Still smiling, he turned. 'Mr Ryan!' It was seamless. 'How are you this bright, almost-spring morning?'

'Well, thank you, Mr Maxwell,' the deputy head said and he did indeed look well these days. With his private life finally in less turmoil, Bernard Ryan had become almost human. But only almost. He turned his attention to Thingee. 'Sarah,' he said, 'have you put all of those notes into pigeonholes as I requested in my email?'

'Yes, Mr Ryan,' she said, all efficiency. It didn't do to slack, not at times like these.

'Colour-coded?'

Oh, oh! 'Um . . . we didn't have any orange paper, Mr Ryan . . .'

He smiled at her and she nearly fainted with shock. 'Never mind,' he said. 'I expect you used the next best thing. Thank you,' and he leaned over a little, patted the reception desk smartly in a rapid tattoo and swung away, into the maelstrom that was developing as the lifeblood of Leighford High, as represented by the student body of the Breakfast Club, began to pour in through the doors. She wasn't to know that, for the first time in his life, Bernard Ryan was truly happy. He had been seen off at his front door that morning by his lover, they had exchanged a loving kiss and who cared who was watching and the feel of him would stay with the deputy headteacher all day, the smell of his cologne, the touch of his hand. Yes, bring on Academy status — Bernard Ryan for one just didn't care.

The staff room was strangely quiet that morning, with a doom-laden air. Maxwell, the historian, was reminded of the Cuban Missile crisis, when the world held its breath. The usual cliques and cabals had formed of course, from the Back Row Element to the Young Mums Corner but, for once, there was not a guffaw, not the click of a knitting needle to be heard. Maxwell was front and centre as always, his legs stuck out in front of him and his arms crossed across his chest. He was Richard, he was Raymond, he was Godfrey at the gate. At the very least, he was Horatius on his bridge; attack or defence, Maxwell had the historical character at his fingertips. It was normally at this point that Sylvia Matthews pointed out he still had his cycle clips on; he could feel her absence like a cold spot in the middle of his back, where she usually sat with the PE staff. He looked behind him. There was no space. They had healed the gap already and his heart gave a sad little lurch. How soon they forget.

He turned back to look at the front with his normal steely gaze, which had been known to reduce James Diamond to gibbering incoherence and he suppressed a small scream. While he had been turned around, Diamond; Ryan; Jane Taylor, the deputy's deputy and a strange woman had entered and were standing, like the four horsemen of the Apocalypse, having left their steeds outside. If Bernard Ryan was Pestilence, Diamond had to be Famine. Jane Taylor, a perfectly pleasant woman but Maxwell believed in taking every metaphor and shaking till its pips squeaked, therefore had to be Death, if only because she was a bit pasty and had a tendency to wear a bit too much eye makeup. But the fourth person who stood there, she just had to be War. She had a combative air even when standing stock still and her smile had swords in it. 'Come,' Maxwell muttered to himself, 'we will meet at Har Megiddo.'

Diamond fixed him with a glare. Maxwell knew there was no chance that he could have read his lips, his mind or the Revelation of St John the Divine, but even so he settled down, chin on chest, to await events. Diamond was quite bucked up — it wasn't like Max to behave himself on such a slight reprimand. However, he already suspected it was too little, too late.

Diamond didn't need to wait as he usually did for the room to quieten. You could hear a pin drop and the small sounds of the largely empty school came tinnily through the door. The clatter of crockery and cutlery from the dining room as the Breakfast Club got outside their Weetabix, the clack of a heel as the office staff ran errands before the madness began. Diamond cleared his throat.

'Ladies,' he said. 'Gentlemen, I would like to introduce Fiona Braymarr to you all. Er . . .' Surely, he couldn't be stuck for words this early in the announcement? And yet, how could he introduce her. Super Head sounded rather too Marvel Comic. 'My replacement' may yet be premature. He cleared his throat again. 'Ms Braymarr comes to us from . . .'

She stepped forward, almost imperceptibly, but it was enough. She had taken over. 'If I may interrupt you there, Mr Diamond,' she said, 'I would like to be clear from the outset, so I think it would be best if I take over from here. Firstly, I am not Mizz. I am *Mrs* Braymarr and so I would like to be called *Mrs* Braymarr at all times. My name as *Mr* Diamond has revealed, is Fiona, but I don't believe in forenames in the workplace. I don't expect to be called by it. It is unlikely that I will be calling you by yours. Where I come to you from is immaterial. I do not judge anywhere by where I was before. I do not expect to be judged by my previous appointment. I come here as over-arching head of Leighford High School and a number of other schools in the catchment which have been given Academy status or have it pending. However, I shall be based here as the most central and the largest of the schools under my care.' She leaned forward and some of the more fanciful staff thought for a moment they saw her eyes glow red. 'There have been changes, as I am sure you are all aware. There will be more. Starting with the Monday meeting. Meetings will from now on be on a daily basis and will take place at four o'clock.'

'But . . .' it was faint, but she was on it like a ninja.

'But?' Her lips straightened so it may have been a smile. 'May I ask who said that?'

The staff at Leighford had been together, by and large, a long time. This woman had just walked in and, for the purposes of the meeting, blood was thicker than water. No one spoke.

'I see. Well, we are all very new to each other, are we not?' she said. 'But to answer the inevitable questions, yes, I can do that. Your contracts allow for hours over and above those stated as required by the senior management — 1265 was, after all, a long time ago — and that would be me, as I think you will soon come to discover. So, we won't have a meeting this afternoon, of course, but they will begin tomorrow.' She shot her cuff and bent her arm at the elbow, looking with ostentatious concentration at the slim gold watch on her wrist. 'I must be off now to my other schools. They have been happy to make arrangements to accommodate Leighford High School's timetable, but let me make it clear, that there *will* be changes made and not all of them will be palatable. The sponsors of this Academy initiative have given me carte blanche and I intend to use it to bring this school kicking and screaming into . . .'

'. . . the Century of the Fruitbat,' Maxwell murmured. He thought a little Terry Pratchett, may he rest in peace, could never hurt, especially when things were getting tense.

And now, as everyone would have attested, her eyes really *did* seem to glow red. 'You would be Mr Maxwell, I assume,' she said, shouldering her very efficient-looking bag and pushing back her chair. 'I didn't quite catch what you said, but unless it was "outstanding status according to Ofsted" then you and I are not thinking along the same lines. I will be interviewing you all in the coming weeks. Perhaps, Mr Maxwell, we could make an early appointment.' She raked the room once more with her basilisk glare and in a clack of heels and the swing of a door, she had gone.

As the door clicked finally into place and everyone could hear their own blood, pounding and susurrating in their ears, it was of course Maxwell's voice which was the first to be raised.

'She wasn't very nice, now, was she, boys and girls?'

CHAPTER FOUR

It isn't always easy to tell what a teacher is thinking. The stone face and the blank eyes are something they cultivate very quickly as a means to survive the whiteboard jungle. The kids can tell, ironically — their rate of evolution is quicker still and for every trick a teacher learns in their attempt at survival of the fittest, there will be a student waiting around the next bend, antennae already tuned to detect it. If they would only learn about the Corn Laws and the latent heat of fusion of ice with such alacrity, the world would be a smarter place.

So the student body of Leighford High School knew to tread warily that Monday. There was a tang in the air that told them that all was not well. As a rattler tastes the air with its tongue, so the many-headed dragon could tell that this was not a day to piss about. No slamming doors as they came into a classroom one by one. No dropping pens in a perfect Mexican wave across the room. Just eyes front, shoulders back, all attention. Mrs Braymarr would have found it hard to fault the little dears. It was temporary, of course, and by early afternoon the cracks would be showing, but for now, all was peace and the more fragile members of the teaching staff took it for what it was; not peace, but the calm before the storm.

The staff too, were on eggshells. After Mrs Braymarr's exit they had quietly gathered up their traps and gone to their classrooms. Diamond, Ryan and Taylor had stood, stone-faced, where their Nemesis had left them and no one had the heart to speak to them as they left the room. A chill wind was blowing and it didn't need a Sherlock Holmes to know where from; or where it might end up.

Peter Maxwell headed for his office, his bolthole, his sanctuary, his home away from home. He looked around the walls, at his posters, lovingly collected and changed each term, to keep the memories fresh. These would go, he felt it in his water. In the world of Mrs Braymarr and her ilk, there was scant regard for individuality. Nothing different. Nothing out of line. The automata that her school . . . no, he corrected himself, *Academy* would be turning out would have no place in their endless rows for anyone who did not conform. George Orwell had got it wrong. It wasn't 1984 they should have dreaded; it was now, over thirty years too late.

He switched on the kettle, by habit. By now, he should have had a quick update with Sylv, been told which of his Own were heading for pregnancy, measles or incipient bulimia. They would have put the world to rights. She would have brought brownies. Instead, the Sylv-shaped gap that had been so evident to him at the meeting now sat mutely at the end of his carefully positioned row of chairs. The chairs he now would always check in case of recumbent headmasters. But there was no one. Not even the usual crew of absconders from other departments who found the air on the Sixth Form Mezzanine more to their liking than the stinks of chemistry or the chill of maths. With a sigh, he made his coffee, stirred it absentmindedly although he had run out of sugar months ago and sat down, staring out of the window into the future.

And it wasn't pretty.

* * *

James Diamond had gone to that place he visited more and more often these days. There weren't quite bluebirds — courtesy of Disney, with little aprons and brooms — tweeting around his head, but they wouldn't have surprised him had they arrived. He had some pills — he wasn't sure what — and was happy, after his own fashion. He had looked into the future too and, although the window gave onto a different view from Maxwell's, he wasn't seeing a happy ending either. Mrs Braymarr didn't get any more likeable with further meetings; she had struck him as scary when he met her first and she was even more scary now. Why she behaved like that he didn't know. He was self-aware enough to know that he didn't always come across as Little Mr Sunshine, but he was sure his staff were fond enough of him, in their fashion. As he was fond of them in his. But Mrs Braymarr? Who on earth could like her?

* * *

Mrs Braymarr straightened her skirt and checked her lipstick in her mirror. She was not an affectionate woman, she knew that, but she did like sex. She liked it a lot. And if it had to happen in a stationery cupboard from time to time, so be it. It was the power that made her this way, she told herself. Every time she wiped the floor with a roomful of stunned teachers, she had only one thing on her mind. The man adjusting the cut of his trousers beside her seemed to be under the impression he was the only one; that was fine by her. If it kept him compliant it did no harm to boost his ego from time to time. And he was good at what he did. Oh, she had no idea of how good he was at running a used car dealership, although she assumed from the amount of spare cash he had he was no slouch. No, what she was interested in was how he could push her buttons whenever she demanded it. That, and how he could control a board of school governors.

'That was amazing, darling,' she said, mechanically. And it had been — she didn't lie. She just wasn't given to mad enthusing.

He nodded, panting. He wasn't getting any younger and Fiona was getting a little . . . he hesitated to use the word insatiable, because he fancied he could sate any woman breathing, but it was getting a little hard to explain to his rather boot-faced secretary that there must be no calls, no interruptions whenever Mrs Braymarr popped in to discuss the new Academies. 'Amazing,' he agreed. And it had been — he just needed a lie down now.

She gave her skirt a last tug. 'Well, I must be off. I have two more staff rooms to visit before the end of the day.'

He reached for her. He always found her sudden switches to business mode rather enticing. Fatigue forgotten, he pressed against her, but she pushed him away. 'No, Geoff, really. I have to go. But I can see you this evening, if you like. Come round to the hotel, why don't you?'

Yes, he thought, why don't I? Could it be because I have a wife and two stroppy teenagers who were starting to watch him like hawks. Was it that when their hormones started raging, they were hypersensitive to everyone else's? His wife at least was oblivious. If he wasn't a character from *Emmerdale* or *Coronation Street*, he didn't really exist in any meaningful way. Let's see — Monday. Stroppy Teenager One would be at badminton, ST Two would be at oboe; that should give him an hour. 'Lovely,' he said, with his best car salesman's smile firmly in place. 'Seven?'

'Sounds lovely. See you then.' And without another word, she was gone.

He leaned on a stack of blank invoices and winced slightly as his back reminded him he really was too old for this kind of lark. Then he shook himself and followed her at a discreet distance. There were cars to sell, money to make, people to see. He had at least four messages from that whinger Diamond on his desk — but they could wait until another day.

* * *

At Leighford High School, all was not well. Maxwell was in the middle of explaining the Boston Tea Party to Nine Pee

Oh and was getting into his stride, sneaking aboard a ship in the harbour when there was a tap, one could hardly call it a knock, at the door and Thingee Two fell in, looking frantic.

Maxwell looked up mildly. 'Thingee, old thing,' he murmured. 'We're rather engrossed in stuffing the British at the moment. We can't really leave things where they are or we'll never get on to the snowball fights and Paul Revere.'

'Mr Maxwell.' Thingee's eyes were wide, showing the whites like a startled horse. 'I think we need you downstairs. There's an . . . incident.'

'I don't really do incidents, do I, Thingee?' Maxwell remarked kindly. 'That's Mr Diamond, Mr Ryan, Mrs Taylor, people of that nature. You know, the ones who get the big bucks.'

'But Mr *Maxwell*!' Thingee was now speaking with gritted teeth. 'It's an *incident*. In the sick room.'

Maxwell had expected trouble without Sylvia in situ; he just hadn't expected it to come so soon. 'I still don't see . . .'

Thingee took a deep breath. 'It's an angry mob, Mr Maxwell,' she said. 'No one can cope with an angry mob like you, Mr Ryan said. He said to fetch you, quick.'

Maxwell turned for the first time to give her his full attention, holding out an admonitory hand to the class, who were taking the opportunity to get restive. 'Mr Ryan said that?'

The girl nodded, lips compressed, bright spots of excitement high on each cheek.

'Really?' Maxwell turned back to the class. 'Right, you horrible lot,' he said. 'Turn to Chapter Three in your guide to history as rewritten by the Americans. And I shall be asking questions later, make no mistake. Especially along the lines of that politically correct hot potato, why did the rebels dress up as Indians — oops — Native Americans.' Then, shrugging his shoulders so that his jacket sat right, because you can't be untidy when facing an angry mob, he ushered the receptionist through the door and to the top of the stairs. 'Tell me, Thingee, how many constitutes an angry mob, in your opinion?'

'Mr Maxwell,' she clutched his lapel convulsively then let go, patting the tweed back into place, 'it looks like hundreds.'

He raised an eyebrow and inclined his head towards her, smiling,

'I would say at least twenty,' she said, climbing down from the heights of hyperbole. 'But they're all the usuals, you know, the one Mrs Matthews always gets on the first day back.'

Maxwell patted her absently on the shoulder and clattered down the stairs. At the bottom, he looked up at her, only halfway down as she was. 'Thingee,' he said. 'Gather up your colleagues, go into an office and barricade the doors. This isn't going to be pretty!'

Maxwell had seen many films based on hostage situations and as he quickly reprised them in his head, they rarely seemed to end with hearts and flowers. He ran them quickly through his head and try as he might, there wasn't one where everyone went off after for a drink and a laugh. So he gave up on trying to channel Kevin Spacey and be all conciliatory. Only Clint Eastwood would really do.

* * *

The hundred that had already dwindled in Thingee's estimation to twenty were actually fourteen. That was their number; their ages ranged from eleven to fifteen and Maxwell was pleased — and not a little proud — that none of his Own were among them. The Sixth Form knew better than to tangle with Mad Max.

Paula MacBride saw him first, coming down the stairs like Moses from the mountain. Or was it Mohammed? She never really listened in Social and Religious Studies lessons, not until it got on to something interesting, like contraception and she didn't really listen too hard even then. Instinctively, she tugged on her big sister's arm. 'Don't mix it with him,' she whispered. 'He's mad.'

Dee threw her little sister a withering look. 'I'm not scared of him,' she muttered and pushed Alex Caulfield in front of her.

The mob were silent now and they had stopped trying to rip Sylvia Matthew's door off its hinges.

'Alex,' Maxwell said quietly, reaching the stairwell and closing on the boy. It was pure Clint, but any minute he was afraid he would have to put on his dark glasses, rest his hands on his hips and turn into Lt Horatio Crane of the Miami Dade police. 'You look like a man who ought to be in Double French.'

'Spanish, sir.' If Dee MacBride had hoped Caulfield would speak for England, it wasn't working out that way.

'Even better,' Maxwell beamed. 'Think what you're missing. How can you order up that Pina Colada in Ibiza this summer if you skip Monday's lesson?'

That hadn't occurred to Caulfield. He didn't know he was going to Ibiza. He wondered briefly whether his mum and dad knew. Dee knew an idiot when she saw one and had had enough.

'Where's Miss Matthews?' she asked Maxwell. 'Where's the nurse?'

Maxwell looked at her, then beyond to the huddled masses at her elbow. Dee was the spokeswoman, the ring-leader, that much was certain. Her little sister was there, from Year Nine. Caulfield he knew — Grade E GCSE top whack come the summer. There was that fat kid from Year Ten, the one all the others laughed at. Little Tommy somebody . . . Tucker? No, that couldn't be right. There was talk of abuse at home. The three girls at the back he knew by sight. He didn't need to be a school nurse to know why they were there. It would be the usual period pain that came on at the mention of Integrated Science or the morning after pill. No one was there with the perennial problems of his own schooldays; lacerated rugger wounds; cricket-ball testicles; rope burns from the gym. Ah, how the old order changeth.

'I said,' Dee was getting into her stride now, 'where's the nurse?'

'Why don't *you* tell *us*?' Maxwell challenged her.

'Do what?'

'Well,' he said, still smiling, 'with your daddy being Chair of Governors, Paula, I'm sure *he* knows what's going on. Does he not let things slip over the morning muesli?'

There was a snorted laugh from somewhere behind and Dee whirled to see who it was. She was too late and thirteen angelic faces looked at her.

Maxwell sighed. 'Look, everybody,' he said. 'Things are about to change here at Leighford High. I don't know yet how or when. But I promise you, you won't be disadvantaged by it. Not if I can help it.'

Eyes swivelled to left and right. The fight had not gone out of the mob yet and Maxwell knew all about that madness of crowds. 'Alex,' he said. 'Get yourself along to Mr Ryan's office and ask for immediate cover for my Year Nine history class. I've just told them all about revolution and I don't want them acting it out.'

The boy hesitated.

'Now, Alex, please.' There was something in Mad Max's tone that made the boy jump and then he was gone, up the stairs two at a time. Hell did not follow him.

'The rest of you,' Maxwell said and he jabbed his right elbow into Sylvia Matthews' frosted glass door and shattered a pane. He reached in and unhooked the spare key he knew hung there. He clicked it in the lock and flung the door wide. 'The rest of you are welcome to come in. Mind the glass. I know some of you will have had pretty shitty weekends. And I know how much your usual chats with Nurse Matthews mean to you. I can't actually *be* her, but I'll give it my best shot and I can listen for England. What I will *not* be doing is doling out any medicines or sticking on any plasters. It's more than my job's worth.'

They murmured, jostled each other, thought about the offer.

'Tommy,' Maxwell held out his hand. 'How about we start with you?'

Tommy blinked. He hated the limelight but, although he had never been taught by Mr Maxwell, but there was something in the man's voice; in the man's eyes. He walked into Nursie's office.

'If anybody would rather not . . .' Maxwell raised his voice as the muttering started. There was a shuffling that grew to a rumbling and three Year Eleven girls made for the stairs.

'Make sure that gum finds a bin, Elena,' the Head of Sixth Form called after them, 'or we'll be meeting up again later.'

In moments only three people were still there apart from Moses who had parted the Red Sea; the MacBride sisters and little Tommy, already sitting rocking in Mrs Matthews' spare chair.

Maxwell turned to face Paula MacBride. She was a beautiful child under the makeup and clearly overshadowed by her bolshie sister. 'For the record,' he said softly, 'I miss Nurse Matthews too.'

She scowled at him.

'Feel free,' he smiled, 'to tell all your friends on Facebook.'

* * *

It was fair to say that Peter Maxwell had always admired Sylvia Matthews, a calm place on a sea of storms, but after half an hour sharing the hell that was Tommy's life, he admired her even more. He dealt with the MacBrides in short order and was about to mount the stairs, his head still full of what an adult with a heart full of hate and spite could do to a small boy and leave no mark, when he heard his name. He looked around and saw no one but a movement in the corner of his vision coalesced into Thingee, peering through the cracked door of reception.

'Mr Maxwell?' She gestured with an urgent finger. 'Do you have a minute?'

He looked both ways before padding over to the girl. 'You do know I am a teacher, Thingee, do you? Only at the moment, I don't seem to get the opportunity. And, despite all you hear in the news, I do rather like doing it.'

'Yes, Mr Maxwell, I do know that,' she said, 'but we were wondering as you were down here, you might want to come and see us for a minute. Only a minute . . .'

Her big eyes looked so stricken that Maxwell had no choice. He was a sucker for the big eye thing — he would even do almost anything for Antonio Banderas, and he wasn't his usual type at all. 'Well, just a minute, then . . . but I don't really know how I can help.'

He slipped round the door with yet another look both ways. He had a sudden epiphany, that the future would hold a lot of looking, lurking and whispering in corners. He shook his head to clear it of this glimpse of the impending Perfect Day and pinned on a smile with which to comfort the ladies of the office.

'Mr Maxwell.' Legs Diamond's secretary and general Johanna Factotum was, as always, the first to speak her mind. 'What's going on with this Academy nonsense? Surely, we can do something about it, can't we? *You* can do something about it. We can't just have it foisted on us, surely?'

'And that Mrs Braymarr? What's with her? She isn't the boss of us?' This came from the general dogsbody of the office, a pale girl with curtains of paler hair through which she looked malevolently at anything she didn't understand; in practice, everything.

Maxwell raised a hand and brought the rabble to order. Honed as he was at the whetstone of Mrs B., he took the questions in order. 'I believe the Academy nonsense is a government initiative. I don't believe we can, no. No, I can't. Yes, we can. Who knows? I certainly don't have a clue.' And finally, although it wasn't strictly a question, 'I'm afraid she is.' He looked round at them all, every one a woman with worries. Whether they lived for their jobs or simply dragged themselves in for the money like Jodie the dogsbody, they all needed Leighford High School and their jobs. Although none of them had been personally put at risk, there was always that sneaking suspicion that, when axes were wielded, they sometimes took off the wrong head. And, job security or no job security, working for Fiona Braymarr had nothing in common with working for James Diamond. He could be a funny bugger, it was true, but there was nothing funny about Mrs Braymarr. She could suck the joy out of everything and there wasn't much joy to start with in a school office. It was rumoured in the windowless cavern behind the reception desk that some of the benighted souls out there actually enjoyed their jobs, Peter Maxwell being one. But they found it hard to believe. But, as Joni Mitchell often reiterated on Radio Two, you don't know what you've got till it's gone. If Diamond's rule wasn't exactly Paradise, Mrs Braymarr's was going to be the parking lot from Hell.

Their faces said it all. Those few who could afford it would be leaving soon, job or no job. The others would stay, if they were allowed to, but under a cloud. They backed away, leaving Maxwell a clear path to the door. He had been their last hope. And he had given them none. He patted the nearest shoulder and went back into the foyer, then climbed the stairs, with heavy feet.

CHAPTER FIVE

No man lives forever. Dead men rise up never. Even the weariest river winds somewhere safe to sea. The breeze off the beach was cold and mean, cutting through the coat of the woman who stood on the top of the cliff. She had had a shock and, as always when she had something to think over, she had come to the clifftop. Although it always brought the rather sad lines of Swinburne to her mind, she wasn't suicidal these days. She had had her moments, back in the day, but now she was okay. Mostly. She knew she was over-medicated, but she preferred the deadened state she got by in to the churning of her mind when she stopped taking the tablets. She coped. But a shock always brought her back to the cliffs, the wind and the waves. That poem wouldn't leave her head, despite trying to drive it out with something else. 'Dead men rise up never' — she looked out to sea with hollow eyes and shook her head. They could. Oh, yes, they could.

* * *

'Jacquie? Can I have a minute?'

She looked up and had to think for a moment before she could answer. 'Guv. Of course. Sorry, I was miles away.'

'I could tell. I just need to have a bit of a chat — nothing major, just something I could do with talking over with someone, if you don't mind. It's always the same, isn't it, when we're not so busy; things get into your head and you keep on worrying away at them.'

'I know that feeling.' Jacquie had been reading the background on a series of wallet snatches in the town centre and felt she was near an answer — even if it sounded a bit unlikely, even the silence of her own head. Could it really be a ring of pensioners? She knew she would have to address it, but it was such a case of the prey turned predator; little old ladies seemed to be jostling skateboarding teenagers, who later found their wallets, iPhones and other removables had disappeared. It could simply be that an opportunist was jumping in when walking sticks tangled with legs, but . . . again, she gave herself a little shake and suppressed a smile. 'What's your problem?' she asked. 'Mine can certainly wait.'

Henry Hall was not someone given to flights of fancy. The blank face he presented to the world was not a front; he really did have all his ducks in a row but just now, something was bugging him. He sat down opposite Jacquie and she pushed the files aside, so he knew he had her full attention.

'My sister,' he began, to Jacquie's surprise — she had no idea he even had a sister. 'My sister lives next door to a family whose kids go to Leighford High School.'

The DI held up a hand. 'Sorry, guv,' she said. 'No interference with exam results possible, you know that!'

'It would be good if that was the problem,' he said. 'No, the problem is, she hears crying through the wall, every night.'

Jacquie shrugged. 'Nine nine nine,' she said. 'CYPR. Children's services. Job done.' She couldn't quite see where this was going.

'She did all that. Nice clean home. Child has all the trimmings — laptop, iPad, iPhone. Fridge full of appropriate food. Good clothes. Nice parents . . .'

'But?'

'But, she still hears the crying. It's getting her down. Social workers' hands are tied, so are ours. I've got the Children's and Young Persons' Report here . . .' he flicked through the file he carried while Jacquie smiled gently. How like Henry to give it its full title. He found the page and handed it over. She glanced through it and it all bore out what Henry said. The crying was mentioned, with the anonymous caller, but it was marked NFA — no further action.

'So, what would you like me to do?' She knew the answer, but had to ask all the same.

'Can you have a word with Max? See if he knows anything about this kid? Schools often know more than we can find out.'

Jacquie glanced at the boy's date of birth. 'He isn't one of Max's Own, Henry,' she pointed out. 'He's too young. He might not even teach him, you know.'

'Sylvia will know him, though.' Henry had only met her once or twice, but to meet her once was to trust her implicitly.

'She will, no doubt,' Jacquie agreed. 'But she doesn't work at Leighford High any more.'

Hall was staggered. He was surprised to find that Leighford High was still standing, without Sylvia. Maxwell must be bearing all the weight of the crumbling structure on his own now, then. 'Has she retired? She isn't old enough, surely?'

Jacquie sighed. 'No, she is one of the first victims of the new regime.'

He raised his eyebrows. 'Did I know about it?' he asked.

Jacquie told him the sad story of the incipient Academy in a few pithy words. Hall's boys were well beyond that stage, but grandfatherhood beckoned and he was getting interested in schools once again, to be ready. It sounded a bit of a cockamamie plan to him, but he had never really understood teachers, especially Peter Maxwell, although they had come to a working neutrality and in many circumstances he even enjoyed the man's company. As Jacquie came to the end of her tale, he tapped the file on the desk and got up.

'Max might not be able to help me, then,' he said.

'No, no,' Jacquie said. 'I'm sure he still can. It will just mean a bit more digging. If this has been going on for a while . . .' Hall nodded, 'then I am sure that Sylv already knows about it. I'll give her a ring in a minute, and see if she has anything to add.' She flicked over the CYPR and made a note of the name. 'Child at risk — Thomas Ryan Morton'. She handed the sheet back and Hall slipped it into his folder.

'Thanks, Jacquie. Hetty will be relieved.' And he was gone.

Hetty? Oh, surely, Jacquie thought with a smile, Mr and Mrs Hall Snr hadn't called their children Henry and Henrietta? Still chuckling quietly, she picked up the phone and dialled.

'Sylv? Hi, it's Jacquie. How's retirement suiting you?'

'Don't even ask! I'm bored already.'

Jacquie could well believe it. Sylvia was always someone who could fit forty-eight of anyone else's hours into every twenty-four, so she would probably be on her second complete redecoration of the house by now; it had, after all, been a week since she gave up work, or work gave her up, depending on the point of view. 'Well, I wonder if you could do me a favour . . .'

* * *

It was Peter Maxwell's favourite day of the week. On a Monday, he always picked up Nolan from school and they wandered through the town to wait for Mums. Nolan was a child in size only — sometimes, Maxwell was convinced that he was the junior partner in the duo, but he cherished these times, having never expected them to ever come. This late child and his mother had brought joy back into a life which was previously merely content. But Nolan had a flaw — he only ever mentioned any salient fact once. This was fine as long as the recipient was a parent, but as often as not it was the dinner lady or a random parent of a friend, so there had been desperate moments Chez Carpenter-Maxwell when the requisite costume/cake/poem needed to be magicked into being on the morning of, rather than in the weeks ahead as planned by Mrs Whatmough. So Monday was important, not just for lad and dad bonding but also for gathering of vital information. Maxwell could see storms ahead when Mrs Braymarr's regime began to bite, because unless she had some wild horses to hand, she would not be seeing Maxwell on a Monday afternoon, after school.

But that was something for later. For now, they walked hand in hand, Maxwell with his son's satchel hung nonchalantly from his shoulder, his son's cap at a rakish angle over one eye. He waited for the day when Nolan would complain about this bizarre parental behaviour — and hoped that that day would never come.

'Dads?'

'Yes, mate.'

'Do you know your nine times?'

'Sometimes,' Maxwell replied. 'I'm good up to six times nine, after that I have to be having a good day.'

Nolan nodded sagely. 'I'm a bit like that,' he agreed. 'Today was a good day. I did it all.'

Maxwell was impressed. 'All through? Nole, you're a marvel.'

The boy gave a hop. 'I was a bit surprised, if I tell the truth,' he said, sounding so like Mrs B that Maxwell had to smile. 'But I got a gold star and it won't be my turn again for a long time.'

Maxwell did a quick calculation. 'How far up do you go?' he asked. 'In the timeses?'

Nolan was quiet as he looked into the future of fourteen times, fifteen times . . . 'I think we start again when we get to twelve,' he said, more for his own sake than Maxwell's.

'I expect you do,' his father agreed. He hadn't been joking about his prowess with nine times and wasn't looking forward to helping with anything much higher. 'Apart from the tables phenomenon, how was your day?'

Nolan loved new words and pounced on phenomenon with glee. 'Phenonermen?'

'Phenomenon.'

'Phern . . .'

'Phen.'

'Phen!' Nolan loved the ritual.

'Nom'

'Nom!'

'Enon.'

'Enon!'

'Phenomenon.'

'Phenomenon!' And he was off, hopping on one leg then two along the almost deserted shopping centre. 'Phenomenon! Phenomenon! Phenomenon!'

Maxwell smiled and let the boy bounce on ahead. He was a careful parent, but not a smothering one and as long as his boy was in sight, he was happy. Then, almost simultaneously, several things happened. Nolan bounced round a corner, there was a distant scream, a crash, a shout and then silence. Without a second's pause, Maxwell was in full flight, wanting to be at his son's side but also scared to find a pile of mangled humanity around the corner. There had been at least three different voices in the melee, Nolan's among them.

The scene that met his eyes was not instantly clear. Nolan wasn't part of any carnage, so that was all right, Maxwell stepped to his boy's side and patted his shoulder, muttering, 'Are you all right, Nole?'

'Yes, Dads,' he said, sounding puzzled.

Maxwell, satisfied his chick was unhurt, refocused on the pile of humanity some yards ahead on the pedestrian area. It began to resolve as he looked at an elderly woman, complete with walking stick, and a youth of around eighteen. Somewhere in the mix was a scooter, looking somewhat the worse for wear. The human elements looked a little ruffled but otherwise uninjured, but the Public Schoolboy rose up unbidden in Maxwell and he stepped forward, calling, 'Can I help?'

The old dear looked up pathetically. 'Oooh, what a kind gentleman,' she cooed. 'This young man just cannoned into me. I don't know what's coming to the youth of today, I really don't.' She started to struggle to her feet, and Maxwell extended a helpful hand.

'Mad old biddy,' the lad spat. 'She stuck her stick out a purpose.'

The woman's eyes flashed. 'You wicked young lout,' she said, hauling herself upright surprisingly easily using Maxwell's arm as leverage. 'You hit me. Zooming along on that contraption. It's a kid's toy, that is. What are you thinking, playing in the street at your age?'

The lad appealed to a higher authority. 'Mr Maxwell,' he said, jumping up and dusting himself off. 'You know I wouldn't do anything of the kind. I use the scooter to stay eco-friendly. I wouldn't use a fuel-based method of transport. I keep a negative carbon footprint, I do.'

Maxwell looked closer. On inspection, the boy did indeed turn out to be one of his Own, known for his green habits and infamous for his total eschewment of deodorant of any kind. He stepped back. 'Jem,' he said. 'Sorry, I didn't recognise you from this angle. Are you all right?'

'Oh, that's it,' the old crone snapped. 'Be on his side. I might have known the poor old lady would get short shrift.'

'Madam,' Maxwell lifted Nolan's cap in the time-honoured fashion. 'I apologise, but I do know Jem here and I'm sure that this was just an accident. Can I call anyone to help you? I'm afraid I don't drive myself so I can't . . .'

The woman curled her lip. 'You Greens,' she said. 'Hang together, why don't you?'

Maxwell glanced back at Nolan, who shrugged. He was a bit of an expert on old ladies, having honed his skills on Mrs Troubridge and Mrs B, but he knew when he was beaten. He looked pointedly up at the sky, Nolan shorthand for 'leave me out of this — you're on your own'.

Maxwell opened his mouth to speak, but the old lady had straightened her body-warmer and looked in her bag to make sure that there was nothing missing amongst her shopping. Satisfied, she turned to Jem, who was trying to straighten the wheel of his scooter.

'Take more care next time, young man,' she said. 'I could have broken my hip and that might have been the end of me. A broken bone is no joke at my time of life.' And with that, she brushed angrily past him, heading for the bus station.

Jem watched her go. 'I didn't hit her on purpose, Mr Maxwell,' he said, plaintively. 'I would swear she stuck her stick out deliberately.'

Nolan, seeing the old lady leaving, had joined the menfolk. 'She did, Dads,' he said. 'She did stick her stick out.' He paused for a moment. That wasn't the kind of grammar Mrs Whatmough would allow. 'She made him fall off his scooter.'

Maxwell and Jem looked at him in wonder.

'And it was funny. She just walked back in the direction she came from. It's almost as if she was waiting for him. She walked faster before she stuck her stick out than she is doing now and do you know what's funnier still?'

'What?' Maxwell was used to his son but Jem was still a little overawed. It was like Maxwell. Only shorter.

'When she went away, she pinched his wallet. Or it might have been his phone.' The boy patted his back pocket. 'From in there.'

Stricken, Jem did the same and came up empty. 'You're right!' he said to Nolan. 'The old cow has had it away with my phone. I saved up for that. Low impact,' he explained to Maxwell. 'Completely recyclable.'

'Naturally,' Maxwell agreed, whatever that might mean.

Jem thrust the handlebars of his scooter at Nolan, who stood holding them proudly as the lad ran off, following the elderly dip. It wasn't long before he was back, shoulders slumped. 'No sign,' he said. 'The old cow . . .' he looked anxiously at Nolan but the boy didn't flinch. He heard much worse most nights when his father did the ritual fall over the cat on his way to bed. 'I'm going to report it to the police. *And* she's wrecked my scooter. Look!' He held it up and it was indeed in a sorry state. The wheel was bent at right-angles to the handlebars and when he tried to straighten it, it made a rather unpleasant grating noise. He shook his head. 'I saved up for this as well.'

Nolan slipped his hand trustingly into Jem's. 'Come on,' he said. 'We're going to see Mums now. She will sort it out.'

Jem looked uncertain. He was touched the lad thought his mum could put anything right. He remembered when he thought that too.

Maxwell leaned forward and murmured in Jem's ear. 'His mum is Detective Inspector Carpenter-Maxwell, so she really will sort you out! Come on — she always enjoys it when we take her customers.'

Jem hefted his scooter over his shoulder, Maxwell Nolan's satchel and with the brains of the outfit leading the way, singing 'Phenomenon' to the tune of *One Man Went To Mow*, they headed off to the nick.

* * *

The deal on a Monday was that Maxwell and Nolan, having done some window shopping — or, depending on the efficacy of Nolan's big doe eyes, actual shopping — would wait for Jacquie in the coffee shop in the local Tesco on the edge of the shopping centre. After a quick latte and poppy seed muffin, Jacquie would feel less of a detective inspector and more of a human being and they would head off home, often with a special bag of favourites in tow. So she was taken aback when the phone on her desk trilled to tell her that the two of them were waiting downstairs. She checked her watch — no, she wasn't late. Maxwell would surely not have come to her if Nolan had been injured in any way; he would have either called an ambulance or stuck a plaster on it, according to circumstances. Even so, she took the stairs at a rather faster pace than was usual or even advisable.

In the foyer, there was a motley crew, sixty-six point six percent Maxwell. A cursory glance showed her they were both uninjured, so she turned her attention to the boy with them. He was probably about seventeen, she judged and good looking in an etiolated sort of way. He was wearing clothes that were probably considerably older than he was, but whether from a style angle or necessity, it was hard to tell. They were clearly all together and she raised an interrogatory eyebrow.

Nolan was in full official mode and didn't do his usual flying leap at her. 'We're here to report a crime,' he said, importantly. 'I'm a witness.'

So, that explained that. Probably some homework project being squeezed till its pips squeaked.

'I'm a bit busy for the moment . . .' she began.

'Mrs Maxwell,' Jem broke in. 'We really are here to report a crime. I've been . . .' the lad lowered his voice; his street cred was already low, what with the pre-loved clothes and the scooter, not to mention the armpits. He really didn't need the world to know his latest problem. '. . . I've just been mugged by an old lady.' He waited for the laugh, but none came. 'Nolan saw everything.'

'Max?' Jacquie looked at her husband, standing at the back of the tiny mob. 'What happened?'

'I didn't see,' he said, sensing a problem looming. 'Nole had gone round the corner just as Jem was tripped up by the old dear and then he saw her pinch his phone.' He read her face. 'I was only inches behind, I promise.'

Her face promised questions later, but for now it all seemed to be falling into place. Her hunch had been right — but was it a gang or just one person? 'Tell me about this old lady, Jem, is it?'

'Yes, Mrs Maxwell. I go to Leighford High. Mr Maxwell knows I wouldn't have run into her on purpose. She stuck her stick out. It got in the axle of my scooter and I went right over the handlebars. I don't think I even touched her but when I looked, she was lying on the ground.'

'She sat down,' Nolan offered. 'She didn't fall over. She just sat down, like this.' The boy mimed a walking stick and used it to lower himself to the ground.

Jacquie put a friendly arm around Jem then recoiled slightly. 'Come this way, Jem,' she said. 'Are you hurt at all? Would you like to see the First Aid officer?'

'No, thank you, Mrs Maxwell,' Jem said, a little in love. He had always favoured the older woman — more likely to be green, in his experience — and here was one to die for. Mad Max was a bit of a dark horse and no mistake.

'A drink, then. Coke?'

Jem nodded.

Jacquie gestured to the desk sergeant who pressed some buttons on the vending machine and handed over the can. 'Come through, Jem. Nole, can you take Dads home, please? I may be a while here.'

'But what about your poppy seed muffin?' Nolan asked. He worried about his mother, was she eating properly when he wasn't there, what if a burglar got her . . . you couldn't be too careful.

'Why don't you buy me one to take out?' she suggested. 'And something nice for supper. I shouldn't be too long.' She planted a kiss on the top of his head. 'See you soon. I might even be home first, if you two get enravelled in your shopping.' Then, like flicking a switch, she was DI Carpenter-Maxwell again, ushering Jem through the flap in the counter, into the hinterland of the nick.

The Maxwell men turned on their heels and made their way outside, pulling scarves tighter as the cold of the February evening bit.

Nolan was quiet as they walked towards the supermarket, then finally burst out, '*Now* do you see why I don't tell you everything!'

Maxwell laughed and pulled the boy closer. 'Nole,' he said. 'Welcome to my world!'

* * *

'So,' Maxwell said when, finally, the evening got back on track. 'Tell me about the Darby and Joan Gang.'

'No Darbies as far as we can tell,' Jacquie said. 'Just a lot of Joans. I think yours this afternoon was unusual in that she was working alone. There is normally one to stick out the stick, wheelie thing or whatever is to hand and one to take the fall. Perhaps she just saw Jem as a perfect victim and had a go all on her own.'

'Are you likely to catch them?' Maxwell found it hard to take mugging grannies seriously.

'I would like to say yes,' Jacquie said, 'but I think it's doubtful. The public see little old ladies as victims, no matter what they do and in this case there is the built in response which suggests they are just fighting back. But when a nice lad like Jem is turned over, it isn't so clear cut and anyway, from our point of view, it is a crime and we have to sort it out, stop it. When you add up the things they have stolen, it comes to thousands of pounds. It isn't a minor thing at all.'

'She was a bit of a piece of work,' Maxwell said. 'Somebody's granny, no doubt, but more Catherine Tate than anything else.'

'I got that impression from Jem,' Jacquie said. 'And I do feel sorry for the lad; no phone, no scooter and all saved up for too. No indulgent parents for him . . . oh, that reminds me. Do you know a boy called . . . oh, hang on, what's his name?' She tapped her head, annoyed with herself.

'Tommy Morton.'

She opened her eyes wide. 'That's bonkers! How did you know that?'

'I didn't. I just had a rather painful afternoon with him, that's all, doing my best to be Sylv. He's a sad little boy, and no mistake.'

'Henry's sister lives next door.'

'Henry has a sister?'

'Hetty.'

'Not short for Henrietta, I hope.'

They looked at each other for a few moments, in shared horror, then laughed. 'I can't think of anything else.'

Maxwell shook himself and returned to the problem of Thomas Morton. 'It's a problem. He doesn't want to have any police involvement. Apparently, there was a visit . . .'

'Hetty dialled 999.'

'Ah. And that made everything worse. He said the policeman looked around and wrote things down and then nothing else happened. Except that the abuse got worse. Can that be right?'

'I've seen the report. They checked all the usual things — cleanliness, appropriate food, clothing, all that. Thomas seemed to have everything any child could want, he had no bruises they could see. The parents seemed very affectionate towards him . . . their hands were tied.'

'There are no bruises to see. Just mental scars, caused by relentless bullying. Everything they "give" him,' Maxwell made ironic speech marks in the air, 'has to be earned and if he steps out of line, it is taken back. It doesn't take much. If he eats all of his dinner, he is a fat pig; loss of TV rights. If he leaves anything on his plate, he is an ungrateful little bastard, loss of iPad. If he has a bath, he's wasting their hard earned money; if he doesn't, he's dirty. The list goes on. A sad, sad little boy.'

'Hetty said that she hears him crying, but there was no mention of shouting, anything like that. I suppose they are the worst kind of bullies, the ones with smiles on their faces.'

'Bully. Not bullies. Apparently, it is just the mother. Tommy doesn't want to be taken away, though, because when he isn't there, she picks on his dad. When he went away on a school trip, when he came back, his dad was in plaster; she'd broken his arm.'

'I'll have to report this, Max. The child is in danger.'

'With no bruises?'

'But . . . we can get her on domestic abuse. It doesn't all have to be physical these days.'

'Can you promise she would be taken into custody? Never let near the boy and his father again?'

Jacquie didn't answer and that was answer enough.

'Precisely. I think perhaps a visit from a social worker to Tommy, at school, might be a halfway house. I can't believe that Sylv not being there has had repercussions so soon. She's only been gone one day and here we are, trying to pick up the pieces.'

'I gave her a ring after Henry popped in about Hetty's worries and she seems stir crazy already. She sends hers. But she hadn't been able to pin Tommy down to much. Just general misery, which he couldn't quantify.'

'Funnily enough, he opened up to me. On the other hand, I suppose women don't exactly fill him with confidence.'

Jacquie smiled. 'This isn't women, Max. This is Sylv.'

'True. But Sylv to us is Womenkind to Tommy. Still, we're on the case now. You'll leave it till tomorrow though, yes?'

Jacquie sat, half in and half out of her chair. 'I can see now how they crawled under the wire,' she said. 'Comfortable home, nice clothes and surroundings. A woman's touch. A spot visit won't come up with anything different and will make things worse, no doubt. I'll leave it.'

'Oh, yes,' Maxwell said. 'A gilded cage is still a cage. Sometimes it's hard to see the bars, except from the inside.'

CHAPTER SIX

That night, things took their usual course along Columbine. At the end of the road, traffic became intermittent, then stopped. Metternich prowled his favourite beat, leaving little sprayed messages here and there to warn off any strangers that it would be unwise to hang around. He had already played out the ritual of hiding just in the shadow of the third stair from the top, so that Maxwell could fall over him. It was as near to an endearment that the Count would come; women and children always excepted, of course. That little chore complete, he could maraud at will and woe betide any creature, big or small, that crossed his path. He had to keep the road safe for his Boy, after all; you couldn't be too careful.

Mrs Troubridge heard the cat flap's clatter and began to get herself ready for bed. Metternich's movements were better than a clock for her — although they existed in a state of armed neutrality, the great beast had his uses. She warmed up her milk and added a spoonful of honey and a glug of single malt — both for medicinal purposes. She filled her hot water bottle and tucked it under her arm and headed for the stairs. All was quiet from next door on one side and she thanked her lucky stars for the Maxwells, even though that included

Mr Maxwell, a loose cannon if ever there was one. From the other side came the distant howl of the Arctic Monkeys, but she had embraced the benefits of old age and turned down her hearing aid to compensate.

Chez Maxwell, all was peace. Maxwell had bathed his most recent Metternich-induced scratch down his shin with TCP and was sitting up reading the new biography on Rupert Brooke. He was not surprised to find that he was a rather odder person than previous thinking had portrayed him to be; no one with hair that floppy could be quite the thing, in his opinion. Jacquie was already asleep — she had a knack he envied of deciding to go to sleep and simply dropping off. Nolan had inherited that skill and Maxwell never failed to be grateful; he had seen too many colleagues joining the zombie legion of the parents of sleepless children.

Finally, all Rupert Brooked out, Maxwell put his book down and turned over to go to sleep. He reached out and switched off the light and had soon joined the rest of his family in the Land of Nod.

Mrs Troubridge drained her cup of milk and snuggled down, her hot water bottle strategically placed under her knees, to give her arthritis a bit of TLC.

Metternich, out in the frosty dark, pounced on a vole whose luck had finally run out.

The Arctic Monkeys faded away to silence.

Columbine slept.

* * *

Arthur Innes didn't actually like dogs. Come to think of it, he didn't much like his wife, either. And since Jock was his wife's dog, he didn't remember which came first. In a way, they had merged. Sheila didn't demand to be walked three times a day and she didn't go a bundle on charcoal biscuits; yet facially there was something of a resemblance. Didn't they say people start to look like their pets? Sheila had taken to wearing a bow in her hair recently, often of tartan hues.

Mercifully her sartorial tastes had not yet run to a little diamante collar, but it was early days.

Arthur was getting less and less patient with Jock. Not only did he have the most clichéd name possible, as a Skye terrier, he insisted on stopping every half yard to sniff the pavement and cock his leg. Arthur wasn't sleeping well these nights. Sheila had buggered off to her own room years ago, so it wasn't her snoring that kept him awake. He'd done the crossword, found the latest Andy McNab less than gripping, so he thought he'd clear his head and take Jock for a late constitutional.

Leighford was like a graveyard at this time of night, at this season of the year. The nightclubs were all locked and barred and the fairground silent. To be honest, Arthur liked it like this. He didn't know why he'd moved to a seaside town, really. Something to do with the council job and the pension, he supposed.

Jock had found a new lease of life tonight. It was the witching hour and Arthur expected to see Sheila flapping skyward against the clouds any minute, shrieking in that banshee way of hers. The dog was straining at the leash, at least as much as a Skye terrier could strain, his little fluffy feet skidding on the concrete. Suddenly, he stopped. His head and ears were erect. He was staring into the window of the car sales showrooms, the Renault outlet. MacBride's, wasn't it? Arthur had once considered buying a car from there but Sheila hadn't liked anything on offer and didn't care for the snake-oil salesman with the glib patter, so off they went elsewhere.

There was a dim blue light at the back of the showroom and another one in the top left-hand corner of the window. Half a dozen new cars gleamed with their sale prices and today's deals still visible. But it wasn't the consumerism that had stopped Jock in his tracks. It was the long dark smear that ran from the top of the showroom window to the bottom; that ran down to the unmistakeable shape of a woman's body, wedged between a car and the glass. Her cheek and mouth had been compressed, as though she had leaned too close to a mirror and her eyes were wide open in shock.

Jock cocked his head from side to side. Then he cocked his leg and prepared to move on. That was fine if you were a Skye terrier. But Arthur Innes could not let things lie.

* * *

Suddenly, bells seemed to ring from every quarter. The landline phone on the bedside table sprang to life and Jacquie's mobile, stashed under her pillow to cause less annoyance if it rang in the night, pealed urgently, even though a little muffled. As the two sprang awake, groping for handsets, so a frantic ringing of the doorbell joined the fun and for a moment or two, Maxwell had a pang of fellow feeling for Quasimodo.

With her phone clamped to her ear, Jacquie made for the stairs, shrugging one arm into her dressing gown as she went. Maxwell heard her, 'Guv?' as she dived through the door.

He turned his attention to the phone in his hand, still ringing. He pressed the appropriate button, as far as he could identify it through the haze of sleep and spoke. 'Maxwell.' The middle of the night didn't seem appropriate for his usual greeting of 'War Room.'

'Is that Peter Maxwell?' a clipped voice asked.

'It is. May I ask who is speaking?' He could hardly believe it was a cold call at this time of night, but it was hard to second guess them these days — it might well be there were people out there keen to discuss reclaiming mis-sold PPI at gone three o'clock in the morning.

'This is Marilyn Fairbrother. I am the duty social worker and I need an appropriate adult.'

Maxwell wasn't completely up on social work and all its wiles, but he was pretty sure he was on firm ground with his reply. 'Isn't that you?' he asked.

'Isn't it me what?'

'Are you not an appropriate adult?'

'I am, of course. But this particular case has requested you.'

Maxwell tamped down his hackles. A case? A *case*? Presumably, this was a person she was talking about. But nothing would be solved by losing his temper. 'Who is it?' he asked.

There was a rustle of paper which only served to annoy him more. For heaven's sake, how many people did she have in her caseload on this particular shift? Leighford wasn't perfect, he of all people knew that, but her night duty would be something of a sinecure, he would have thought.

'Umm . . . it's Thomas Ryan Morton.'

'Tommy? What's happened?'

'I can't divulge that over the phone, Mr Maxwell. Can you come or not?'

Maxwell was stuck for an answer. Jacquie was obviously in the middle of some kind of crisis of her own and they had Nolan to consider. Although the Count would be back in by now, he was hardly the babysitter of choice. And Mrs Troubridge would be well away, snoring to beat the band and she couldn't be disturbed at this hour. 'I'm afraid it may be a bit difficult. My wife has just had a call and . . .'

'Would that be Detective Inspector Carpenter-Maxwell?'

'It would.'

'I see. I understand there is a case which will involve a large number of staff currently off duty. This does make it . . . excuse me.' Mrs, Miss or Ms Fairbrother was clearly talking to someone over her shoulder. 'We can arrange for someone to come and sit with your son, Mr Maxwell. It really is very important that you come to the police station, if you possibly can.'

'I don't understand why . . .'

The social worker put her mouth much nearer to the phone and dropped her voice. 'Tommy really does need you, Mr Maxwell,' she hissed. 'You see, we think he has killed his mother.'

Maxwell was both gobsmacked and not at all surprised. It was a crime waiting to happen; he just hadn't expected it so soon. Assured by the woman that the sitter was on her way — and was, not unusually in Leighford one of his very Own from way back — he rang off and started to dress. Slowly, he became aware of voices from the floor below and started down to meet the next crisis which was clearly blowing up. He met Jacquie on the stairs.

'I've got to go out, Max,' she said, looking up into his face and then letting her eyes travel down, taking in his fully clothed state. 'Why are you dressed?'

'I've got to go out too,' he said.

'But . . .' she gestured to Nolan's room.

'Someone's on their way. A duty social work assistant — I'm needed as an appropriate adult.' He held up his hand to circumvent her questions. 'I expect that's where you're going too, is it? The Nick? Tommy Morton's in there, accused of murdering his mother.'

'What?' Her eyes popped. 'No, I'm going to look at a body, just found in town.'

He frowned. 'Isn't that a bit . . . ?' Overkill didn't seem the right word, in the circumstances.

'I know what you mean,' she said. 'It looked like a jumper at first, but then the ambulance guys noticed her nails were all torn and she seemed to have a lot of damage to her clothes — rips and so on — that suggested she had struggled with someone before she died. It looks like murder.'

'Even so . . . the call from Henry. The heavies at the door. Wouldn't a preliminary report and a meeting tomorrow be more appropriate?' Appropriate seemed to be tonight's word.

'Yes. In normal circumstances. But these circumstances are a bit out of the ordinary.'

'How so?' The Maxwells were edging up the stairs, so that the DI could get dressed and they wouldn't have to whisper.

'It's the wife of what the newspapers like to call "a prominent citizen".'

'How exciting.' Maxwell couldn't disguise the gleam in his eyes. 'Who?'

Jacquie shrugged out of her pyjamas and dressed with practiced ease, slipping a jumper over tee and jeans to be the epitome of efficient policedom. 'Don't ask, Max, and I won't have to refuse to tell you,' she said. 'It will be in the papers soon enough.'

'I told you mine,' he wheedled.

'I'm a detective inspector, Max,' she said, bending to Velcro up her trainers. 'I get to know everything. You, not so much.'

He chuckled.

'Well, yes, you do get to know everything. But not necessarily first. Be patient.'

Down below, the bell pealed.

'That's for you,' she said. 'Are they sending her out with a driver?'

'I believe that's the plan.'

'In that case, don't keep them waiting. I can show her where everything is before I go.'

'What about if we're not here when Nole wakes up?'

'I'll get her to get Mrs T in for breakfast. You know she's always up at sparrowfart. Now, go.'

And the appropriate adult scooted off, making for the stairs.

* * *

Peter Maxwell had been in Leighford nick at almost every hour of the day or night over the years, but night time always struck him as the worst. It was now he believed the doubtless apocryphal story that more people died at three a.m. than at any other single hour of the day or night. There was a feeling that the air had been breathed in and out too many times, that the clocks were running on special, extra-slow ticks, that the doors had healed up and there would be no way out of the flickering, neon-lit hell they were all trapped in. He was met in the foyer by the social worker. She was tiny, perhaps not even five feet tall, but there was steel in her eye that was hard to miss. Her fluffy hair framed a heart shaped face and Maxwell could see that she was an iron fist in a little, curly glove; the scariest kind.

'Mr Maxwell?' She stepped forward, arm extended. 'Hello. I'm Marilyn. Thank you so much for coming. Poor Tommy, he is in such a state, as you can probably imagine . . . well, no, of course you can't. How can anyone imagine what it's like to have killed your mother?'

Maxwell thought back to his own mother, dead and gone for far too long. To the gentle woman with the kindly eyes, who would kiss him to sleep every night, then wake him with another kiss every morning. Nasty thoughts may sometimes have entered her head, but none that he would know about. He and his sister had been loved unconditionally and he still missed her, even after all the years since she had died. He gave a shorthand agreement with a shake of the head.

'He's through here,' the social worker said. 'We haven't put him in an interview room; he's in the family suite.'

The room was self-consciously decorated in child friendly colours, bright and breezy but managing somehow to still be thoroughly institution — the cream and green of the twenty teens. A couch was pushed against one wall and some bean bags were scattered around. A box of rather grubby soft toys were in one corner, a box of Lego in another. Curled up against one arm of the couch was Tommy Morton, looking somehow smaller in this alien room. He looked up with enormous, tear-reddened eyes as the door opened. He stiffened as he saw Maxwell and Marilyn Fairbrother. Maxwell knew that he had to play this one right or they might not get another chance.

'Tommy,' he said, as though they were meeting casually in a corridor. 'How're you doing?' Normally, such grammar would make Maxwell's soft palate curdle, but he was prepared to bend the rules a little, circumstances being what they were.

'Mr Maxwell,' Tommy said. 'I killed my mum.'

'I don't think we want to be saying that kind of thing, Tommy,' the social worker said. 'Not until the duty solicitor gets here.'

'I did, though,' the boy said. 'It's all my fault.'

Maxwell saw the loophole and spoke quietly in the woman's ear. 'Can we have a word?'

She pinned on a bright smile and said, 'I'm just going to have a chat with Mr Maxwell, Tommy. He'll be right back.'

Outside, she said, testily, 'We can't keep dodging in and out, Mr Maxwell,' she said. 'The boy is not in a good place.'

She could say that again — the family suite was definitely well down there in the circles of Hell. But Maxwell had other things on his mind and couldn't take up the subject of family suites and their décor. 'I didn't think I would hear the magic words so soon, Miss Fairbrother,' he said.

'That's Ms,' she inevitably corrected him. 'And what magic words would they be?'

'"It's all my fault",' he told her. 'When you are trying to find out who dunnit, as opposed to who is taking the fall for it, you listen out for those words. They mean that the person feels culpable, but they rarely mean they actually wielded the spade, or whatever the murder weapon of choice might have been.'

'Have many cases of murder in Leighford High School, do you, Mr Maxwell?'

The voice came from behind him and had hostility written all over it.

'You'd be surprised,' Maxwell said, without turning round.

'Yes, that's right,' the voice agreed, coming closer and coalescing into the unattractive exterior of Rick Shopley. The newest sergeant on the block had not endeared himself to Jacquie or indeed to anyone else in Leighford, but the good news was he was on secondment and would soon be gone. 'I have heard about you and your little hobby. Sleuths R Us.' He turned to the social worker. 'Why is he here?'

'Appropriate adult,' she said. 'Requested by Tommy. He has that right, you know.'

'Is he on the list?'

'He doesn't have to be. He has enhanced CRB and that's all it needs. And he knows Tommy; the poor boy needs a friendly face.'

'Yeah, well, he should have thought of that before he stabbed his mother with the bread knife, don't you think?' the sergeant sneered.

'When did this happen?' Maxwell asked mildly. 'I only ask because, well, I have reason to believe that Tommy is usually packed off upstairs by eight o'clock at the outside and it would be unusual to say the least if he had a bread knife in the bed with him.'

The sergeant looked at him with contempt. 'The stairs aren't landmined, Mr Maxwell,' he said. 'Just being sent to bed doesn't mean he had to stay there.'

'But it does,' Maxwell said. 'Tommy was completely dominated by his mother. He would never go against her orders.'

'All the more reason for him to snap. I've looked at the CYPR,' he said, speaking now to the social worker. 'It's marked NFA.' It was clearly his intention to exclude Maxwell by using initials for everything, but Heads of Sixth Form were as up on children's services jargon as the next man, except that perhaps he had a different set of words for NFA.

'So, as I was saying,' Maxwell also concentrated on the social worker, '"It's all my fault" means something very different from "I did it". Where is Tommy's dad, by the way?'

'He wasn't there,' she said. 'Tommy doesn't seem to know where he is.'

'Away on business, we heard,' the sergeant said.

'Heard? From whom?'

The sergeant curled his lip. '"From whom"?' he mimicked. 'From Tommy.'

'Really?' Marilyn Fairbrother was beginning to take sides and she certainly wasn't aligned with the sergeant. She flicked open the file she had been clutching to her chest. 'It says here that he works for the bus company as a route planner.'

'And?'

'And so I don't see how he can be away on business. Even the most dedicated route planner wouldn't be out planning routes in the middle of the night, would he?'

Shopley looked uncomfortable. 'He could be on a course,' he blustered.

Ms Fairbrother pulled herself up to her full height and stared him straight in the tie-knot. 'I think before we question

Tommy any more, we find his father, don't you? I believe, as does Mr Maxwell, that Tommy feels responsible, but that doesn't mean he did it. In my capacity as the representative of the child protection department of Leighford, I must insist that you postpone any further interviews until every effort has been made to find Mr Morton.'

It was a little like being faced off by a hamster, but Rick Shopley knew when he was beaten. He slouched off down the corridor and slammed through the double doors at the end, leaving them swinging like a larger version of Metternich's cat flap, and with much the same acrid scent of threat wafting in his wake.

* * *

'Can we get some lights on in here?' Jacquie called, her voice echoing slightly in the saleroom. She could picture Maxwell's sense of disappointment. As an avid watcher of the CSI Franchise, he expected policemen (who also appeared to be SOCO to save on the expense of paying extra extras) to bob around corners at crime scenes, a powerful torch balanced on the rigid wrists of their gun hands, just in case the perp was still there.

There was a loud clunk and the neon popped into light. Jacquie was aware of the PR problem immediately. 'Close those blinds, somebody. We'll have half of Leighford gawping in.'

'Jacquie.' She heard the DCI murmur her name. 'What have we got?'

Henry Hall looked like shit. He was in the grip of his annual cold and nobody could deny he put the 'Man' into Man Flu. He had been feeling sorry for himself before he left home, but there was nothing like sudden death for jolting him out of that.

'It's Denise MacBride,' she told him, edging round the gleaming pale blue Megane to the front of the shop. 'Wife of the owner.' It was not the most pure form of police procedure but the rookie constable who had responded to Arthur Innes' phone call had moved the dead woman. It was all too horrific to leave her where she was. They had carried her to the back of the car where there was space and laid her flat on her back. Her face was a mask of blood and two of her teeth had shattered with the impact of the fall.

'Your best guess?' Hall asked his favourite inspector. Jacquie knew that Hall didn't do guesses. Later he'd want t's crossed and i's dotted but for now the big picture would do.

Jacquie squatted alongside the Megane, then looked up at the showroom roof.

'I think she fell from there,' she said. 'The gallery.'

The gallery was where Geoff MacBride took his special clients, those with more money than sense. He showed them glossy brochures here, flipped on his laptop with all the specifications. He knew his business. Traditionally, the men were fascinated by woofers and tweeters, overhead camshafts, sat-nav capabilities and smart parking. It was the women who stressed over the shade of the interior and where the vanity mirror was. While he was explaining this, MacBride was popping a champagne cork (special deal from Asda in the High Street) and relieving the unsuspecting clients of a substantial amount of money.

Hall crouched beside the car. Behind him, SOCO had arrived with their Outbreak suits, as though Ebola had come to Leighford. They were not best pleased to see Hall and Jacquie already contaminating their precious crime scene, but they knew that those two knew their business and would tread as lightly as possible.

'We had an unusually observant paramedic on duty,' Jacquie told Hall. 'Everybody assumed suicide at first. Nasty fall — the steps up there are a bit of a challenge; the main access is from the office, which is still locked, so she must have taken the emergency stairs and there's only a very low rail. Then, he saw this,' she stepped backwards and crouched beside the dead woman, carefully lifting up one hand with gloved fingers. 'Broken nails.'

'A fight,' Hall nodded grimly. He stood up. Henry Hall was ageing well, but hours of crouching alongside bodies he could do without. 'A fight started up there . . .' He looked down again. 'There could be debris under those nails. She was pushed or thrown and ended up here. She must have bounced off the Megane,' and he ran his gloved hands over the roof, feeling the dent, 'and gravity brought her down between it and the glass.'

They looked at the corpse again. The dead woman was fully clothed, in jeans and a jumper. Her face was too much of a mess to see individual wounds and the blood had smeared over her shoulder and left breast. Her hair, dark and curly, was matted with blood.

All in all, it was not the most positive advertisement for MacBride's Motors, the Best on the South Coast.

* * *

Back in the nick, Tommy Morton was not saying anything and this was only partially because he was curled up asleep on the sofa in the Family Suite. Maxwell and Marilyn Fairbrother were sitting in the two armchairs, watching him. In a dim light, they could have passed for doting parents watching their only chick, even though he was more goose than swan. There was no clock in the suite, but Maxwell's inner timer knew it was not far short of five o'clock, or possibly even worse. They had talked to Tommy, asked over and over where his father was, but the only answer was 'away', or variations on that theme. Then he had suddenly curled up and gone to sleep, as only children can; even children with the weight of the world on their shoulders.

Maxwell leaned over and touched the social worker lightly on her arm. She jumped and confirmed his suspicion that she had been asleep for almost as long as Tommy. She blinked at him and licked her lips, mouthing, 'Sorry.' She sat up and ran her fingers through her hair and pointed to the door. They crept out into the corridor, propping the door open with a cushion.

'I think I'll get off home now, Marilyn, if you don't mind,' Maxwell said, just above a whisper.

'What if he wakes up?' she asked.

'Do you have children, Marilyn?'

'Well . . . no, not as yet.'

'As the owner of one,' Maxwell said, offering up a silent apology to Nolan, who had been owned by no man since he first opened his eyes, 'I can assure you that that child won't be awake for hours. In fact, if you can arrange it, let him sleep. I don't think he has slept properly for years.'

'We don't have a file on him,' she complained. 'Not until today, that is.'

'No.' Maxwell patted her arm. 'There is no blame to be laid here, Marilyn, unless it is at the feet of a dead woman. And then, it could belong at her mother's feet, or hers . . . who knows where these things begin? We just need to make sure that Tommy comes out of this as unscathed as possible. When he wakes up, if he still wants me, I'll come. But meanwhile, I have a boy who needs not to wake up and find both his parents have done a runner. Fair?'

She looked up at him. She had wondered why Tommy had asked for this man, who she had heard tended to be a bit of a loose cannon. But now she knew. She nodded, and slid back round the door, kicking the cushion aside and holding down the handle so there was no click. Maxwell watched her go, then turned for the foyer, and then the exit.

CHAPTER SEVEN

Jim Astley should have retired. Almost every joint in his body ached these days, it didn't matter how early he went to bed, he still woke up exhausted every morning. When he had decided, long aeons ago, to opt for pathology instead of the nuisance of working with the living, he had never thought he would be doing it for so long. He had never reached the heights of fame of Keith Simpson and Francis Camps and now he knew he never would; he was doomed to spend the rest of his life — and many mornings he hoped that would be measured in hours — cutting up the deceased of Leighford, checking for the incompetence of his peers. Donald, his assistant, had over the years taken much of the basic work off his hands and in fact had become a damn fine postmortem practitioner, but it would stick in Astley's throat to tell him as much. It came as no surprise therefore on that Tuesday morning to find that the day's customer was already prepped on the table and Donald was standing, gowned, masked and gloved, ready to begin when Astley was still in his overcoat.

The pathologist peered at the woman, laid out with her bagged hands by her side. 'Violent death, Donald?' he asked. 'Why was I not called?'

'It was dealt with on call, Dr A,' Donald said, breezily. Best not to let the old geezer know that they were watching his back these days. There had been a few howlers in his reports just lately and a middle of the night call wasn't going to make him any more accurate. But then, even the great Bernard Spilsbury had gone the same way. Sometimes, Donald wondered if there was such a thing as second-hand drinking; if so, Astley's home life would make him a prime candidate.

'Is there an identification yet?' Astley was trying to regain the upper hand.

'It's Denise MacBride,' Donald said, as though that should mean something.

It didn't, but Astley waited a moment before asking. Donald didn't offer any further information — it was all part of the game that made up their working day.

Astley sighed. 'Denise MacBride,' he said. 'Should I know her? It does sound faintly familiar.'

'MacBride's Motors. In town. You know, the big Renault dealership.'

'Ah, yes.' It was all starting to fall into place. 'Isn't her old man a JP or something.'

'A JP, exactly,' Donald said. 'Also he is on the Council, though not leader, much to his annoyance. He is also Chair of Governors at Leighford High School and a number of junior ones as well; basically, with Geoff MacBride, if there is a chair, he likes to have his arse in it. Rumour is, he wants to be our next MP.'

'Yes.' Astley had him now. Superficially good looking, though going over a bit. Had to take care these days which direction the photos were taken from. Slimy, snake-oil salesman type. Had been a bit of a pain in the neck when Mrs Astley had been picked up one night drunk and disorderly in charge of a pushbike. It wasn't the drunk and disorderly that was a problem so much as the fact that she thought the bike was a buggy and she had lost the baby out of it. Hushing up had been the order of the day, but MacBride had been a hard nut to crack — he wore his JP hat rather literally. 'So, what happened? Hit and run?'

'Funny you should say that,' Donald said, with his usual mordant humour. 'She was hit by a car. Or rather, she hit it.'

Astley blew out his cheeks in exasperation. 'I'm going to change now, Donald. When I come back, do you think you could have marshalled your thoughts sufficiently to be able to tell me what happened without any puns or similar jocundities?'

Oh, oh. He'd started using words which Donald doubted actually existed. That was never a good sign. The big pathology assistant lined up the instruments yet again and stood back from the table in an attitude of muted attention.

When Astley returned, he was in full kit, from his wellies to the natty little hat holding back his few remaining hairs. He flexed his latexed fingers and looked at Donald again, an eyebrow cocked in query.

'Denise MacBride,' Donald intoned. 'Date of birth to be confirmed when her records come up but believed to be forty-two years old. Wife of Geoffrey MacBride, mother of two girls. Found last night — perhaps I should say seen last night, as she was inside the building and the passer-by was outside — at around midnight, by a man walking his dog.'

'Bit of a cliché,' Astley remarked, half to himself.

'Where would we be without them, though?' Donald said and Astley smiled his agreement. Donald relaxed a little. The old man was starting to enjoy himself, as far as their job could ever be said to be enjoyable.

'Where was she?' Astley asked. 'How could the dog walker see her if she was inside? Is he a peeping tom as well as dog lover?'

'No, no, nothing like that,' Donald said. 'She was in the car showroom; she'd fallen from the gallery, like a kind of mezzanine extension they use as an office, and bounced off a Megane and landed up against the window. I've seen the pictures — it was a hell of a fall.'

'So . . . since we seem to be doing clichés this morning; did she fall or was she pushed?'

Donald looked across at the brief notes at his elbow, but before he could answer, a buzzer sounded. Someone was in the office and needed a word.

'Nip and see who that is, Donald,' Astley said. 'I'll just do the preliminary external description.'

Donald had already done that, but forbore to say. He pulled off his gloves and went through the swing doors out to the office. He wasn't gone long before he shouldered his way back in, reading a fat file as he did so. He stood in the middle of the floor, humming to himself under his breath and nodding.

After a minute or two, Astley could stand it no longer. 'Donald, can you share, do you think? I'm on tenterhooks, here.'

'Mm?' The big man looked up and refocused his eyes. 'Sorry, got a bit engrossed there. This,' and he hefted the fat file, 'is Mrs MacBride's notes.'

'Anything helpful?'

'Not sure,' said Donald, wrinkling his brow. 'The first thought of the police was suicide, then a paramedic noticed torn nails, hence the bagged hands. So, murder, they thought. Now . . . well, I dunno.'

Astley tutted. He was working on making Donald a proper professional, but every now and again he lapsed. 'Why don't you know?' he asked, the implied criticism laid on with a trowel.

'Well, this file is almost all from Psych. She has a few other bits; the kids, you know, and a broken arm at some point. But mostly Psych.'

Astley knew what was coming.

'She's red flagged here. Suicidal ideation, on more than one occasion. Bit of a bugger, isn't it? Makes the whole thing a bit more complicated.'

'Or simpler,' Astley said. 'Perhaps she chucked herself over then changed her mind, grabbed at something, you know?'

'The crime scene pics are quite clear,' Donald said. 'Just a smooth, low rail to grab at. The most that might happen is a cleanly broken nail, not the ragged look we have here. It looks to me as though it was staged to look like a suicide. Most people would assume it would be a shoo-in with her record.'

Astley winced. He opened his mouth and then closed it again. Some things just weren't worth arguing over. Instead, he reached over to the tray Donald had already prepared for him and chose a reamer and a petri dish.

'Let's see what she has under these nails, then, shall we?' he said and bent to his task. After a moment or two, he looked up at Donald. 'I wish you wouldn't do that, Donald,' he said, peevishly.

'What?' Donald had been toying with a small and hopefully undetected passing of wind, but hadn't yet quite followed through on his intention. Could the old bugger predict the future these days?

Astley gestured to the petri dish. 'Clean the nails, that kind of thing. You've been watching too much CSI, my lad, that's your problem.'

Donald looked aggrieved. 'I haven't done any such thing,' he said, his voice a petulant whine. 'All I did was measure, examine, you know the drill. I wouldn't . . .'

Astley cut him short. 'Well, that's odd, then,' he said. 'Because someone has cleaned these nails, and since she died. It's a rough job and yet there is no bleeding or bruising.'

Donald tried to stop his eyes from lighting up. A woman was dead after all. But still . . . 'Murder,' he breathed.

* * *

Long before Astley and Donald had met over his wife's body, Geoff MacBride had been told she was dead. In fact, it had not been as simple as that. He had been phoned by the police to tell him that there had been an incident at MacBride Motors. Then they had added the fact that it was a fatality. Only then had they added the fact that it was his wife. It was almost an afterthought on their part when they asked where he might be, please? They had phoned his home and found his daughters there alone and, whilst not against the law, they were surprised that he was not present. Unless, of course, he was out of town . . . ?

He had taken the first sentence of the call lying in bed, his still sweaty arm across Fiona Braymarr's body. The second sentence had him on his feet and the rest on his knees, bent over as if in pain. Fiona looked over her shoulder at him and she languidly swung her legs over her side of the bed and came round to him, patting him absently on the shoulder. Even in the circumstances he was in, the sight and smell of her naked body had its usual effect but for once he kept it to himself. Somehow, it struck even him that it wasn't quite seemly to be told of the death of your wife when in the throes of an erection.

'No,' he said, eventually. 'I'm here in Leighford. I . . . I had a meeting and had a little too much to drink. I . . . well, obviously in my position, I can't drink and drive . . .'

'That applies to everyone, sir,' the dry, cold police voice informed him.

'Yes, yes, of course. Well, I decided to stay here, until the morning, you know. Until I could drive.'

'If you could give me your location, sir,' the police voice said, 'we can send a car for you?'

'No, no, it's fine,' he said, not thinking, but noticing that Fiona had walked away on silent feet and gone into the bathroom, closing the door firmly behind her.

'Well, surely not, sir,' the voice went on. 'You will still be over the limit, unless you finished drinking very early in the evening. Our squad car has just dropped a social worker off with your girls; obviously, they were concerned when you weren't at home and we felt it would be best if someone was there. In the . . .' and the voice paused for the first time, 'circumstances.'

* * *

And shortly after that, Jacquie Maxwell had slid into bed beside her husband. In some ways, it hardly seemed worth it; in about an hour it would be time to be up and about, but there was something about the chance to warm her cold feet on his warm bum, to feel the solidity of him, that couldn't be passed up. He gave a little scream as her icy soles connected, then he turned over and enveloped her in his arms. She lay there for a moment, enjoying the warmth and comfort then said, not knowing whether he was awake enough to hear, 'Have you ever felt like killing me, Max?'

'Only when you put your cold feet on my nice warm bum,' he said.

She chuckled into his chest. 'So, that would be yes, then?'

'Mm.'

She lay there for a few more minutes, then said, in a different voice, 'Will Nolan ever want to kill me?'

There was no answer to that, except a kiss on top of her head. As usual, she had managed to tap into his thoughts. Tommy Morton had been in Maxwell's head, waking and sleeping, since he had left the police station. The little boy peering out from the pale face, the need to know that his father was safe, that his one solid mooring in his life would still be there for him. Tommy thought he knew the score. He had watched hours of *Law and Order*, both UK and otherwise and he knew that the DA would cut him a deal. He knew that he would be sent to a juvenile facility and then come out the other end unscathed. And if his dad was out there, waiting, it would all be fine.

Except, it wouldn't be fine. There were two likelihoods. They wouldn't find his dad and Tommy would be sent somewhere horrendous from which he would emerge broken and damaged. Or, they *would* find his dad and then he would be sent somewhere horrendous. Etcetera. Etcetera.

Maxwell had never knowingly met Mrs Morton. But he had a feeling that, had he had the dubious pleasure, he would have happily knifed her himself.

'No,' he muttered finally into his sleeping wife's hair. 'No, he won't ever want to kill you.' And he lay, awake, keeping her safe, until the dawn. The next day held some difficult interviews for Maxwell, but none would be as difficult as the one Geoff MacBride would undergo. He had been collected from Fiona Braymarr's hotel foyer in the wee small hours by a police driver with a face like a hatchet. The man had not exchanged a single word with MacBride on the way to the police station but that put him on a level playing field with Fiona; she had not emerged from the bathroom while he had dressed hurriedly and had not replied to his goodbyes through the door. He knew, as surely as if she had put it in writing, that his new status as widower had been somewhat of a game changer. He seemed to be carrying a stone in his chest, but whether it was grief for Denise or for Fiona he couldn't tell. He had always prided himself on being king of the love 'em and leave 'em brigade, but now, he wasn't so sure.

His arrival at the nick was low key, but not as low key as he had hoped. A photographer from the *Leighford Advertiser*, pyjama leg visibly poking out from under his jeans, had jumped out from the shadows as the car made the turn into the car park. MacBride knew that his startled face would not appear in print just yet — he had tangled with the editor often enough to make that gentleman a little wary — but this was not going well. In fact, he felt a little sick and as woozy as he would have had he had so much as a sip of alcohol. To his surprise, he realised it was probably shock.

He was escorted into the police station by his silent guardian, who punched a code into the pad by the door, which quietly opened inwards on a brief puff of warm, stale air. The desk sergeant looked up from his keyboard and nodded to the driver, who left his charge standing there as he went back out to his lonely vigil, tucked into the layby below the Dam, with a flask of coffee, a bag of Krispy Kremes and a well-thumbed copy of *Fifty Shades of Grey* he had found tucked under his wife's pillow. He gave a little chuckle as he turned back to page four hundred and sixty, clearly, if the fingernail marks were any guide, his wife's favourite bit. Boy, did she have a surprise coming when he got home! Kill his wife? Not just yet, at any rate.

* * *

The desk sergeant took his time checking Geoff MacBride's credentials. He reached under the desk and foraged around for a minute or so, not taking his eyes off the man's face. Finally, he came up with a breathalyser machine and took his own sweet time fitting a mouthpiece. He handed it over.

'Take two deep breaths, please, sir, then blow steadily into this until you hear the beep.'

MacBride didn't take it from him. 'Why? I haven't been driving.'

'No, sir,' the desk sergeant didn't waver. 'It's just routine. We don't want anyone to say we took advantage of you when you were under the influence. Ha.' It may have been a laugh, but it was hard to tell.

MacBride decided to mount his high horse. 'Am I under arrest?' he asked. 'I am in some distress, you know. My wife . . .' he paused as it suddenly hit him full force, '. . . my wife is dead.'

'Yes, sir. I am sorry for your loss.' The sergeant might as well have been reading from a cue card, such was the lack of empathy in his voice. 'But we have to follow procedure, even so. Please take two deep breaths and . . .'

'Blow steadily, yes, I know the score.' MacBride blew until the beep went and handed the gizmo back across the counter.

The desk sergeant looked at the meter quizzically.

'Well?' MacBride was starting to get testy now.

'Well, sir,' the policeman said, levelly. 'It would appear that your alcohol level is . . .' he gave the meter another glance, '. . . zero.' He shared a wintry smile. 'Perhaps you would like a repeat? That is your right, of course.'

'Why would I want a repeat?' As soon as the words were out of his mouth, MacBride saw his error.

'I really don't know, sir. Except that perhaps you would expect it to be higher, as you had to check in to a hotel because you were not fit to drive.' Again, he smiled but it had no humour in it. 'If you would just like to take a seat over there, someone will be with you shortly.'

'Good.' MacBride's high horse, having briefly thrown him to the ground, had cantered back up and he was firmly in its saddle. 'I do want to see my girls. They will be distraught.'

The desk sergeant made a brief note and nodded. 'Naturally, sir. We will be as quick as we can. Meanwhile, your girls are being looked after in their home by social services, so please don't worry on that score.'

The clock in the foyer had a very annoying tick. It did one very loud one, then two quiet ones followed by three counts of silence. Geoff MacBride became a little mesmerised by it after a while and, as happened to so many people sitting in the foyer of Leighford nick, waiting to learn their fate, he finally slept.

The desk sergeant, hearing his faint snores, ducked down behind his desk and quietly picked up the phone and jabbed some numbers.

'Yes?' Hall sounded tired, but who wouldn't at this god-forsaken hour on the cusp of dawn?

'Guv? It's Mason. On the desk.'

'Mason. Can't you speak up a bit? You're very quiet.'

'Not really,' Mason mouthed. 'I've got MacBride here. He's asleep in a chair. Zero alcohol and doesn't seem too cut up about the missus. Just thought I'd let you know.'

There was a silence. In any other person but Henry Hall, it would have been filled with a satisfied smile. 'Thanks, Mason. Good to know. Let's let him sleep. Nothing like a crick in the neck for making an interview go with a swing.' And with a click, the phone went down.

* * *

Breakfast chez Maxwell happened as breakfasts will and it was testament to Nolan's reliable sleep patterns that the dramas of the night had all passed him by. He ate his Coco Pops, recited his homework poem under his breath and was mildly surprised, though pleased, that Dads and Mums seemed more than usually happy to see him. A bit of parental adoration never came amiss, after all.

Jacquie got up and kissed him one last time. Maxwell raised a cheek to her and got a hug for his pains. She was the only one in the house who shared her family position with two dead women — wife and mother; it was more dangerous than you might think.

'Ring me when you have a moment, about . . . you know,' Maxwell said as she went out of the door.

'As soon as I know anything,' she said and dashed headlong down the stairs, having just seen the time. There would be enough to do this morning, without being late.

Nolan watched her go. 'Is everything all right, Dads?' he asked.

Maxwell looked at him, startled. 'Yes, mate,' he said, ruffling his hair and then hastily stroking it flat. 'Why do you ask?'

'Well, all the kissing and cuddling. I like it, I really do, but there was a lot of it this morning.'

Maxwell forbore to add to the count of hugs and kisses. 'It's just work, Nole. You know how it can be.'

Nolan sighed and shovelled in some more brown goo. 'Yes,' he said. 'I know it's important. But I do worry about you two sometimes.'

'Don't worry, mate,' Maxwell said. 'We're fine. It's just . . .'

'Yes?' Nolan's huge brown eyes were on him and he knew it was useless to lie. That kid had been able to spot a prevarication almost since birth.

'Mums had to go out last night, to see about a poor lady who had had an accident. And one of the children at school, well, his mum was killed.'

Nolan thought about it for a minute. 'Same lady?'

'No. Two different people.'

'Well, that's very sad,' Nolan announced at last. 'No wonder Mums was feeling a bit cuddly.' He glanced up. 'But you're all right, though?'

'Never better.' So, Maxwell thought, here we are. The kid is worrying about us and we're not even in a home yet.

There was a toot from a car horn down in the street. 'Oops.' Saved by the toot. 'Mrs Plocker. Come on, let's get weaving.'

Nolan gave him a shove as he slid down from his chair. 'No time for weaving, Dads. We've got to get to school.'

Pausing only to pick an errant Coco Pop from his son's jumper, Maxwell jumped to it. No time for weaving, indeed. 'Scarf? Gloves? Lunchbox? Do you know your poem?'

Four nods and his boy was off, down the stairs and out into the frosty morning. 'February's ice and sleet,' warbled Maxwell as he dashed along behind him, 'Freeze the toes right off your feet.'

Nolan was clambering into Mrs P's 4x4 as he reached the door and he could tell that he and Plocker were already hard at it. How those boys still had stuff to say to each other day after day, he had no idea. But he thanked his lucky star they did — Nolan wasn't an only child while Plocker was around. The two boys gave him a perfunctory wave and Mrs P held up her thumb, the morning shorthand which meant, more or less, 'I will pick him up and take him back to mine tonight if that's okay. Ring me if you want him to stay over.' The woman was a saint — Saint Mrs Plocker; he could almost see the window in the chancel now.

'Bye,' he called and went back in to fish White Surrey out of the garage. It was cold for riding a bike, but it would soon be spring. If he said it often enough, it might be true. Jamming his hat on his head and giving his scarf an extra turn, he pedalled up the hill to the main road.

* * *

DI Jacquie Carpenter-Maxwell, as she became moments before she walked into Leighford Police Station every morning, was surprised to see what looked like a pile of old clothes in the corner of the foyer as she signed in and she raised an eyebrow at the desk sergeant, all squeaky clean and alert at the beginning of his shift.

'Mr MacBride,' he said, reading her eyebrow like the pro that he was.

'Still?' She leaned over and checked. Yes, definitely MacBride, if a little more dishevelled than one normally saw him, leering out of the pages of the *Advertiser*. 'Shouldn't he have been sent home last night, with an appointment for today? His wife has just died, you know — he has children.'

The desk sergeant picked up a post-it and showed it to her, stuck to the end of his forefinger.

'GM came in stone cold sober,' it read. 'Went to sleep and so left him there. PS He clearly did it — put me down for a tenner.'

'Would you like to explain that last bit?' she said, icily.

The desk man turned it round and blushed to the roots of his hair. 'Oh, I think that is . . . ooh, what's her name, you know, whatsit, in the office, pregnant. We've got a bit of a book on when it will be born.' He smiled, but without much hope.

'"He clearly did it"?'

'Oh. Ha ha. That's a bit of a joke, we've been joshing her, you know how you do. Her old man . . . he clearly did it. Hah.'

'And the date?'

'What date? I think she's married. It wouldn't be the date . . .'

'The date of birth?'

He knew he had lost but for some reason carried on regardless. 'I think he must have already filled that in. I don't expect he had put down the bet.'

'Well, do him a favour,' Jacquie said. 'Don't put the bet on. Tanya had a lovely little boy Wednesday before last.'

'Oh, yes, *Tanya* did. But what about . . . ?' The hope died in his eyes and he looked down, beaten. 'Sorry, guv.'

'Yes, well, let's pretend this never happened. But what about the sober? What does that mean?'

The desk man nodded over her shoulder and as she turned around, the old pile of clothes became more recognizably

JP, councillor and school governor extraordinaire, Geoffrey MacBride. 'His excuse was he was drunk,' he hurriedly said, 'when they found him in a hotel. But his level was zero.'

She nodded and patted his hand, still stuck to the post-it. 'Thanks,' she said. 'Useful. Get rid of the post-it, there's a good sergeant.' Then, pinning on the smile, she turned to where Geoff MacBride was unravelling himself from his slumped position. 'Mr MacBride,' she said, advancing with her hand extended. 'Thank you so much for coming in.'

'I didn't so much come in as was dragged,' he said, running his tongue over his teeth. 'My mouth is like the bottom of a budgie's cage,' he said.

'I suppose that's the drink,' she said, still with a smile.

He looked at her, assessing, deciding whether she would be susceptible, even though he was unshaven and rather tousled. He knew this woman. She was married to that mad old bugger Maxwell, from up at the school . . . sorry, Academy. She was probably ripe for a bit of a tumble, he had to be over the hill in that way, surely. And she was a tasty bit of . . .

'I said,' she spoke slowly and clearly, 'I suppose that's the drink.'

'Sorry.' MacBride had messed up already and he had only been awake two minutes. This was no time to lay on the charm. Denise was dead. God knew where the kids were. He had been caught out in a lie. And he knew that Fiona Braymarr would not be giving him an alibi any time soon. He decided to fall on his sword. 'The drink was a lie. I was . . . I'm not proud of this, erm . . .'

'DI Carpenter-Maxwell,' she told him, although she knew he was perfectly well aware who she was.

'DI Carpenter-Maxwell. My wife is . . . was . . . a lovely woman in many ways, but we didn't get on, if you catch my drift.'

'Shall we go through into an interview room?' Jacquie interrupted. 'This isn't really a conversation for the foyer, is it?'

'No, perhaps not.' MacBride collected his overcoat which he had been using as a pillow and allowed himself to be ushered through the door. 'But . . . well, long story cut short, DI Carpenter-Maxwell, my wife didn't understand me. I was with . . .'

'Interview room,' Jacquie said, shortly. 'Please, Mr MacBride, don't make me ask again.'

She opened another door, showed him in and stood in the doorway. 'Tea? Coffee?'

'Oh, yes, thank you. Coffee, black, one sugar.' He ran a hand over his hair. They always came round in the end. She was bringing him a drink. He was home and dry.

'I'll send it in,' she said and closed the door behind her. If there was any possible way she could avoid doing the first interview with the slimy little toad, she would take it. She was just making for the foyer for a token for the machine when, with a clatter of feet, Rick Shopley appeared in the bottom of the stairwell.

'Ma'am,' he said, with a nod. 'Seen your old man today? We met last night.'

Jacquie had heard the truncated version — no doubt there would be more detail that evening. 'So I understand. Umm, Rick? Can you do me a favour?'

'I was up all night, guv,' he whined. 'With that little toe . . . lad who knifed his mum. Might have knifed his mum.' The correction was swift and seamless.

'I was also up for much of the night,' she told him, 'but of course, if you need to get off home, I do understand. I can find someone else.'

Shopley could hear the edge in a voice as well as the next man. Rumour had it that this tart was a bit of a favourite with Old Man Hall, so best play nice. 'No, no, I can help. What's the problem?'

'In there,' she jerked a thumb at the interview room, 'is Mr Geoffrey MacBride, widower of this parish. He became a widower last night because his wife took a header onto a Renault Megane, low mileage, one careful owner. Have a word with the desk, then have a chat with him. Oh, and can you take him a tea. White, three sugars? Thanks, Rick. I owe you one.'

'No problem,' he said, to her retreating back. 'It's a pleasure.' At least that was his good deed done early — he could be as much of a bastard as he liked now for the rest of the day, no harm, no foul, no Karmic damage. Lucky, lucky Geoffrey MacBride.

* * *

Peter Maxwell walked into the foyer of his place of work humming a little tune. He had remembered to remove his cycle clips two days running and so far the day hadn't hit him round the back of the head with anything unpleasant. True, the night's traumas had left his eyes a little baggy, but he still had a spring in his step as he put his foot on the first step of the stairs to his mezzanine eyrie.

'Mr Maxwell.' A crisp voice behind him made him pause, but when nothing else came, he lifted the next foot.

'Mr Maxwell. Could you step into my office for a moment, please? I think we could take this chance to place our meeting in the schedule, if you have a moment.'

'Mrs Braymarr.' Maxwell delayed turning round. He could feel the chill already, as the Ice Giants moved out of their usual home of Niflheim and took up residence in Leighford High. 'How can I help you?' He turned and was again surprised to see an attractive woman standing there, rather than the Medusa he had feared.

'By stepping into my office. Did I not make myself clear?' He realised what was odd about her. She moved very little, like a reptile conserving energy on a sunless day. 'I have you at the top of my list for meetings and there's no time like the present.'

The historian in Maxwell might have disagreed with her, but he chose to let it go. 'Indeed not.' Maxwell looked with extravagant over-acting to right and left. 'I do seem to be free as it happens. Where is your office?'

She gestured to James Diamond's door.

'Legs not here today, then?' Maxwell said, blandly.

'If by "Legs" you mean Mr Diamond — an amusing epithet, I should say, Mr Maxwell — then he is away today, yes. He is looking around other schools in the academy family here in Leighford, to see if anything suits.'

'Ah. Family; that sounds warm and fuzzy enough, I suppose. Let's have this meeting, then, Mrs Braymarr. Why put off until tomorrow what we can do today, hmm? Lead the way.'

Fiona Braymarr pushed open James Diamond's door (as Maxwell promised himself he would always call it) and walked around and sat behind the desk. It was James Diamond's room and yet it wasn't — the walls were the same, Maxwell was pretty sure, but after that, it was moot. The desk was now angled so that the daylight made a nimbus around Fiona Braymarr's head, making it hard to see her expression. All of the pictures had gone, to be replaced by charts and calendars in various colours. The desk was bare. Diamond had always kept a small amount of chaos on his desk, just enough to make it look as though he was working. Now, all it held was a tablet, angled just so to prevent anyone reading it upside down, and Fiona Braymarr's hand, one finger tapping as she looked at Maxwell with her head on one side.

'So, Mr Maxwell . . . may I call you Peter?'

'Well, you can,' he conceded, 'but no one since my mother has called me that. Everyone calls me Max.'

'I see. A nickname.' She tapped on the tablet and frowned slightly. 'I'm afraid I don't really approve of that kind of thing, Mr Maxwell. So we'll keep it formal, shall we?'

'Perfect.' It wasn't like Maxwell to use one word where a thousand would do, but this woman was beginning to rile him.

'I had you at the top of my interview list for several reasons, Mr Maxwell and I think it only fair that we take them one by one, so you can explain or rebut as you think fit.'

A smile was all he could manage. Peter Maxwell was that unusual man, a multi-tasker, but even he found it hard to make polite noises whilst imagining beating someone around the head with a frying pan.

'Firstly, I have got the impression that you are somewhat of the school clown.'

In the silence, Maxwell lifted his chin to let the metaphorical bow tie whizz round and shifted his feet slightly in his size 26 shoes.

'Do you have any comment?' Her smile was acid.

'I lighten the mood if I can,' he said. 'Sometimes it makes the world spin a little easier. But clown . . . no, I take exception to that. Wit. Raconteur. But not clown.'

'I understand you leapt upon Mr Diamond a week or so ago. In your office.'

'A misunderstanding.' How in heaven's name had she got hold of that? It wasn't Sylv, and he knew it wasn't Helen. It could only be Diamond. The stupid man had surely not entered it in the accident book, had he?

'I read the details in the accident book.'

Bingo.

'It could have been very serious.'

'Can we just say,' he said, still just keeping the frying pan out of sight, 'that it was not intentional, and leave it at that?'

She tapped her tablet again and peered at it. 'The next thing I need to raise is exam results.'

His hackles rose so high he felt that he must look like a cockatoo. 'My results are the best in the school,' he pointed out as calmly as he could. 'Always have been. Always will be, while I am here.'

'There has been no improvement,' she said coldly, 'as laid down in the action plan. Can you explain?'

Maxwell looked at her in stunned disbelief. He was not exactly a byword where statisticians gathered, this he knew, but he felt he was on safe ground. 'How can I improve on best?' he asked. 'And besides, I don't think in terms of results; it's the kids who count, surely. If they do their best, how much more can we expect? You get good years, you get great years. I've never really known how that works, but every teacher will agree that that's the way the cookie crumbles.'

He had hoped that appealing to her inner teacher might help, but she didn't seem to have one.

'It isn't the position which needs improvement,' she said, ignoring him almost entirely, 'but the number of As and A stars. There are a number of fail grades, which need attention.'

Maxwell mentally added her hazy grasp of grammar to his reasons to hate the woman with a passion. 'Fail grades?' He cast his mind back. 'Three. In the whole GCSE cohort. None at A level. Are you seriously expecting one hundred percent success?'

She raised an eyebrow. 'It is that attitude, Mr Maxwell, that has brought Leighford High School to the state it is in. However, if we can't reach consensus on this point, I will move on.' Again, she tapped the tablet and read her notes. 'Ah, yes. Your popularity with the student body.'

Maxwell shrugged. He had never gone out for popularity. He didn't want to be friends with the kids. They were just . . . well . . . kids. He wanted to do his best for them. He wanted them to do their best for him. If that ended up with them liking him, that was a bonus. If they didn't, it was their loss. 'Is that a question?'

'Apparently, they have names for you that they use quite openly. Mad Max, for example.'

'Bound to, really, wouldn't you think? Especially with the new franchise.'

'I beg your pardon?' She leaned forward, a pained, eager to understand smile on her face. Now he knew who she reminded him of — Maggie Thatcher at the height of her powers. And she was as dangerous.

'Mad Max. Beyond the Hippodrome — sorry, Thunderdome, I should say. Mel Gibson. Tina Turner. Now repackaged with Tom Hardy.'

She shook her head. Perhaps she was confusing the actor with the author of Wessex or the captain of the *Victory*. Then again . . .

'Charlize Theron.' He waited for a response. 'Well, not to worry. You clearly aren't a film fan. But yes, they call me Mad Max. But it could be worse.'

Again, the tap. Then she raised her head and leaned forward, pushing the tablet aside and lacing her fingers together as though in prayer. 'I'm glad you mentioned films, Mr Maxwell, because it brings me on to my final point. I have been looking around the premises and I notice you have . . . personalised your office. With film posters.'

'I have.'

'They will have to go.'

'May I ask why?'

'Mr Maxwell, there is no room for individuality in my academy.'

'*Your* academy?' This was clearly not a slip of the tongue. Maxwell doubted that Fiona Braymarr ever made one of those.

'My academy. I am a reasonable woman, Mr Maxwell,' she said, with what Maxwell considered was an admirably straight face, 'so I will give you until the end of term to remove them. But if, at that point, they are still present, they will be removed and destroyed.'

'I will send the bill,' he said. 'Some of those posters are worth rather a lot of money.' As soon as he said it, he knew he had made a tactical error.

'In that case,' she smiled, 'all the more reason to remove them. Along with the posters, you will also remove your kettle and all coffee and tea making paraphernalia. All foodstuffs. All non-regulation furniture. In fact, all items which were not issued by the education authority are to be gone by the end of term. But before, if possible.'

'And if they are not gone by then?' He knew the answer.

'Frankly, Mr Maxwell, I don't expect that to be an outcome. Besides, the whole thing may be moot anyway.' She stood up and walked round him to open the door. 'I wouldn't expect you to leave your valuable belongings behind. And at current showing, I somehow doubt you will still be here after Easter.'

Maxwell had seen a lot in his millennia of teaching, but this took the biscuit — banned from the premises though they were. 'A threat, Mrs Braymarr?'

'A promise, Mr Maxwell.' Ah, the dependable cliché. She left the door open and went back to her desk and looked out of the window. Without turning round, she said, 'Please close the door on your way out.'

* * *

'What's this?' Geoffrey MacBride peered into the khaki liquid in the police polystyrene.

Rick Shopley looked at him. He thought this man was a JP, car showroom owner and all-round smartarse. Rather an odd question, but maybe it was the shock of the night's events. 'It's tea, sir.'

'But . . . oh, never mind. Who are you?'

'DS Shopley, sir.'

'Where's DI Carpenter-Maxwell?'

'Called away, I'm afraid.' Rick Shopley's smile was like the silver plate on a coffin, but he could lie for England. 'I'm sorry for your loss, by the way.'

Geoff MacBride doubted that. Shopley's flat delivery sounded so much like every US cop show going, except that this sneering sergeant didn't exactly have the curves of Marissa Hargitty from *Law and Order SVU*. Shopley reached over and switched on the tape recorder. 'What are you doing?' MacBride asked, suddenly alarmed.

'Just routine, sir,' Shopley smiled thinly.

'I'm a fucking JP, sergeant,' MacBride reminded him, 'and it's not routine at all. Unless, of course, I'm a suspect . . .'

'Like I said, sir,' Shopley said, in a tight voice around his tight smile, 'just routine.'

MacBride folded his arms and sat back. 'If I am a suspect,' he said blandly, 'I'd like my solicitor present.'

The sergeant's smirk gave way to a proper smile and he flicked the machine off. 'All right, sir,' he said sweetly. 'No need for us to get heavy. Just a few points — for the record, you understand?' He pulled a notebook from his pocket and clicked his biro. 'When did you see your wife last?'

'When do I get to see my girls?' MacBride countered.

'As soon as possible, sir,' Shopley told him. 'This won't take long.'

'Er,' Geoff MacBride was trying to concentrate, clear his mind of the demons crowded into it. 'I don't know. Eight? Seven? Last night, not late — that's as accurate as I can be. It was just an ordinary evening. I didn't know . . .'

Shopley ignored the potential histrionics. 'Where was this, sir?' he started scribbling.

'At home, of course.'

'Did you go out, sir?'

'Out?' MacBride was tapping his finger on the polystyrene cup, watching the ripples on the greasy surface of the tea as though the answer lay there. 'Um, yes. Yes. I went for a drive.' He had come close to spilling his guts to that rather lovely DI, but he had himself a little more in hand now. This guy didn't look the type to understand that a man's wife didn't understand him. Judging by his clothes, rumpled and lived in, he didn't even have a wife, let alone an extra-mural sex life of Byzantine complexity.

'On your own?'

'Of course.'

'Do you often do that, sir?'

MacBride felt the red mist rising. Every question this shaven-headed shit asked him was like a needle in his testicles. *Christ,* he realized as his skin crawled, *he thinks I killed her.* 'No.' The distraught widower was trying to keep it all together but everything was unravelling fast. His old granny used to recite some guff about when first we practice to deceive — well, he thought he had had plenty of practice, but he was making a right hash of this, he knew it in his bones. 'No, I had a new Captur,' — how he wished he hadn't chosen that model out of the many in his head. A psychologist would make hay with that — 'I needed to try out.'

'At night, sir?'

'Yes,' MacBride shouted, suddenly tired of the Torquemada thing. 'Checking the lights, the performance in frosty conditions. It's just a little extra service I give my clients.'

Shopley nodded. 'I'm sure they appreciate it, sir,' he smiled. 'Tell me, was your wife going out too? As far as you know?'

'She didn't say so,' MacBride told him.

'Perhaps she went to the showroom to meet you,' Shopley suggested. 'When you took the car back.'

MacBride was silent and Shopley made a note.

'So,' the DS filled the gap in the conversation, 'you expected to find her at home when you got back?'

Geoffrey MacBride was a far from stupid man. Sergeant Shopley was digging a big hole for him to fall into.

'Ordinarily, yes, but I didn't go home. I went for a drink.'

'Where was that, sir?' Shopley sat poised, pen in hand.

'The Ellisdon.'

'Ah,' Shopley nodded. 'The new hotel, overlooking the Dam. Very nice.'

'Yes.' MacBride's mind was racing. 'Yes. I got talking to some people. Had a couple too many; you know how it is. A few years ago, I'd have risked it. But these days . . . well, you boys in blue; CCTV. Can't be too careful.'

'No, indeed, sir. Er . . . these people you met at the Ellisdon, could you give me their names, please?'

'Oh, God.' MacBride took a swig of tea, as classic a case of displacement activity as Shopley had ever seen. 'Um, now you've asked me. I didn't know them. One of them was Alan, I think. The other . . . no, it's gone.'

'Locals, were they?'

'No,' MacBride shook his head, then realised he was being too emphatic and stopped abruptly. 'No, reps. Moved on by now, I shouldn't wonder.'

'Never mind,' Shopley said, with another of his disconcerting smiles. 'No doubt they will be in the hotel register. What room were you in, sir? Just for the record, you know.'

MacBride had no option but to throw his toys out of the pram. He was so far in the shit now that a tantrum was his only recourse. This hatchet-faced idiot was not an idiot at all — in fact, as he looked into the DS's eyes, he saw contempt there and he just lost it. In his panic, he almost sounded sincere. 'Look here, sergeant,' he blustered. 'Enough is enough. I don't understand why I am being treated like some kind of criminal here, just because I had a few drinks with some strangers.' Was it his imagination, or did Shopley's eyebrow raise just a tad? 'My wife is dead. My girls must be distraught. I must get home.' He got up, knocking the table so the tepid tea spilled over and ran over the edge and on to his trousers. 'I must go home.'

Shopley skilfully avoided the spilt tea and closed his notebook carefully. 'Yes, sir, of course.' He opened the door and called to a passing policeman. 'Constable, show Mr MacBride to the car park, will you?' He turned to the car salesman. 'A car is waiting for you, sir. We'll be in touch.'

MacBride's smile was little more than a grimace. Rick Shopley leaned against the wall and watched him go, then opened his notebook again. This was not the one he used in court, not the one he left out on his desk. This was the one he used to jot down what was really going on. And he smiled as he clicked his biro and wrote — 'guilty as fuck.'

CHAPTER EIGHT

That February Tuesday was treating no one very well. Maxwell simmered through the rest of the day planning, as were many of the staff, to boycott the daily meeting called by Fiona Braymarr. James Diamond had not even returned to the building after his day of looking around the other schools. Long, long ago he had decided that he was not really cut out for teaching 5-year-olds. He had never understood the paroxysms of delight some of his colleagues went into when speaking of their enthusiasm, their eagerness to learn, the sheer joy of being in a room with thirty wriggling, weeing, snot-streaked kids at once. So he had not had a great day.

Bernard Ryan had had a much better day. He had spent most of it at home, having pleaded the headaches before morning break. The only one of the SLT left standing was poor beleaguered Jane Taylor, who really *did* have a headache, but hadn't been as fast as Ryan when it came to skiving off. Amongst the rest of the staff, panic, bloody-mindedness and insane levels of stress spun their toxic web and tangled them in it.

Watching from his balcony, Maxwell could almost smell the fear. Had the staff been a herd of wildebeest, Fiona Braymarr was the lioness, stalking them through the grasses of the Serengeti. Maxwell had just reached the point of decorating the scene with a whispering David Attenborough when his phone rang in his office, he answered it with less than his usual elan. 'Maxwell.'

'Max?' Jacquie was immediately on edge. Where was Mr Burns' 'Ahoy ahoy'? What about 'War Office'? 'Are you all right? Is someone with you?'

'Yes, I'm all right. No, not a soul is here. And I mean that literally. And as you know, when I say literally, it is literally true.'

'As long as . . .'

'Can I tell you about this when we get home? We've been Braymarred. If there isn't such a word, there should be. I'm sure it will be in the Oxford Inconcise by the next edition. How are you? It's nice to hear a human voice.'

'As bad as that? My day is not going too well, but at least I haven't been Braymarred. We will need you this afternoon, if you can manage it. Tommy Morton's dad still hasn't turned up and we'll need to get him sorted. As his appropriate adult last night, some continuity would be good. But only if . . .'

'I'll come now, if you want me to.'

'Ah. Well, around three would be early enough. But now would be better, if that's what you want.'

'Better put it in writing, but I am on my way. How's Tommy?'

'Still saying it's all his fault.'

'And how is Mr MacBride? The girls aren't in today; I checked.'

'Max, we'll have you wearing Sylv's uniform as soon as you like. You may have missed your calling.'

His chuckle made her feel a bit better. She worried when he was down. 'Second nature, woman policeman, second nature.'

'He went home. He told a complete tarradiddle when it came to his movements and the man is as slimy a git as you would meet in a long march, but even so, I don't see him doing it. He might talk her off a balcony, but I can't picture him doing any shoving. And anyway . . .' in the distance, Maxwell could hear a door opening and a voice, but not the words. 'Anyway, it's not always easy to make a hair appointment when I'm so busy, so if I could ring you back?'

'Yes, modom,' Maxwell said. 'We'll soon have those roots up to snuff. See you soon.'

But she had gone.

* * *

Jacquie turned to face her visitor. It was only Henry; she needn't have prevaricated on the phone. Time was, you could almost get Henry Hall riled — but not quite — by letting him know that Maxwell was on the case, but not now. Not only had Henry mellowed over the years, but Maxwell had been right too often to be ignored.

'Have you got a minute, Jacquie?' he asked. 'We'll be having a meeting about this MacBride business shortly and a press conference this afternoon. We've already got twitterings from above. The man is too high profile to ignore but not high profile enough to be able to farm the investigation out, worse luck. I've got Jim Astley's preliminary report here. Can you give it a quick once-over and then do me a précis? I'm up to my eyes with this poor kid who's stabbed his mother. Hetty is in bits, to add to my woes.'

Jacquie took the file and opened it, to show willing, but she needed to put the record straight. 'Max doesn't think . . . *I* don't think that Tommy killed his mother.'

'He wouldn't,' Henry said. 'A Leighford High kid.'

'Not one of His Own, though,' Jacquie said. 'He hadn't really met him until yesterday. It's just his teacher's nose. And my cop's nose, come to that. And don't forget Hetty.'

'They *were* on their own in the house,' Henry began.

'Exactly. So, where is the dad? And who made the call?'

'We haven't found the dad. And it was the boy who made the call.'

'There you are, then.' She swivelled her chair back to face the desk. 'He didn't do it. The dad did it. Now, I'll just flick through this and send you an email. When's the meeting?'

Hall looked at his watch, then at the clock above the door. Ever since Jacquie had known him he had done that. Belt and braces. Good old Henry. 'In an hour. I'll give you a ring just before.'

'Thanks.' Jacquie felt sorry for him. He had a cold — or flu as he would insist — and his sister was giving him grief. He had two murders in one night. Leighford was not always the quiet backwater it seemed on the surface, but two was pushing it, even so. She focussed on the file. It was typed by Donald, she could tell, judging by the rather exotic spelling and sentence construction, but it seemed straightforward enough. Head injuries. Anti-depressive drugs in system, consistent with prescribed dose. History of suicidal thoughts . . . cleaned fingernails. What on earth did that mean? She thought for a moment and then pulled the keyboard closer. 'Dear Henry,' she wrote. If Hall had been staked out over an anthill and asked to list what he loved about Jacquie Carpenter-Maxwell, near the top of the list would be the fact that she treated every email as though it were a proper letter. No 'hi' for her. No plunging straight in with no preamble. Always 'Dear Henry' and always 'best wishes, Jacquie' at the end. After the salutation, she paused. She didn't want to give the fingernails undue prominence, but, still . . . cleaned fingernails? Who would do that when the dead woman was displayed like the latest coupe in the lit window of a car saleroom? It meant that she was killed elsewhere . . . she began to type. This was going to be one of those cases, she could tell.

* * *

Thomas Morton was not a brave man. Even his best friend would say that, except that Thomas Morton had no best friend. Or any kind of friend, come to think of it. Once, he had. He remembered those days. When he had just left school and was working for the bus company. He was too young to be a driver, so he worked in the office; he didn't know then that scheduling the buses that circled Leighford like some kind of demented prayer wheel would sop up fifteen years of his life. But when he had started there, everything was new and bright. He and his mates would go out on payday and have a moderately raucous time, always leaving enough in their pay packets to give to their mums for rent and food. Then, one day, he looked up from his desk and a vision of loveliness walked in and took his breath away.

A tear ran down his cheek as he remembered his first view of the woman who became his wife. She was tall, taller than him by perhaps an inch, but he still had some growing left in him, his mother would always say, as she kissed him goodbye in the mornings. She was blonde, she was blue-eyed, she was gorgeous in all the right places. It didn't take five minutes for Thomas Morton to be in love. It didn't take five days for Louise the lovely temp to have him in the stationery cupboard, shagging his brains out. It didn't take five weeks for her to tell him she was up the spout, the kid was his and they had better get married. It didn't take six months until the kid was born but long before then, Thomas Morton knew he had been had. She was a shrew, a harridan, a bitch in blonde's clothing. He had wanted to die, but one look into the worried eyes of little Tommy as the midwife placed him in his arms was enough to keep him living. He might not be his, but they were in it together. Essentially, they were all they had.

Then, last night, he had come home late. He had muttered to himself all the way home, gathering some rather odd looks from passers-by. It had been a colleague's leaving do. He had known him since they had started work together, back in the days when he was happy, before he knew a hen could peck so hard and so deep. He had asked permission of course that morning, asked Louise whether he could go out. He could rerun the conversation word for word in his head. He supposed it was because they were the last words he heard her speak. Or perhaps it was because he had heard them, or something like them, over and over and over since he said 'I do'.

He had dropped the question in amongst the breakfast banalities. 'Old Mike is leaving the office. It's his leaving do tonight. I thought I might go, unless we've something planned.' He said this as though their social calendar was chock full, but for the last fourteen years to his knowledge, no one had willingly stepped over his threshold.

'He's got a promotion, I expect,' she had said. 'More than you'll ever get, you worthless heap of shit.'

'Lou, not in front of the boy,' he had said.

She had looked the child up and down, a sneer pulling up one side of her lip. How had he never noticed how thin, how hateful her mouth was, not seen it before it was too late? 'He doesn't care,' she said. 'He knows you're crap. Don't you, Tommy? You know he's crap?'

Tommy had concentrated hard on his cornflakes, his eyes behind his glasses full of tears.

'Don't nag the lad,' his father said. 'If you're angry with me, take it out on me. Not him.'

She stood back from the table, hands on hips. 'Ooh,' she said, in a mocking voice. 'Big man, all of a sudden. Because you're going out with the boys tonight.'

'So, I can go, then?' He knew he sounded like a whining teenager, but in so many ways that was how she had kept him. She had found herself a spineless 19-year-old and that's how she had kept him, all this time.

'Of course you can't, arsehole,' she said. 'You!' She poked their son in the ribs. 'Bugger off to school. I need to talk to your dad.'

Tommy had slipped off his chair and slid from the room without another word, glad to be gone.

His mother turned to the stove and picked up a skewer, kept alongside for the purpose. She lit the gas and Thomas Morton rolled up his sleeve, resignation having taken the place of fear and pain long before . . .

He found he was clenching the cheap quilt of the B&B in his fists. The latest weal still hurt, but not as much as the first had done. It had been hurting more when he had come home and had trouble opening the front door. It was because his wife's body was sprawled in the hall, a knife buried in her chest. And on the stairs, his boy who was not his boy, his Tommy. They had looked at each other and in the horror, there was relief. Before he had even got inside the hall properly, Tommy had given him his orders. He was good at taking orders.

'Dad,' the boy had said. 'It wasn't me, honest. I found her like this. But you'll have to go, Dad. When they see the marks, what will they think? I'll call the police. Just go, Dad. I'll be all right.'

And, because he was so very good at taking orders, Thomas Morton had left his boy sitting on the stairs, waiting for the police to come and take him away.

So, no, Thomas Morton was not a brave man. But it was time he did something about that. He stood up, put on his anorak, the one his wife had bought him from the charity shop, the one he had to wear rather than the good one his mum had given him for Christmas. He squared his shoulders and went to find his boy.

* * *

Peter Maxwell was not really a taxi person. True, he didn't drive, hadn't sat behind the wheel of a car, except once, a couple of years before in a dire emergency, since his little family — he refused to think of them as his 'first' family; they had come first, but that was in another country, the country of the past — had died on a wet road, so many years ago. He got around through the medium of lifts and bike, but White Surrey was not the way to arrive when one was an Appropriate Adult — the messages given out by cycle clips, soaking wet hair and trouser bottoms from the unrelenting winter weather and lips so cold it was hard to speak, where just somehow so . . . inappropriate. So, taxi it was. At one time, not so long ago, he would have inveigled a lift from Sylvia Matthews. At one time, he would have stayed until the end of school, no matter what. But Sylv wasn't there and time at Leighford High School was something that Maxwell would rather not have too much of — so, taxi it had to be. But a man has his pride, so he paid the taxi off at the kerb outside the nick.

'That's . . .' the driver checked the meter, 'four fifty to you, guv,' the driver said.

Maxwell rummaged in his pocket and came up empty. With a tut, he swivelled the other way, to release the other buttock and hence his wallet. As he did so, he heard a faint click. It was either his hip or the central locking and a quick glance at the cabbie's face in the rear view mirror told him which.

'Can't be too careful,' the driver said. 'I had a bloke in here the other day . . .'

But before he could complete his fascinating tale, Maxwell had found a fiver, which he passed across, waving away the reluctant offer of change. The central locking clicked off again and Maxwell clambered out. Whoever thought that an ordinary saloon car was a good idea for a taxi, he wondered. Emerging in a half crouch with one leg tangled in the front seat belt did nothing for anyone's gravitas.

Straightening up, he made for the gate and got there with another taxi-delivered man, small and apologetic-looking. It was one of those awkward social moments never covered in the etiquette manuals. When approaching a police station and another person is on the same errand, how does a person avoid looking as though one of the two is escorting or chasing the other? Walking side by side is obviously out. Walking in line looks too much like a very short chain gang. The journey from the kerb to the door is too short to begin an animated conversation — what *is* the answer?

In this case, the problem resolved itself just inside the foyer. The desk sergeant looked up and two expressions crossed his face in quick succession. The first one said, as clearly as if he had spoken, 'Oh, bugger. It's Maxwell here to bend his missus' ear about something which will mean work for us all, I expect.' The other was even clearer and to make things even simpler for the casual bystander, was accompanied by speech. 'Mr Morton, I presume. Stay where you are, please. Lockdown.' And he pressed a button on the desk. This time, the click was clearly not Maxwell's hip — unless incipient arthritis was accompanied these days by a siren and flashing blue lights.

* * *

That evening, with Nolan in bed and Metternich limbering up for a night's voling by sleeping along Jacquie's outstretched legs, Maxwell was nonetheless feeling a little dystopian. His world had been turned upside down more than once, but there was something about this latest crisis which felt more permanent somehow, as though a switch had been flicked on which could not be switched off. He nursed his Southern Comfort and glowered at the fire.

Jacquie looked up from her book. 'I refuse to offer you a penny for your thoughts,' she said. 'Why pay good money for something I know already?'

He looked at her without turning his head. 'Do you?'

'I think so,' she said. 'You've had a rubbish day, one way and another. It hasn't been great anywhere, as far as I can tell. Two murders. Another granny mugging, except that now I know who is mugging who things are a little simpler. One slimy git at home in what currently seems to be the clear. Another sudden widower in the nick for further questioning.'

As if in answer, Maxwell pointed the remote at the TV and brought up the text. As a technological achievement, it wasn't first flight, but he was still proud of it. Choosing 'local news' he pointed wordlessly to the screen.

'Local Man Held,' the headline said. 'A man is being questioned this evening by police in connection with the death by stabbing of mother of one Louise Morton, 37, in her home last night. Mrs Morton was discovered by her son, 14, who cannot be named for legal reasons. Her husband, Thomas Morton, 33, was unavailable for comment. A man, 33, is currently helping police with their enquiries.'

He flicked the TV off again and waited.

'I wish they wouldn't do that,' Jacquie said, 'that "man thirty-three" business. I know it looks as though they are keeping the identity secret, but they might just as well stick a badge on him.'

'I can't believe he's thirty-three,' Maxwell said. 'He looks fifty if he's a day.'

'Being married to Louise Morton will do that to a person, I should imagine.' She looked up at him and smiled. 'Can we skip all the usual things about strictly between you and me, all that kind of stuff?'

'Consider it skup.' He smiled back at her. They had come a long way since the Red House, that was for sure, since that day when one of Maxwell's Own had died and Jacquie Carpenter was a very new and rather scared DC.

'We haven't arrested him, of course, but we are questioning him as someone who may be a suspect in the death of his wife. Speaking for myself, I don't think he did it, but that only leaves Tommy in the frame.'

'And he definitely didn't do it.'

'No.' She stroked the cat's flank absently and he flexed a warning claw. 'He came in, not to give himself up, as that idiot on the desk seemed to think . . .'

'That siren really gave me a start,' Maxwell observed. 'Thank heavens I had my brown trousers on.'

'I know,' she chuckled. 'It's his latest toy. We're going to have to relocate the button — I think it's because it's near his hand. Anyway, Thomas Morton came in because he was worried about Tommy. Who isn't his, by the way, although he is on the birth certificate.'

'Really?' Maxwell's interest was piqued. 'Do we know who the actual father is?'

'No. And according to Thomas, we probably never will, now. She threw a lot of her past behaviour in his face over the years, but never that. No names at all, in fact. It was more a case of . . . well, dimensions. Stamina. That kind of thing. She was a horrible woman, there's no doubt of that. It's a wonder she lived this long.'

'I expect there are still a couple of florist shops outside the house,' Maxwell remarked.

'And candles, or so I believe,' Jacquie said. 'She kept all her nastiness for the family. Her neighbours have all made the usual noises.'

'Except Hetty.'

Jacquie chuckled. 'I'd forgotten Hetty. Yes, except her.'

'Seriously, has either you or Henry had a proper sit down with Hetty . . .' Maxwell looked at Jacquie wide-eyed. 'I can't get away from the fact that her name is Henrietta.'

'I don't know that it is. But what else could it be?'

'Étienne?' Too French. Too male.

'Hepzibah?' Too . . .

'That would be Heppy, though, wouldn't it? Herriot?'

Jacquie guffawed and Metternich took off in a rake of claws, all high dudgeon. In fact, he had overslept and should have been away hours ago. His memory for poetry was far below that of Nolan, but somewhere in his furry brain, Sir Walter Scott urged him on: Breathes there a cat with vole so dead . . .

'Are you all right, heart?' Maxwell said as Jacquie massaged her shin. 'Can I bring you something? Iodine? Savlon? TCP? All of the above?'

'What is it with that animal?' she said, settling back against the cushions with a wince. 'One minute he's spark out, the next he's behaving like some kind of homicidal maniac.'

'He's a cat,' Maxwell shrugged. 'All mouse and trousers.'

'Seriously, though,' Jacquie said, 'you are quite right. I will have a word with Hetty. She might have seen someone at the house.'

'And you can find out what her name is at the same time, can't you?'

'It won't be priority, but,' and she spluttered another laugh, 'it would be nice to know.'

Without being asked, Maxwell got up and left the room, coming back with his glass replenished and a gin and tonic for his wife. After a good mauling by Metternich, sometimes only alcohol would do.

'Oh, thank you,' she said, puckering up for a kiss. 'Just what a clawed person needs.' Then, she was straight back into the conversation. 'Of course, the unlovely Mr MacBride was let go. Now him, I'm not so sure about.'

'Didn't you say he had an alibi?'

'He has a *story*, yes. I wouldn't call it an alibi as such. He says he had taken a new car out for a spin, stopped at the Ellisdon for a drink, got talking with some reps and went over the limit, so stayed over. He doesn't appear to have rung his wife to tell her, he had a zero alcohol level when we brought him in . . .' she blew out her cheeks, 'I really don't know. Can we arrest him for being a slimy, lying git?'

'Perhaps if all lying, slimy gits were rounded up, the world would be a better place. A little subjective, though; one woman's slimy git is another's Prince Charming.'

Jacquie watched the bubbles in her drink for a while, before nodding. 'Yes,' she said, looking up with a smile. 'You may be right.'

'I'm not sure I have ever been thought of as a slimy git. Mad as a snake, perhaps, but snakes aren't really slimy.'

'Mad as a newt?' she ventured. 'Newts are slimy. I can vouch for that.' Over the Christmas holidays, Nolan had been proud custodian of the Class Newt, the Franz von Werra of the amphibian world; the wretched creature could escape from the tank in the time it took to throw in some nourishment.

Maxwell was serious again. It wasn't often that three Leighford Highenas became motherless in one evening. 'You've checked his story?'

'As best we can. It won't hold up, but we need to get more evidence on him before we can test it, really. He was seen at the Ellisdon, and was indeed talking to some reps. We've managed to contact three of the four, but the fourth wasn't staying there and isn't known to the others. Also, MacBride was on tonic, ice and a slice. The blokes thought it was gin, but it wasn't, according to the barman. Then he just drops off the radar. He left the bar, but didn't get a room. So, he either went somewhere else he isn't prepared to tell us about, or . . .'

'Or, what? He went off to kill his wife.'

'Well . . . yes, I suppose that is an option. But forensics is almost useless. His DNA and fingerprints will obviously be all over the crime scene, because he works there. Ditto his wife. Although he did have the lack of taste to tell me she didn't understand him . . .'

Maxwell blinked. 'He actually said those words?'

'Yes. He didn't use them later to Rick Shopley, which is either interesting or typical, depending on how you look at it. However, whether or not she understood him, there was bound to be his DNA etcetera on her body. It would be strange if there wasn't. But the one odd thing was . . . her fingernails had been cleaned.'

Maxwell perked up. 'That must mean another person involved, then, surely? If she had scratched him, he could always have said it was done earlier.'

'Yes. Or he could have cleaned them out precisely so we thought it was another person.'

'Hmm.' He subsided again. 'Is Geoff MacBride that clever, though? He's cunning, shrewd, ambitious, all that I know, but clever? As in, intelligent enough to plan a red herring like that.'

'Do you watch *CSI*?'

'Does the Pope shit in the woods?'

'Exactly. Although I don't expect Geoff MacBride has much time for TV, what with all his committees . . .'

'. . . and women,' Maxwell added.

'Really? I assumed as much, but . . . I have to ask, Max. Is that a fact or just some staffroom scuttlebutt?'

'The latter,' he admitted. 'Make the most of it. I don't think there will be much more of it. Mrs Braymarr isn't a fan of gossip. I understand she is planning to fit us all with scolds' bridles, only removing them as we enter a class. But, yes, back in the day, there was a lot of talk of our esteemed Head of Governors and his undoubted inability to keep it in his trousers.'

'Anyone in particular?'

Maxwell laughed. 'Me? Details about who is doing what to whom?'

'You can remember it if it happened in eighteen something,' she pointed out.

'True. But I doubt I will be bumping into Prinnie and Mrs Fitzherbert next time I am in Tesco. Hmm, let me think . . . I do believe there was a bit of chat about MacBride and, ooh, you know, thing . . . that supply teacher we had when . . . oh, don't tell me.' He closed his eyes and sketched what seemed to be rough dimensions on the air. His eyes flew open. 'Sandra! No, sorry, heart, we'll have to agree that I never remember the details. But isn't that what you police people are for? Digging? Delving? Getting all the dirt?'

She would have been disappointed had he known — she would have immediately started a search for her real husband, as opposed to the clone who knew all the dirt and could dish it like a pro. 'That's all right,' she smiled. 'Just having some gossip gives us a start. No one current though, as far as you know?'

Maxwell shrugged. It covered a multitude of sins.

'Well,' she drained her glass, 'bed for me, I think. Come and cuddle up and tell me all about Fiona Braymarr. I think such stories are best told in the dark.'

'Too scary,' he said. 'Let's just say she and I have agreed to agree.'

She spun round. That was unexpected. 'What?'

'I hate her; she hates me. So we have that in common. Other than that, I can't get a handle on her at all. Apparently, when you Google her, which apparently isn't as painful as it sounds, she comes up empty. She isn't a Googlewhack as such . . .'

Jacquie shook her head. 'How many times have I told Nolan not to use words he doesn't understand? It applies to you as well.'

'I know what that means,' Maxwell said, hurt. 'It doesn't really apply to people, but it is two words which only get one hit when you Google them. I was . . . stretching the envelope.'

'Stop it!' She hit out at him with the newspaper, folded ready for the crossword in bed. 'You're scaring me.'

'Anyhoo, apparently, the only entries on anyone with that name are just two about someone called Fiona Braymarr who was run over aged six in Tasmania in 1951.'

'That's insane,' Jacquie said. 'Everyone's got more than that on Google.'

'I haven't,' he said, smugly.

She looked at him, disbelievingly. 'Max, have you no idea? Google you and it goes for pages. Most of it good . . . at least no trolls.'

'That's good,' he said, dubiously. 'The only place for trolls is under the rickety-rackety bridge, waiting for the three billy goats gruff.'

She let that one go. She was too young for Uncle Mack but had fond memories of Ed 'Stewpot' Stewart; she had even written in to have a record played for her birthday, but it wasn't picked — perhaps Dexy's Midnight Runners had been a step too far for Ed.

'Well, at any rate, she isn't on Google.'

'But she *should* be, Max. She's supposed to be some sort of superhead, isn't she? Goes around the country making good schools into a seething bed of intrigue and despair?'

He put an arm round her and hugged her close. 'That's my girl,' he said, kissing her cheek. 'Cut straight to the chase.' He reached out with his other hand and switched out the light. 'Bed for you — you've got grieving husbands to grill tomorrow.'

But his face was thoughtful as he closed the door and headed for the stairs.

CHAPTER NINE

Maxwell was still thoughtful as he pedalled through the gates of Leighford High School that morning. He barely registered the fact that Mavis, rather than standing like Achilles in the trench as was her wont, was actually on the pavement, in a small huddle with some assorted adults, some of whom he recognised vaguely as he whizzed past, his dopplering 'Morning, Mavis,' lost on their unhearing ears. BB (Before Braymarr) he could have taken his problem to the IT department, albeit reluctantly. He had become almost used to their expressions when he entered their sanctum; a mixture of exasperation and exaggerated patience, the kind of look always seen on the carers' faces in newspaper photos of 'the oldest resident's birthday'. But those days were gone. The IT department was no more. When the computers broke down in future, Mrs Braymarr had decreed, the member of staff in question would have to call the academy helpline, where a dedicated IT professional would be able to talk them through any fixes necessary. Any member of staff experiencing more than three breakdowns in a term — on reading the memo, Maxwell had chosen to believe she meant computer breakdowns, but the other kind was no doubt implied as well — would have the cost of repair removed from their next pay.

Maxwell didn't worry unduly. He never used his computer anyway, so it was unlikely to break down.

So, what to do? Fiona Braymarr's absence from the Google searches had struck him as possibly odd, but when Jacquie was also struck by it, he began to see it for what it was; very strange indeed. So strange, that it must be deliberate. But once he had used the term 'Google', Maxwell had used up all the computer knowledge at his disposal. Asking a kid was one other way to enlightenment, but he had his dinosaur reputation to uphold, so, no.

He was deep in thought as he crossed the foyer and was suddenly stopped in his tracks when he cannoned into something wiry, angry and smelling like an ashtray.

'Oy!' it said.

He focussed his eyes and saw, to his amazement, Mrs B. Seeing her at Leighford High School in the morning was like seeing the sky darkened by a flock of passenger pigeon or the bird table — always vacant, perhaps unsurprisingly, Chez Maxwell — inundated by dozens of *Zitting Cisticolae.* Unlikely, unexpected but, especially with the thoughts going through his head, very welcome.

'Mrs B! What are you doing here?' He knew he was not at risk of being shot, even with a forefinger, by Mrs B. The only TV she watched was the soaps and the gadget programmes. Which was why he was so glad to see her. He leaned nearer. 'Tell me later,' he hissed. 'I need your help on a technical matter.'

She looked at him, all ears. 'I'm here to see that Braymarr woman,' she said. 'We all got a memo yesterday, said we has to come and do in the mornings before six and evenings after seven.'

'Which?'

'Both! We're not having that! We've got homes to go to, lives to lead. She can't change our working hours just like that. I've come to represent the entire hygiene staff to tell her where to stuff it.'

If there was just one place Maxwell wanted to be that day, it was to be masquerading as a fly on the wall in that meeting. But he had something more urgent for her attention and it wasn't just selfish. She might learn something to her advantage. 'Can you just give me half an hour or so? I'm assuming you don't have an appointment.'

'No, I bleeding well do not have an appointment, 'scuse my French,' she said. 'If she won't see me, she just won't have a clean school no more, that's all. My girls and Daniel ain't putting up with it. It's not right, is it? Messing about with our schedules.'

It wasn't like Mrs B to only have one question in a speech, but Maxwell couldn't help it. 'No, it's not,' he said. 'Who's Daniel, by the way?'

'He does the rough,' she replied, enigmatically. She stalked into the reception area and tapped on the counter. Maxwell couldn't hear her exact words, but the gist was clear. Sadly, Mrs Braymarr seemed to be currently at one of her other schools — this piece of information eliciting a snort from Mrs B that made Thingee's hair ruffle — but if Mrs B would like to wait . . . ?

'Wait? Wait for that trollop?' she said, returning to Maxwell in a state of the highest dudgeon. 'No, I will not wait.' She looked at him again and cocked her head. 'So, what d'you want me to have a look at? Not that ancient thing in your office, I hope? There's nothing can help that old rubbish, is there?'

'I should think not,' Maxwell was almost weak with relief. For a moment, he thought that Mrs B had disappeared for ever beneath the mantle of a political firebrand. 'Not for a trollop like her, certainly. I need your internet expertise. No, it isn't. Probably not; you know best.'

'Just as well I've got me tablet,' she said, patting her huge handbag.

Maxwell's heart did a little lurch. Was the woman ill? Mrs B was immortal, surely?

'It's Android,' she said, inexplicably, 'so you'll recognise some of the commands.'

He nodded and shook his head by turns. She probably knew what she was talking about. Since her emergence some years before as a computer geek, nothing she did could ever surprise him again.

'We'll go to your office, shall we?' she said, and led the way, hauling herself up each step with a grunt. Mrs B had spent years cultivating her persona and even righteous anger couldn't make a dent in it. Once ensconced at Maxwell's desk and with a steaming cup of builder's tea in front of her, she delved into her bag and fished out her tablet, complete with detachable keyboard.

'Oh!' Gautama Buddha had never had a more profound experience. 'A laptop.'

For a moment, Mrs B considered patting him, condescendingly, the way the shop assistants in PC World had once done to her, but she decided against it. 'Yes, Mr M. Sort of. Let's call it that, if that makes you comfy. Now, what did you want me to show you?'

'It's not so much show me as . . . it's a bit difficult for me, because I don't really know the jargon.'

Bless him! This time, Mrs B did pat him. This man had a brain as big as the great outdoors, but when it came to computing, it was just as empty. 'Don't worry about the words, Mr M,' she said, kindly, as though to a child. 'Just tell me what you need.'

Maxwell tried never to condescend, but he recognised it when he saw it. Never mind, it might make his task easier if he started from a position of idiot. The savant could come later. 'I understand that people have Googled Mrs Braymarr, but she doesn't come up in the searches.'

Mrs B raised an eyebrow. 'That don't seem very likely,' she said, turning to her tablet. 'She's one of them super heads, ain't she?' She swiped the screen a couple of times and then applied herself to the keyboard. 'How'd you spell her name again?'

'B-R-A-Y-M-A-R-R.'

'There you are, y'see, loads of . . . wait a minute.' She peered more closely. 'No, that can't be right . . . hang on, I'll check again.' She tapped and swiped, then tapped and swiped and swore. 'Bugger me, Mr M, excuse as always, but you're right. There isn't even a Fiona Braymarr on LinkedIn. Facebook. Nuthin. It's not normal. She strikes me as the kind of woman as can't keep her hands off Twitter. But even if she doesn't do social media . . .' Mrs B's hands were on the keys again, 'where's her other schools? Where's . . . well, anything?'

'So, it is unusual, Mrs B?'

'Not so much unusual, as . . . well, I never seen it before. Let me show you something.' She typed and turned the tablet's screen to face him. 'Got your glasses?'

'I don't wear glasses, Mrs B.'

'Hmmm.' She looked at him appraisingly. 'Good for your age.'

'Thank you.' And he really meant it. Mrs B of all people was not given to praise.

'Have a look then. D'you know what that is?'

'A list of . . . websites?'

'Correct. About . . . ?'

'I don't know him. Should I? Is he famous? I'm really bad at singers and so on.' The man didn't look like a singer, but that didn't seem to have anything to do with the music business these days. 'Britain's Got Talent runner up? Sorry.'

She gave another snort and shook her head. 'You wouldn't know him, but it's my old man. Rest his soul, I suppose I oughter say.'

Maxwell peered closer. He had never met the man, who seemed to most people who knew Mrs B to be as legendary as any unicorn. There were images, there were websites about long-ago darts matches — the list went on and on. 'But . . . ?'

'Exactly,' she said, triumphant. 'If you Googled me, you, Mrs M, little Nole, even that bleeding cat of yours, I bet there are pages of hits.' She looked up and quickly translated. 'Websites with their name on at the very least, but often a picture or a bit of news. But Mrs Bloody Hitler Braymarr, nothing. It's not right.'

'So, what is it, then?' Maxwell stopped looming over her and pulled up a chair. 'How can she not be on the web?'

'You *can* do it,' Mrs B said, ruminatively. 'The new Google rules mean you can ask them to remove sites you don't want there, but it takes a while and they still get to decide what stays and what goes. There is software . . .' a few more clicks and she was pointing to the screen again, 'but I dunno how well they work. You can overload your name. Put loads of the same article up with your name in and Google will think you're a spammer and take you to the bottom of the rankings. But still . . . can you give me a while, Mr M? You've got some teaching to do anyway, haven't you, I expect?'

Maxwell looked over his shoulder at the clock, which stood at a rather disconcerting nine fifteen. 'Oh, bugger and poo, Mrs B. I should be with Ten Zed Ex Oh! They will have ripped the windows out of the frames by now; I'm late!'

'Off you go, then,' she said, already hunched over the keyboard, a woman on a mission. 'I'll winkle this tart out if it's the last thing I do!'

Although winkle tart sounded rather unappetising, Maxwell applauded her enthusiasm and raced down the corridor, jacket flapping, to quell the riot he could hear dimly from below. Even without Dee MacBride, ring leader extraordinary, it wasn't going to be pretty in there.

* * *

The MacBride house, like 10ZXO was totally MacBride-free. Jacquie had rung to check before she arrived, but the answerphone simply asked her to leave a message. She checked the dealership and he wasn't there either. Council offices; the same. Jacquie had always suspected that Geoff MacBride was a slippery customer, able to play both ends against the middle and this was proof positive. What she needed was a warrant and her next stop had been the Law Courts, to get a magistrate to sign the paperwork. And here was where the embarrassment had begun because, contrary to popular opinion, Geoff MacBride was not hiding under the nearest rock, he was in court, his turn on the JP roster having come around. Keeping her head down, Jacquie had got one of his colleagues to put pen to paper. Then, all she had to do was get to the house and meet the forensics team, before giving it the once-over. No one expected to find anything, but they had to go through the motions. A similar team, led by Rick Shopley, were combing the dealership. Jacquie hated this rif-fling through someone else's stuff. It wasn't like a quick pat down, this was seriously intrusive. She always had in the back of her mind the thought of what anyone would think of 38 Columbine, should they decide to do a search. Maxwell's attic diorama, for a start, with his beloved Light Brigade drawn up before the Heights. What did that say about a grown man, that he spent a considerable amount of time, energy and money on what most people would think of as toys? Would they check the garden over, drawn by the clear signs of digging? They would only find out later that it was only Nolan trying to find Troy. And the final nail in the cof-fin would be when they checked with the neighbours; what on earth would Mrs Troubridge have to say about them?

The house would have been easy to find even without the SOCO van parked outside. A couple of forensics staff were lounging in the open rear, one hurriedly pinching out a cigarette as she drew up behind them.

'Morning, guv,' he said, snapping on his latex gloves and trying to look all attention. 'Bit warmer this morning, don't you think? Feels a bit like spring at last.'

Jacquie looked around. It was true that the garden of the MacBride house was a colourful sight. The deep Mediterranean blue of grape hyacinths edged the brick driveway and the daffodils had put in an appearance, just in time for St David's Day. A couple of hanging baskets in the rather over-large porch were full of winter pansies and in tubs beneath, crocuses were just getting past their best. Someone loved this garden and Jacquie felt sad when she realised it was almost certainly Denise MacBride who had lavished the attention on it and that it would never look this good again. It was a pleasant change to be able to do her work without a gaggle of gawping neighbours foregathered, but this was simply not that kind of road; any peeping was being done discreetly from behind net curtains or, more likely in these affluent homes, bespoke vertical blinds.

She rubbed her hands together and smiled at the men. 'It does feel a bit warmer, Josh, now you come to mention it. Right, let's get this started.' she looked at each man in turn and they suddenly felt like a million dollars. A smile from DI Jacquie Carpenter-Maxwell could do that to a man, even when he was encased in a disposable white suit that made him look like a mixture of Baymax from *Big Hero 6* and the Staypuft Marshmallow Man from *Ghostbusters*. Before Jacquie lived with the Maxwell boys, a film analogy would have been completely alien to her, but now it was a shorthand she couldn't have avoided had she tried.

She walked up the drive, taking in the house frontage as she did so. The place was as good an advertisement for MacBride Motors as the showroom itself. It said 'success' with every brick — there had to be five bedrooms if there was one. She guessed there would be rather a lot of bathrooms too. She turned to the forensics guys. 'Sorry,' she said, 'I don't think I was expecting the house to be this big. Do you want to call for more help? I'll sign it off when I get back to the nick.'

'Nah,' Josh turned to his silent friend, who nodded his agreement. 'There's nobody in, is there?'

'No. The girls are with their grandmother, or so I understand. That was all arranged yesterday. And I know Geoff MacBride is at the courts — I nearly bumped into him when I went to get this.' She brandished the warrant.

'Got the keys?' So, he could speak after all. His name was Robert and he deliberately modelled himself on the silent one of the same name.

'I have.' Jacquie fished the keys out of her bag, a Yale and a Chubb on a piece of string and with a brown label attached. 'Mrs MacBride thoughtfully provided them.'

Behind her back, the two men looked at each other. It wasn't like Jacquie Carpenter-Maxwell to indulge in gallows humour. They both correctly guessed that she didn't like the widower; what they couldn't work out was whether the man was in the frame.

'Got anything in mind, guv?' Josh asked.

'No.' She pushed the door open and a waft of warm, slightly stale air came out to greet them. 'Just look around. Especially bedrooms. I want to know who sleeps where.'

Robert raised an eyebrow.

'Apparently,' Jacquie said, 'his wife didn't understand him.'

'Gotchya.' Robert's wife often kicked him out of her bed, but in their flat his only recourse was the sofa.

The forensics team split up at the foot of the stairs, Robert going up to dig what dirt he could, Josh heading for the kitchen. Although this wasn't the scene of crime according to first impressions, he had read the PM notes and, like everyone, found the cleaned fingernails to be a red flag. If she had been killed or at least rendered unconscious here, he would find proof.

Jacquie paused in the hall, getting her bearings. A slim unit holding a phone caught her eye. As might be expected in this house, the whole thing was state of the art. The phone, though clearly a landline, looked like a mobile, with a blank screen waiting to spring to life. She put out a latex-gloved finger and felt around for buttons on the base unit, but it all seemed to be housed in the phone. For a moment, she saw the world through Maxwell's eyes — it could be a cold and technological place, that was certain. She picked the phone itself up and it did indeed spring to life. The screen was simpler than a mobile, she could see now, with numbers along the bottom and a few app style logos along the top. One was two circles joined by a line and she smiled to herself. How very retro — a whole generation was growing up not knowing a tape recorder from a hole in the ground, and yet the go-to logo for a recording was still based on a tape. But, and more to the point, there was a red dot in the right hand circle, and it was slowly flashing. A message. She touched the logo and the screen changed.

'You have . . . three . . . messages and . . . one . . . caller who left no message. To hear your messages, press or say one.'

'One.' Jacquie had to admit it, she still loved voice technology, although it rarely worked.

Nothing happened.

'Sorry,' the condescending woman continued after a pause. 'I didn't catch that. To hear . . .'

'For God's sake,' Jacquie muttered, and jabbed the 'one'.

'First message. Message received . . . Monday, 23 February at . . . thirteen hundred hours.'

There was a buzz and a pause and then a man's voice filled the hallway. 'Mrs MacBride, I think we ought to talk. I'm not sure whether you are aware of this, but your husband is seeing my wife . . . and of course you will understand that I use the word in its biblical sense. Now, I don't know how you feel about this, but it is making me rather annoyed.' The caller gave a neighing laugh that could have been genuine or could have been his idea of ironic banter. 'I think it would be good if we could meet, to chat over what's going on. I know my wife and she won't have thought of this despicable behaviour on her own. It's your husband who is to blame and I also feel you are not totally innocent in all this.' The voice was rising, becoming less controlled and then, almost as if he knew it, the man brought himself back to his first pleasant tones and gave a little laugh. 'Mrs MacBride, I don't want to talk about this on the phone, but if you meet me tonight at the corner nearest your husband's car dealership at nine thirty, perhaps we can plan where we can go from here? I know what you look like, so don't worry about recognizing me; I'll recognise you. Although we have met, in fact, some time ago. You may be surprised when you see who I am. Perhaps the name Freeman might give you a clue. Goodbye.'

Jacquie looked up to see Josh standing in the kitchen doorway. She widened her eyes at him and he shrugged. The language of SOCO, in miniature.

'End of message. Next message.' The woman sounded as imperturbable as ever. 'Message received . . . Monday, 23 February at . . . twenty-two twenty-seven.'

This time the voice was clearly that of Geoff MacBride, but not the usual honeyed tones he used in public. He was clearly speaking from some public space, because there was a babble of voices in the background, two of them closer than the others.

'Denise,' he snapped. 'Where the bloody hell are you? Drugged up to the bloody eyes I suppose, as per usual. Well, if you get this message you do, if you don't, you don't.' He heaved a sigh and said something over his shoulder to one of the closer voices, who laughed. 'Something's come up . . .' more laughter, 'and I won't be home tonight. I'll be calling in for a shirt in the morning, but don't get up specially, will you?' He almost spat the words and Jacquie wondered, as she so often did when dealing with domestic disputes, how parents could possibly think it was good for their children to let them live with such hatred. 'So . . . you're not going to pick up, I can see that, so . . . that's the message. Say goodnight to the girls for me if they're still up.' And that was clearly that.

'End of message. Next message.' The woman was unstoppable. 'Message received . . . Monday, 23 February at . . . twenty-three thirty-five.'

Jacquie listened carefully, expecting it to be MacBride again, if not apologizing at least explaining a bit more now he was not in the company of his cronies. But no — it was another voice, but one she recognised nonetheless.

'Denise? Sorry, I know it's late. Can you ring me when you get this? Something's happened. Umm . . . Bye. Oh, I'm on the mobile. Bye.'

Jacquie looked at the phone in amazement. She couldn't have been more surprised had it grown wings and flown away. The caller had not identified himself, always a sign of either malice, as in the first call, or friendship. And this was definitely a friendly call. And it came from Thomas Morton.

Josh appeared again in the kitchen doorway, snapping the wrist of his glove in a rather irritating manner. 'Anything important, guv?' he asked.

'Yes.' Jacquie sounded distant. 'I think it must be, but . . . Josh, how often has there been a night with two murders in Leighford?'

'Murders as opposed to deaths?' Like all forensics geeks, Josh was a stickler for accuracy.

'Yes. Murders.'

The forensics man cast his eyes up, lips muttering soundlessly. 'Since I've been here, which is, as you know, for ever . . . never.'

'As I thought. So what are the odds of one murder victim having a call from the husband of the other?'

Robert had come soundlessly down the stairs. He was the department statistics man. 'Disappointingly boring, actually,' he said. This was the longest statement anyone had heard from him in years, so was statistically important in itself.

Josh took over. 'It's the birthday paradox,' he said. 'The murdered bit is immaterial. The chances are the same as they would be for any two other people and that is fifty-fifty.'

'But . . .' Jacquie didn't like coincidences. She wanted to think there was something more important than sheer chance at work here. There was no point in going back to Henry Hall with a coincidence as part of her thinking. There was something about the word that made him go deaf. But if statistically it wasn't unusual, what else could it be? She decided to change the subject. 'Anything in the rest of the house?' she asked.

'Nothing downstairs,' Josh said. 'The kitchen is freakishly tidy. Either the deceased was a complete nutter when it comes to tidiness and was also on the verge of an almighty top-up shop or this family lives on takeaways and frozen ready meals. The cupboard is bare.' Josh fancied himself as a bit of a gourmet chef, modelling himself on an amalgam of Rick Stein and Jamie Oliver, whilst managing to look a lot more like Marguerite Patten.

'Upstairs the same,' Robert agreed. 'Socks colour coded. Two bedrooms, guv. His and hers. Girls' bedrooms like operating theatres, just a few drawers messed, but they left in a hurry. We won't find anything here. I did find this, though,' he brandished a pigskin manicure set, 'in the old man's bedroom. I've bagged it for the lab.'

With a sigh, Jacquie snapped off her gloves. 'Tell them to get back to me asap with whatever they find — MacBride's DNA won't be much help as evidence though, will it? Never mind, well done for finding it. Was it hidden?'

Silent Robert, reverting to his nickname, shook his head.

'We'll get IT over here for this phone,' she said. 'Without knowing a bit more about it, I don't know whether the message will travel or if it is linked to the line. Otherwise, that's it, boys. Onwards and upwards; it's the Morton house next.'

* * *

'Well, it's not on the syllabus, Idris, but did I ever tell you about the Defenestration of Prague?'

Idris nearly died of fright. It wasn't his real name, of course. No one east of Offa's Dyke is ever called Idris. But he was big and black and laconic and the girls of Ten Zed Ex Oh who drooled over Mr Elba couldn't resist giving him the nickname.

Maxwell swept past the boy and shut the window. 'Prague, anybody?'

They were all, suddenly, in their seats now, models of scholarly rectitude. Thirty-one blank faces. 'Remind me to have a word with that nice Mr Cutter in the Geography Department,' he went on. 'If asked, he would tell you that

Prague is the capital city of the Czech Republic, once called Czechoslovakia, but should really be called Bohemia. This glass and metal thing behind me, Idris, the thing you were just leaning out of, despite the inclemency of the weather — what do we call that?'

'A window, sir.'

'Spot on, my boy,' Maxwell said, prowling the class. 'It's Baliol for you or my name's not Steen Steensen Bilcher. Know what the Romans called such a gizmo, Idris?'

The Baliol scholar was stumped.

'Anybody?'

Anybody was stumped too.

'Fenestra,' Maxwell told them. 'First declension, if memory serves.' There had never been a Classics Department at Leighford High School, so there was no nice teacher there to talk to. 'So, you see, *de*fenestration means jumping, or falling, or being pushed out of a window. There, now, who says History isn't fascinating?'

Thirty-one people were trying to fathom what all this had to do with Women in Nazi Germany, which the Lesson That Maxwell Forgot was supposed to be about.

'What has this, I hear you all cry, to do with Women in Nazi Germany? Absolutely nothing. Unless . . .' he quietly confiscated Jade's mobile phone, 'you follow the notion that it was just such an enforced defenestration which led directly to the Thirty Years War, which led to the rise of a powerful Prussia which became a United Germany in which the Nazi Party proliferated. Cause and effect, eh? So, for that delicious piece of historicity, we all have to thank Idris. All together, now . . .'

And Mad Max's fingers twirled in the air as they chorused, 'Thank you, Idris.'

* * *

Mrs B was no longer hunched like something at lunch on the Serengeti when Maxwell finally returned to his office. She was leaning back in his chair, chin tucked in, nursing another cup of tea in lieu of a much-overdue cigarette.

'Any luck?' Master of body language though he was, Maxwell couldn't quite work out whether her look was one of complacent success or complete dejected failure.

'Nah.' She didn't look at him, just at the screen. 'Tried everything. She didn't exist before the end of January this year.'

'But . . .'

'Don't you but me, Mr M. I'm stumped. I never seen this before, I really haven't. I'll have a word with my sister's lad, well, grandson I suppose you'd say . . .'

Mrs B's family relationships were so byzantine it was probably well not to enquire too closely.

'. . . see if he has any ideas, but I think we'll have to agree that she's got us beat.' Suddenly springing up, she slammed the mug on the table and swept up her tablet, slipping it back into her bag. 'I'll go and see if the lying cow is back in the building. If not . . .' she looked around the office, drinking in the detail as she did so, 'I reckon this place can go about two days before it sinks under the weight of its own rubbish and filth. No offence. Then see where she is then.'

'The trouble is, Mrs B,' Maxwell said sadly, 'I think that Mrs Braymarr may be one of those honoured mortals to whom shit does not stick.'

'Hah!' The woman's derision was palpable. 'I don't reckon she's even mortal, Mr M, since you mention it. Still, I'll still see you at yours, won't I? From time to time?'

'Yes,' he said, answering her first question. 'Oftener than you think,' in answer to the second.

She was hardly out of the door when Helen Maitland took her place. 'Coffee?' She waggled the kettle at him.

'Yes, please. While we can.'

Helen had read the memo. All extraneous means of making beverages were now not allowed, following academy protocol. All snacks brought in by staff must comply with rules dictating the contents of students' snack boxes, viz and to wit, they had to be healthy and no chocolate was the law of the jungle from now on. Helen wasn't sure whether she had ever gone, waking or sleeping, for longer than three hours without chocolate and was already feeling the pinch, though her secret stashes remained, for now, secret. But she knew it was only a matter of time.

Helen set the coffee down on the table between them and sat, looking moodily into the grey-beige depths of her mug. Instant coffee wasn't good for her, it made her stomach acid and rebellious even without the stress they were all under, but even so it worked on her like a drug. How she was going to get through the day without it, she couldn't imagine. A vending machine somehow wasn't going to cut the mustard, even ignoring the fact that there was no possible way that it could cater for the disgruntled staff of what had once been a happy school. She lost herself in watching the milk form a greasy slick on the surface of her drink and so when Maxwell spoke, she jumped and slopped it all down her front.

'For God's sake, Max!' she screamed. 'Look what you made me do!' She dabbed at the stain with a tissue from her pocket, already disintegrating from an inadvertent turn in the tumble drier. It left gouts of fluff on her jumper and she burst into tears, pointing at the mess incoherently.

Maxwell, public schoolboy to the core, leapt up to close the door and draw the blind. He handed her the cleanest of the tea towels to hand and sat down again to wait for her to calm down. Years of Helen Maitland, calm and imperturbable in the worst crisis, had not trained him for this; centuries of hormonal girls of all sizes had. Waiting was the only game in town. Finally, his strategy bore fruit. She blew her nose on the tea towel and then looked at it in horror, holding it out to him as the man who could sort it out. He took it and dropped it on the floor. That was for later.

'Better?' he asked and she nodded, with a final sniff. 'It was time you had a good bawl,' he said. 'You've been taking this on the chin and it's no way to run a railroad, is it?'

She shook her head. 'I feel dreadful, really. I don't have half the problems some of the staff here have. I still have my job, for one thing. And even if I didn't, we wouldn't starve. But . . .' the tears welled up again.

He leaned forward and patted her hand. 'I know,' he said. 'It's been like being hit by a truck. I can't believe this method has ever worked. I've had Mrs B on the case.'

Helen looked at him through tear-clotted lashes. 'Mrs B? What's she going to do, hoover her to death?'

Maxwell reflected how quickly Fiona Braymarr had become 'her' — speak of the devil and she's bound to appear. 'No, although that is a plan, I suppose . . .' he appeared to give it sober reflection, imagining the woman's head, Tarantino-style, whizzing around with the fluff in the vacuum cleaner's innards. 'No, Mrs B is my secret IT weapon. She is a whizz on computers of all kinds and like a truffle hound if you need something found out.'

'There's a rumour that . . . she . . . isn't on Google,' Helen sniffed.

'Not a rumour, in fact. She really isn't, and that's why I have Mrs B on the case. She's already done some digging this morning, now she's off to find her sister's grandson . . .'

'Her great nephew, then.' Helen was doing Mendelian genetics with her Year Eleven and was in a bit of a groove.

'In any other family, almost certainly,' Maxwell agreed with a smile. He gave Helen's hand a final pat and sat up straight. The old back wasn't up to long-term care giving these days. 'Suffice to say, she'll find anything that's there to be found. And meanwhile, we'll all just have to sit tight and try to ride the whirlwind.' He looked up, lips moving, then added, 'If that's even possible, of course. Perhaps if you could grab hold of something as it whirls past . . .'

Helen laughed and took a swig from what remained of her cooling coffee. 'I don't think we're in Kansas any more, Toto,' she said.

Anyone less like a Munchkin than Helen Maitland it was hard to imagine, but Maxwell grinned at her. 'As long as we can get rid of the Wicked Witch of the West with no bones broken, we can be anywhere we like, can't we?'

Helen Maitland was an expert at Maxwell-reading and now she changed the subject, right on cue. 'Any news about Tommy Morton? Or the MacBride girls, come to that?'

'I went to see Tommy yesterday, as you know . . . was I missed at the meeting last night, by the way?'

Helen looked down and took another sip of her coffee. 'I don't know. I wasn't there.'

He raised his eyebrows. 'Was anyone?'

She chuckled deep in her throat. 'I don't know that either. It's hard to find anyone qualified to ask.'

'Dearie me,' he smiled. 'Poor Mrs Braymarr, all on her lonesome.'

'Well, no. Some people went. Just not people I talk too. Brown noses are so unattractive.'

'Indeed. Well, yes, Tommy; in the end, I didn't see him. His dad . . .'

'Man, thirty-three . . . is he *really* thirty-three? He looks . . .'

'Fifty, yes, I know. He arrived as I did and gave himself up.'

'That's that one, then.'

'I don't think so. I still think this case will run and run. But I can't say more, of course.'

'Of course.' Helen could have shaken him — there was nothing worse than someone with the need to gossip all but flashing in a neon sign on their heads who nevertheless was keeping schtum.

'The MacBride girls . . . that one is complicated but the short answer is they're with their granny somewhere. I must say that Ten Zed Ex Oh were a little more subdued than normal without Dee.'

'I teach the younger one. Not quite so obnoxious but with those two, you always have to remember who their dad is.'

'That's true. I understand he's a bit . . .' Although Maxwell was no byword when political correctness was being discussed, he searched for an acceptable word to describe

Geoff MacBride with some care. With so much of his information coming covertly from Jacquie, he had to remember who knew what about who.

'Oh, God, yes!' Helen cast her eyes heavenward. 'Anything with a pulse, flirting, you know, just to keep his hand in. But when it comes to . . .' she blushed a little, 'the full monty, as it were, his women are in two categories. Powerful or airheads. He usually runs one of each, as I understand it.'

'Really?' Maxwell nodded, ruminatively. 'That's interesting. I wonder who fills which niche at the moment?'

Helen leaned forward and dropped her voice. 'It very much depends on who you listen to,' she said and wriggled into a more comfortable position. Maxwell loved this woman, but even so was horribly reminded of Les Dawson swapping goss with Roy Barraclough. 'I know for a *fact* he was having it away with that woman, you know, thingie, leader of the council a while back.'

'Yes, I remember her,' Maxwell nodded. 'So that accounts for the airhead. What about the powerful woman?'

Helen leaned back, laughing. 'Point taken,' she said. 'I'll tell you one thing, though. He'll never crack Fiona Braymarr. She wouldn't give him a second glance.'

Maxwell chewed his lip. She was probably right; and he wouldn't want to be in Geoff MacBride's shoes when she turned him down. She was a whole new breed of spider, one who ate her mates *before* the deed was done, rather than after. Not a good long-term survival strategy, perhaps, but it didn't seem to be doing her much harm thus far.

'Are you going to today's meeting?' she said, a propos of nothing in particular.

'Is there one? After yesterday?'

'That's a good point. If I were . . . her . . . I wouldn't demean myself. But who knows what she's thinking?'

'I may be needed at the nick, of course. Tommy . . . well, you know the drill.'

She looked at him, eyes narrowed. 'What about Man, Thirty-three?'

'Ah, that's true. But Woman, Don't Ask Her Age If You Value Your Life has let slip that she doesn't really have him seriously in the frame.'

Helen was intrigued. 'So it *is* Tommy, then, after all?'

'Well, Man, One Thousand, doesn't think so,' Maxwell said.

'Max, you are a softie really,' she said. 'Don't worry — I'll make sure the kids don't find out.'

'No, no, nothing to do with being soft hearted. He used the magic words.'

'Which are . . . ?'

'In this case, "It was all my fault".'

Helen Maitland hadn't been in the business quite as long as Maxwell, but she knew the code. 'That clinches it, then,' she said. 'He didn't do it. Know who did?'

He pulled a rueful face. 'Not as yet.' Then he brightened. 'But I will.'

CHAPTER TEN

The Morton house could hardly have been more different from the MacBride one. It was tidy, with a minute brick-laid area in front neatly swept and with a small pot of crocuses in the porch, but everything about it was a little sad, a little mean as though whoever lived there was going through the motions for the sake of what the neighbours might say. Along the fence were ranged a few cellophane wrapped bunches of flowers and, unaccountably, a teddy bear, already rather bedraggled. Jacquie and the SOCO team drew up in echelon outside and she led the way round to the back door, the only one for which she had the key.

'Did either of you attend the scene?' she asked, over her shoulder.

Both men shook their heads, with a rustle of their paper suits.

'She had fallen against the front door, more or less. Her husband had difficulty getting in, or so he says.'

'Or difficulty getting out,' Josh added.

'Indeed. Well, lads, I don't have to tell you your jobs. Usual thing. Upstairs, check for who sleeps where. I would like you to check the boy's room carefully, though. I have . . .

well, a little inside info which makes me wonder about abuse. I'll check down here.'

She had no real hopes of finding such gold on the answering machine and in fact it was even more disappointing than she expected; there was no answering machine. 1571 just informed her that there were no new messages. The few bits of post on the mat were catalogues and offers of cheap life insurance, which in the circumstances were rather redundant. The Mortons seemed to live in a vacuum of their own misery, with no real friends or even acquaintances, the flowers and teddy outside notwithstanding. Jacquie looked around downstairs, touching nothing, but apart from the dried pool of blood on the hall carpet, there was nothing that said anything about what had happened. The fingerprint powder from the first SOCO sweep was still evident, but with a quick wipe and a blast of Mr Muscle, the house was good to go.

Time to speak to Hetty.

Jacquie went to the bottom of the stairs and called up. 'Josh? Are you there?'

There was a muffled response and a bump then he appeared, hanging over the banister. 'Yes, guv. Found anything? I was under the kid's bed.'

'Oh, sorry. No, nothing down here. I'm popping next door. Apparently, the neighbours called in possible child abuse a while ago.'

'Really?' Josh's eyebrows disappeared under the hood of his suit. 'That's interesting. So the kid did do it, then?'

'Let's not rush to judgement, Josh,' Jacquie told him. 'The CYP report said there was nothing amiss.'

Muffled though it was through the mask he wore, Josh's response was unmistakeable.

Ignoring it, Jacquie said, 'The neighbour just happens to be DCI Hall's sister, so we do have a bit more fore-knowledge than usual. At least we know it isn't a mad old biddy with a grudge and a glass to the wall.'

'True. Shall we leave the door when we go, if you're not back?'

'You might as well lock up. I won't need to get back in. Email me if you find anything.'

'Will do, guv,' and Josh was gone, back to the dubious pleasure of the underbed secrets of Tommy Morton.

* * *

As she walked down the Morton's tiny drive, along the small stretch of pavement and back up Hetty's path, Jacquie tried to imagine what the woman would be like. Would she be like Henry, bland and inscrutable behind outsize, reflecting glasses? Were they twins, as she and Maxwell had imagined? And what on earth was her name? She rang the bell and stood back. Although this house was the other half of the Morton's semi, the differences were clear. The windowsill was full of photographs in various different frames, scattered willy-nilly along its length. An old birthday card was wedged between two at the side and Jacquie imagined that from inside it was invisible behind the curtain and had just been left behind. A dog lead and a pair of wellies were stashed in a corner of the porch, a handful of poop scoop bags shoved down inside one boot. A single strand of left-behind Christmas tinsel was caught in a drawing-pin at the very top of the doorframe. Not neglected or dirty, Jacquie decided. Just a proper house, lived in by real people.

The bell was greeted by the yapping of a very small, very irate dog, clearly bouncing up and down just inside the door. Jacquie looked again at the lead, which was thick enough to tether a wild ox and was attached to a harness. A plaque on the front read 'Killer'. So, either Hetty had just lost a dog or she had a sense of humour. Jacquie hoped it would be the latter.

And it was. The barking stopped abruptly and the door was flung open. The woman who stood there was the complete antithesis of Henry Hall. She was little and round and her hair fluffed up crazily around her head. She held a minute Yorkie in one hand, almost absentmindedly. She *was* wearing glasses, but they were tiny, gold-framed and perched on the end of her ski-jump nose. 'Excuse Killer,' she said. 'He's all talk.' She looked her visitor up and down. 'You must be Jacquie. Henry's told me so much about you, I feel we're friends already.' She stepped aside, gesturing with Killer for Jacquie to go down the hall. 'Go down into the kitchen. It's warmer and I've just got some brownies out of the oven. We can have one while we chat.'

Jacquie found herself herded down the hall into a warm and welcoming kitchen. Pictures were stuck up on the fridge, of crooked houses, flowers the size of trees, people the size of giraffes. Hetty saw her glance and chuckled. 'The joys of grandparentdom,' she said. 'The other joy being you can give them back. Now,' she gestured with Killer again then, suddenly realising she still had him in her hand, put him down. 'Basket!' she said and with a warning yap, the little creature scuttled away to a minute basket in the corner by an Aga which had been shoehorned into the room. The whole atmosphere was of a farmhouse kitchen and Jacquie almost expected a couple of chickens to wander in from the yard outside. It was hard to remember that this house was one in a road of identical houses in the backend of Leighford.

Hetty sat down, picked up a knife and carved off a huge slab of brownie. 'Now,' she began again, 'you're obviously here about next door.'

Jacquie grasped this first opportunity she had been given to speak. 'Yes. Henry showed me the report from your phone call.'

'A disgrace!' The little woman fairly bristled with annoyance. 'I had a visit from some chit of a thing from Social Services and that was that. I had to change the bedroom round. I know that sounds cowardly, but I couldn't bear to hear what was going on any more.'

'I do understand,' Jacquie said. 'Sometimes the wheels come off the system. You did what you could.'

Hetty shrugged, tears in her eyes. 'I don't know what everyone is thinking, putting flowers outside. That woman was poison. Just poison.'

Jacquie got out her notebook. 'Do you mind if I jot a few things down?' she asked.

'Not at all. My husband is a policeman, or was before he retired. And Henry, of course. He's done so well.' She smiled. 'I bet you didn't even know he had a sister, did you?'

Jacquie smiled back. It was hard not to. 'DCI Hall keeps himself to himself,' she said, diplomatically.

'I'm older than him, of course,' Hetty reminisced. 'Not by that much, but enough to mean we were never in the same school together, that kind of gap.'

Jacquie understood. Maxwell and his sister Sandie were the same and although they loved each other, they had few terms of reference in common. She often wondered if Nolan was going to remain an only — time to do something about it if not . . . she tuned back in to Hetty.

'. . . so, I was something of a surrogate mother to Henry in many ways.' She walked over to a coffee machine on the worktop. 'Coffee? Or tea? It's only a matter of which pod to put in, I'm afraid. I haven't used a teapot in years.'

'Coffee, please,' Jacquie said, picking absently at the brownie, which was totally amazing. It stopped her in her tracks. 'This,' she said, pointing, 'this . . .'

'I know,' Hetty said, smugly. 'It's my own recipe. It always takes people like that. Sugar?'

Jacquie shook her head and flattened out her notebook, trying to look like someone who meant business. 'Can I just have your full name, please?' she said. 'For the record.'

Henry's big sister sat down and looked solemn. 'Really?' she said. 'Won't Hetty do?'

'Well, it will if it's your name.' Jacquie was quite excited. She was finally going to find out.

'I suppose you're right. If this goes to court, it has to be correct. The name is Ethel. Ethel Hampshire.'

Jacquie wrote it down, trying to swallow her disappointment.

'I was named after my grandmother,' Hetty said. 'As soon as it was done, my parents were sorry, so I have been Hetty ever since. And do you know,' she said, leaning forward, 'it's funny but lots of people think it's short for Henrietta.' She laughed. 'As if anyone would call one child Henrietta and another Henry. Madness!'

Jacquie laughed as well. 'Madness, you're quite right,' she said. 'Right, now . . . do you mind if I call you Hetty?'

'Oh, please! Mrs Hampshire is my mother-in-law in my book, even though she's been dead nearly twenty years, thank the lord.'

'Right.' Jacquie could see that there would be no problem with getting the truth out of Hetty Hampshire. She just opened her mouth and everything just fell out. 'I won't take you back through the entire history of next door, what you've heard and so on. I would just like the gist, if that's all right, with a bit more detail over the last . . . shall we say week or so?'

Hetty took a bite of brownie and frowned. 'It's hard to know where to start . . . We lived here already when they moved in. They'd only been married a month or so then and she was so pregnant she was ready to pop. She wasn't very friendly, but I went round, with some clothes of the boys', you know, baby things to help them along. They didn't seem to have much and they were very young. He wasn't even twenty, I shouldn't think, though she was obviously quite a bit older. From the start, he was besotted by the baby, although from things she dropped in conversation, he wasn't his.'

'She told you about that? Did she say who the father was?'

Hetty laughed and sprayed brownie crumbs across the table. 'Sorry. No, she never said. But she was very inappropriate about poor Thomas.' The older woman blushed. 'Comparisons. That kind of thing.'

'To you — face to face?' Jacquie thought she had better check. 'It wasn't just things you might overhear?'

'Oh, no. The overhearing was different. I never could hear the words. Just the tone. And then that poor little boy — well, not so little, now, I suppose — crying. Sobbing all night long. It broke my heart. That's why my husband moved the bedroom round. So we couldn't hear.'

'I do understand, Hetty.' Jacquie could see she was beginning to get upset and she knew gossip usually dried up when tears flowed. 'Did you notice any change lately? More shouting? Less? Visitors?'

'Well, of course, Louise didn't go out to work.' Hetty said this as though it explained it all.

'No, I knew she was a stay at home mum.'

'I think that gives the wrong impression,' Hetty said, setting her lips primly. 'I was a stay at home mum. I am now a stay at home granny. That means you keep the house nice, you cook, you bake. I personally like to write. Blogs, mainly, but I am getting a bit of a name for myself, in the blogging fraternity.' She dropped her lids modestly for a moment, then her eyes flashed up and met Jacquie's. 'But *her*? Louise? No, she was stay at home, but not really a mum. She was more a stay at home tart.' Her hand flew to her mouth. 'I'm sorry. I shouldn't have said that. Evil to he who evil thinks, you know.'

'Honi soit qui mal y pense. My husband would be proud of you.'

'Not "Honey, your silk stocking's falling down"?'

'Prouder still — it's not everyone who reads *1066 And All That* these days.'

'Henry has often said we would be kindred spirits. He's very fond of your husband.'

Jacquie had always suspected it, but it was nice to have confirmation. 'So, when you say "tart" . . .'

'I don't mean the house was always full of men or even that they formed an orderly queue.' Hetty pushed the brownie tray nearer and Jacquie cut another piece. 'But there *were* men that came quite regularly. Almost . . . but . . .'

'Hetty. I know all about not speaking ill of the dead, but this is a murder enquiry.'

The woman sighed and nodded. 'Yes, of course, I'm sorry. I just think of Thomas and that poor child.'

'Were you going to say "almost by appointment"?'

She nodded. 'I didn't always see them arrive, but it's hard not to notice the cars. Most of them would pull up off the road and as you saw when you got here, that means it's almost under our window. The same ones, by and large, on the same day. But not usually more than once a week, sometimes as infrequently as once a fortnight or less. Colin — my husband — he used to say he should report it. That it wouldn't do his career any good to live next door to a knocking shop. Excuse the phrase, but that's what he said. Then he always said that at least he didn't work nearby . . .'

'Where was he based?' Jacquie couldn't remember ever meeting a Colin Hampshire.

'He worked almost all his career in Southampton,' she said. 'He always had a horror of working and living in the same town. He used to say that Henry had to step carefully because of that. And you too, my dear . . . sorry, I feel I know you . . .'

'Don't worry,' Jacquie smiled. 'I've been called worse. I have it double, because teachers have to toe the line even more than the police.' And one day, she thought, mine might actually start doing it. 'But Colin really thought that, did he? That it was a brothel?'

'Not a brothel, I suppose. She didn't have . . . staff. It was just her and a few select men. Very select, judging by the cars.'

'Did you recognise anyone?'

'Do you know,' Hetty leaned forward, in full gossip mode, 'I did in a few cases. Not that they were famous or anything. Just reasonably well known. You know that bloke who bought up all those little corner shops and opened them 24 hours a day, sold them for millions a few months later.'

'Yes.'

'Well, him. And the one who used to run the buses.'

'I wouldn't have thought he was that well off.'

'Perhaps not. But he was her boss for a while, according to Thomas. Back when they met first. I expect it was for old time's sake.' Hetty chuckled. Now the gossip was off her chest, she felt better.

'So Thomas knew?'

'Pardon?' Hetty didn't remember saying that.

'You said Thomas told you about their boss.'

'No, that was in another conversation. No, he didn't know, I don't think. Although he must have wondered where the money came from, surely.'

'So money did change hands?' This was interesting, but it made the suspect list very long; or very short, depending on how jealous Thomas Morton could get.

'I think it must have done, don't you?' Hetty sat back, with arms folded. 'Some of them were okay to look at. One in particular . . . but that's another matter altogether. But some of them were really no great shakes. Older, if you know what I mean. My age. Colin's age. Not someone you would have sex with for nothing.' She blushed crimson. 'Oh!'

'Don't worry, Hetty,' Jacquie said. 'I won't tell Colin you said that. But Louise, if she was older than Thomas, she must be knocking forty.'

'Well preserved, though,' Hetty said. 'And young by the standards of some of the men. And then there was the . . . enthusiasm. I had to turn the hoover on sometimes, to drown them out.'

'Goodness.' Jacquie sat back in her seat.

'So, I can't say I'm sorry she's dead. I'm many things, but not a hypocrite, I hope.'

Jacquie made a note. 'Did you see anyone different over the last week or so?'

'Hard to tell. And I haven't been here as much during the day since Christmas. My daughter's youngest, called Maple for some reason known only to her parents, poor little soul, has had a bad chest, so I have been going there to do the granny stuff, rather than have her here. I did hear raised voices last week . . .'

'So you had to switch the hoover on?' Jacquie thought she would check.

'No, no, not that kind of raised voices. I mean an argument. The door slammed and a man came out and drove away. He went over the grass verge. Made quite a mess; it was after that last sharp frost and the ground was soggy.'

'Excuse me.' Jacquie saw a clue materialise in front of her. She took out her mobile and chose a number. Distant sounds of the theme tune from *CSI: Miami* reached them through the wall. 'Oh, good,' she said to Hetty, 'they're still there . . . Josh? Still here.'

Her phone made plaintive squawks.

'No, I don't have a tracker on you. I could hear your phone through the wall. Before you go, can you have a look outside, see if there are any tyre tracks on the grass outside? If so, can you take a cast or something?'

This time, her phone was indignant.

'Well, why don't you carry it in your kit? This is important. Leave Robert here and go and get some if you have to, but don't leave it to the crime scene tape. That's just asking for tampering.'

Sulky quacking.

'Thank you. Let me know how you get on. Bye.' And she put the phone down. 'They watch too much TV,' she said with a smile.

'I hope I haven't given that nice young man a difficult job,' Hetty said. 'But I don't think anyone else has parked up on the verge since then. Anyway, after that, it was quiet for a day or so, then they started again. It's usually just one a day . . . *was* I suppose I should say. It's hard to remember what's happened.' She stopped for a moment, not tearful but clearly shocked. 'This is a nice road. Not very expensive, these houses, but nice people. Mostly. I think though, since then there's been . . . let me think. The bus chap. I know he's been. Somebody else I know . . . I can't place him, though, but I definitely know his face. And . . . that's it. Quiet week.'

Jacquie put a few final touches to her notes and then closed the book. 'Nothing on Monday night?'

Hetty shook her head. 'No. Colin was at the golf club, it was some farewell do, I don't usually go to those. And I was in here, baking.' She saw Jacquie's face. 'I don't spend my life baking, but my David's eldest has a cake stall at school every

Tuesday, so I try to do my bit. So, I didn't hear anything, although now I think about it, I didn't hear as much hectoring from Louise as normal.' She went white and raised her eyes to meet Jacquie's. 'Was she . . . was she already dead?'

'We believe she died somewhere around eleven,' Jacquie told her.

'I was in bed by then,' Hetty said, relieved. 'And Colin came in around twelve and said there was a lot of kerfuffle next door, but I didn't really take much notice. I just thought perhaps someone else had called the police.'

'They had,' Jacquie said, simply. 'Tommy called, to say his mother had been stabbed.' She popped the last bite of brownie into her mouth and stood up, brushing crumbs off her skirt. 'Well, thanks so much, Hetty, for the information and the delicious brownie.' Killer sat up and growled, in a falsetto.

'Killer!' Hetty admonished. 'He won't hurt you,' she said, 'but then I suppose you had already guessed that. But we like to indulge him, bless him. He means well.' And still whittering, Hetty bustled Jacquie to the front door and out into the wild March day.

* * *

Henry Hall was waiting in Jacquie's office when she got back. He was sitting in her visitor's chair, in an attitude which in anyone else would be rapt attention, but in Henry Hall's case was complete relaxation. He looked round as she came in.

'Hello,' he said. 'Where've you been? You left Hetty's ages ago.'

'Dear me,' she said, unravelling her scarf and hanging it and her coat on the hook behind the door. 'So now you've got a policeperson manqué in your family, too. And a real one, of course, counting Colin.'

He smiled his tiny, fleeting smile. 'She's taken to you. Hetty does have . . . her enthusiasms. She also has her . . . is there an opposite to enthusiasms?'

Jacquie sat down behind her desk and leaned back. 'Are you trying to tell me something, guv? That what I got from your sister may be a little inaccurate, for example?'

Hall had the grace to look a little abashed. 'Not inaccurate, no. But she has been known to indulge in hyperbole.'

Jacquie smiled. 'The dog is called Killer — but as far as I recall, that was the only hyperbole I noticed, really. Everything she said seemed to chime with what we know from other sources and apart from the fact that she said she had to turn the hoover on to drown Louise and her gentleman callers out . . .'

'Oh, no,' Hall said. 'I've been there when she had to do that. It was quite something, I can tell you. Poor old Colin, he's a bit strait-laced; he got in quite a stew.'

'Guv! I'm sorry,' she snorted with laughter, 'I'm just trying to picture it . . .'

'It wasn't funny at the time,' he said, and allowed himself a small laugh, 'but it was in retrospect, I have to grant you that. It sounded like a badly dubbed porn film. But I suppose she was just giving the client what he was after . . . so to speak.'

'So,' Jacquie brought the conversation back to the job in hand, 'she really was on the game, you think?'

Hall took a deep breath and expelled it slowly. 'Hmm, that's hard to say. It's always difficult, as you know yourself, to bring these talented amateurs to court. But I should say as near as makes no difference, yes.'

'Apart from what Hetty told me,' Jacquie said, 'I have made a bit of headway today, but I don't know really how to tell you . . .'

Hall looked at her through blank lenses. 'What?'

'Well . . . it's the C word . . .'

'Coincidence?' He got up from the visitor's hard chair and made for the door. 'When it's more than coincidence, tell me then.'

'I'll email you,' Jacquie said. 'When I've thought it through.'

'Look forward to it,' Hall said and left, closing the door carefully behind him, as ever. But she nevertheless heard him snort to himself as he walked away. 'Coincidence! Hah!'

* * *

The desk sergeant looked up and his heart fell. He toyed with pressing his button, but it had been taped over by maintenance, pending its removal. He would miss his button.

'Mr Maxwell,' he said, with false bonhomie. 'Can I help you?'

'If you could just ask my wife to step down into the foyer for a moment,' Maxwell's smile was equally false, 'that would be simply marvellous. I promise I won't keep her long.'

Without taking his eyes off Maxwell, the desk sergeant picked up the phone and punched a number. 'Ma'am? I have your husband here . . . Yes, of course.' With a sour expression, the man looked Maxwell up and down one last time, then pressed a switch. The door into the inner sancta swung inwards, accompanied by a persistent buzz. 'She says go up.'

Maxwell tipped his hat and sketched a bow. 'Thank you. Usual offices?'

This was an old joke and the desk sergeant ignored it. 'Third on the right, top of the stairs, yes, sir.'

Maxwell wondered if the man had had drama lessons some time in his dim and distant past. It wasn't easy to put so much venom into one three letter word, but he did it with aplomb. He climbed the stairs, wondering quite why he had come. He had sorted it out by the time he tapped on his wife's door. In the absence of Sylvia, the only place he could go when he needed a bit of a detox from Leighford High School was wherever his wife was — and at four in the afternoon, that place was here.

Jacquie was still behind her desk, but her whole demeanour was that of a woman ready to leap into action. Master of body language that he was, Maxwell immediately put out a restraining hand. 'He's all right. I'm all right. The Count is all right, as far as I know. Mrs Troubridge is all right . . . um . . . is that everyone?'

His wife visibly relaxed. 'I don't usually see you here at this time, that's all.' She glanced at the calendar icon on her laptop. 'Wednesday?' she ventured.

'In all probability. It's Beavers, as far as I remember. And if it isn't Wednesday, it's soccer or choir. Say one thing for the kid, he's a busy little devil.'

She laughed. As an only child, she had been determined that Nolan would never want for company. He had taken the decision out of her hands, by being naturally gregarious and also nosy — there was no club that he hadn't tried, including, for one hilarious week, ballet. But that was the only one that had beaten him, although the ballet teacher may have said that he had beaten it. With her worries allayed, she pushed her chair back and looked across the desk at her husband, rather more dishevelled as to hair than normal after a rather blustery ride over on White Surrey. 'So why *are* you here?'

He shrugged. 'Lonely?'

'You? Since when have you been lonely?' She could have bitten her tongue as soon as the words were out of her mouth. She could only imagine what it had been like for him when his wife and daughter had died, long years ago. But he took her words as she had meant them and answered accordingly.

'Since Sylv left. Since Attila the Hen took over.' He smiled at her. 'So, I suppose, since Monday. But it seems longer. Much, *much* longer. The school isn't the same. Mrs B and all her ladies and Daniel have downed hoovers; almost everyone is boycotting the daily meetings, which, don't misunderstand me, is a *good* thing, but it does mean that the staff are split as never before. I mean, we have had the Huge Parking Space crisis of 1992, the Don't Get Me Started Debacle of Oh Five, but this is more than anything that has gone before. No one is speaking, except in huddles. Even Mavis didn't try to kill me this morning and that isn't something I'm used to, believe me.' He sighed and ran his hands through his hair, to its detriment. 'And in all this, three of our kids have been made motherless and no one seems to have noticed. What are we becoming?'

Jacquie looked at the man sitting across from her and wondered, as she often did, how many layers he had. He had grown shells over the years to protect himself from life's boulders raining down on him from on high, but the real, essential Maxwell couldn't help peeping out, usually daily. She got up and went round the desk, just to give him a peck on the cheek, then went and sat again.

Maxwell grinned at her. 'Small, but perfectly formed,' he said, gesturing to his cheek. 'You see, that's all I needed. Maxwell's himself again.' As ever, his Richard III, channelled through Laurence Olivier, was perfection. 'No, what I really came for — apart from a lovely kiss and to see your face in the hours of daylight, of course — was to see what's what about the aforementioned deceased parents. Those of the staff who can still see anything beyond the ends of their own noses have been asking — although why they would think *I* know anything . . .' His voice trailed away and he adjusted an imaginary skirt, took off imaginary glasses and tossed back imaginary flowing platinum hair.

'Why, Miss Smith, you're lovely,' Jacquie said, automatically. Then, more business-like, 'I can't tell you anything you don't know already, Max. Man, thirty-three, remember?'

'Yes, yes,' he waved a dismissive hand. 'We all know *that*. But I know you, Detective Inspector Carpenter-Maxwell. You have not been sitting on your admittedly very attractive arse all day. You have more info or I'm a Dutchman.'

'I still can't tell you what it is, Mijnheer van Dijk.'

'Droll. Very droll.' Maxwell narrowed his eyes at his wife. 'Do you mean you really can't tell me, or you can't tell me . . .' and he lowered his voice, '. . . here?'

'Look,' she also lowered her voice, 'you know you always get it out of me in the end and I promise I'll tell you everything when we get home. But I have a few emails to send, a few reports to read and then I'll be done. Are you on Surrey?'

He nodded and raised a leg, pointing to his cycle clips.

'Right, well, you get on home, start something scrummy for dinner and I'll pick up Nole from whatever he's doing today and when everyone is fed and ready for bed, I'll tell you what I know.'

He smiled and bounced up and down.

'If you're good.'

'As gold. Bitterballen and patats, to continue the Dutch theme?'

'Why not? Rissoles and chips always go down a treat. But I think on balance, I'd rather have something I can just lie in and inhale. It's been quite a day.'

'Paella?' Maxwell gave his scarf a twirl and headed for the door.

'Perfect. You may have to pick up some rice on the way home. Other than that, it's all there in the freezer.'

'Right you are — see you later for something hot, yellow and Spanish.' He flung the door open and cannoned into Henry Hall coming the other way. 'That's paella I'm talking about, Henry,' he said. 'In case you were wondering.'

Hall shook his hand — it had been a while but neither man was much of a social hugger. 'I never wonder when you are around, Max. I was just coming in to try to steal your wife for the evening, but it looks as though you already have plans.'

'No,' Maxwell said, trying to conceal his disappointment. 'You can have her if you want her. One careful owner, you know the drill.'

Hall looked at the man and dithered for a moment or two. Over the years, they had clashed it was true, but when they had stopped crashing antlers, they had found they had much in common. They both loved Jacquie, for a start — and as starts go, it was as good a one as they could wish. Hall had had to concede, too, that usually Maxwell had his finger on the pulse of the beating heart of Leighford and had often beaten the police to the punchline; so he came to a decision.

'Paella?' he said. 'Enough for one more?'

Maxwell looked over his shoulder at Jacquie. 'You'd have to ask the Mem,' he said. 'I cook it, but she buys it. Only she knows if there is enough.' It was an elegant let-out if she wanted one, leaving no bones broken.

'Of course there's enough,' she said, smiling. 'Just you, or is this a family invite?'

'Oh, no — it's work, really.' Hall saw Maxwell's face. 'And you're included, of course, though keep that bit to yourself. I would appreciate your input, actually. Call it a professional consultation.'

'Oooh!' Maxwell's eyes lit up. 'Expenses!' He clapped a hand down on Hall's shoulder and whirled out, turning back only to cry, 'Krupuk?'

'Why not,' Jacquie said, laughing.

Hall sat down in Maxwell's recently vacated chair. 'Krupuk?'

'Giant prawn crackers,' she said. 'You would need to have a printout of the previous conversation to really get the gist of that. But . . . I'm surprised, guv, to tell you the truth. You don't usually involve Max so . . . overtly.'

Hall sighed. 'I've read your emails, and heard the voicemails. I don't do coincidences, as you know, and yet . . . are these murders connected? How can they be?'

'How can they *not* be?' Jacquie was as sure of her ground as he was. 'Max will clear the view,' she said. 'He can pick the bones out of anything. And he does a darn fine paella, too.'

CHAPTER ELEVEN

The room at the Ellisdon had, like hotel rooms the world over, windows which opened a meagre inch at the bottom. Geoff MacBride struggled with it for a moment or two, then gave up.

'Whatever are you doing?' Fiona Braymarr said, sleepily, from the bed. 'Those windows don't open any more than that. And anyway, it's March. What do you want to open the window for, anyway? It's not hot in here.'

MacBride thumped his hand on the glass and turned back to her, pulling the curtains closed behind him. 'I'm not hot,' he said, peevishly. 'I just feel . . . I feel a bit shut in. I'm not very well.' He sat on the bed and suddenly shouted, 'My wife has just been murdered, you know!'

She looked at him, her head on one side. 'I do know,' she said. 'I've had several rather high-powered meetings about it today, as it happens.'

He was working himself up into a fury, one which had been a long time coming. 'Meetings?' he spat. 'You've had *meetings*? Oh, well, dearie me. Poor little you. I, on the other hand, I have been quizzed by the police. I have driven over to the home of the rancid old bat I must call my ex-mother-in-law, I suppose, now, and asked . . . no, begged her to let me see my children. Apparently, they are too traumatised to see me, so I had to come away, as she threatened to call the police if I carried on shouting at her front door. And you, you've had *meetings*?' He subsided, the sweat sticking his rather meagre hair to his brow. A vein pulsed unattractively at a temple and he was a rather disconcerting shade of purple.

'You should try to calm down,' she remarked. 'You won't get anywhere by having a stroke, will you?'

He looked at her, nostrils dilated, panting.

She could cope with him. She could cope with all men. It didn't matter whether it was in a boardroom or a bedroom, she could cope with them and eventually bend them to her will. She put the thoughts of Maxwell to the back of her mind. He was proving less susceptible than most, but she would get there in the end. But this man; she gave a little smile. This man she could cope with any day of the week.

'Don't smirk!' he snapped.

'Darling,' she purred. 'I wasn't smirking. I was smiling. When I said "stroke" it just reminded me of something.'

'Oh, really?' He really was in a *very* bad mood. 'Some poor old buffer at one of your high-level meetings, was it? Some old git had a stroke?'

'No, silly.' She didn't trot out the girlish laugh more often than she had to. It turned her stomach, but needs must, sometimes. 'I was thinking about you and having a stroke.' She whipped back the bedclothes. 'Stroke this, why don't you?' It was a cliché, but it was one which had always worked thus far.

He curled his lip and leaned forward. 'Are you serious? *Are you serious*? I am telling you about my . . . my *life*. It's unravelling, woman. And you lie there with your fanny out, like some tart. No, I do *not* want to stroke that! I don't ever want to touch or see anything of yours, ever again. If I speak to you, you'll be lucky.' He stood up and looked at her with disgust all over his face. 'I don't know what I was thinking,' he said, half to himself.

She pulled the covers back up and sat up against the pillows, her folded arms keeping the duvet tucked in tight. 'I know what you *were* thinking, though,' she said. 'I know what you're thinking *now*. There's a nice bit of . . . what did you call it, you suburban little oik? There's a nice bit of *fanny*. I'll have some of that.'

He was putting on his coat, checking his hair in the mirror. 'And you didn't complain,' he remarked.

'Indeed not,' she said. 'There's no need to be unpleasant. You're a damned good lay, as it happens. Lots of little tricks. But don't think I went along with this for the sake of your dick, darling. I did it because you are Chair of Governors at Leighford High School and chair of lord knows what else besides. I know you screw over anyone you want to, but I thought you might not screw me over if you were screwing me as well. And I was right.' She gave him a smug smile. 'You can't go back now on anything you said or did. Because I *will* wash my dirty linen in public, don't you fret. Your alibi for the night your lovely spouse took a header off the balcony — gone. And I don't mean that farrago of lies you spouted to the police; I mean the *real* alibi, the one you'll need sooner or later. So, bugger off if you're going. Stay if you want to. But don't just stand there in your coat — you look like an idiot.'

Geoff MacBride was many things. He was a brilliant car salesman. He was an excellent chairman of any number of committees. He was a bad father and worse husband. And when he opened his flies, his brains fell out. He looked at her, lying there, outraged belligerence personified, red spots of anger on her cheeks, her eyes sparkling and her lips damp and parted.

And he unbuttoned his coat.

* * *

Metternich loved paella night. He wasn't one for people food as a rule, but as Nolan didn't consider mussels to be people food and so passed them under the table, the cat was happy to oblige with their discreet removal. It was a manoeuvre which Maxwell and Jacquie were happy to live with; it certainly beat stepping on a last night's mussel in bare feet over breakfast into a cocked hat.

When the last grain of rice had been chased round the plate and the last drops of saffrony juice had been mopped up, Nolan asked politely if he may leave the table and did so, smiling beatifically at Henry Hall as he left the room.

Hall was impressed. Jacquie of course and by definition always obeyed the rules; even as he said that in the quiet of his brain, he knew that to not be strictly true, but to all intents and purposes, it was the case. Nolan's father, on the other hand, was a card so wild it was impossible to know what he might do next and, although mostly pleasant to those he brushed up in his daily meanderings, Hall had also seen him cut through rubbish, fools, bureaucracy and similar irritants like a knife through butter. And no one knew when or where the Maxwell axe would fall, the secret, though Hall didn't know it, of his success in the classroom. A class on tenterhooks was a class which wouldn't explode — yet.

'He is such a great kid,' Hall said, a little wistfully. He remembered his boys as nice kids too, but had far too few memories of them for his liking.

'We like him,' Maxwell remarked. 'We're thinking of keeping him.'

'I heard that!' a small voice called, from the landing above.

Hall looked stricken.

'Don't worry, Henry,' Jacquie soothed. 'Nolan has many failings, but one is always being a little slow to leave earshot. We've learned to adjust to it.'

'But . . . don't you worry he might . . .' he looked from one to the other, '. . . overhear? I know you two talk about . . .' he couldn't keep his eyes from the door, 'things.'

'No things until we know he is fast asleep,' Maxwell said firmly. 'He only lingers. He doesn't use anything more dastardly than that. He's just hoping to be invited to stay for dessert. But no such luck. He can hardly move as it is.'

'He is a good little trencherman,' Hall agreed. His youngest had gone through three horrendous years of eating only cold chicken and bread.

'He's always liked his food,' Jacquie said, gathering the plates and taking them to the side. 'He knows if he doesn't eat it, the cat might have it. It's a great incentive.' She flicked the switch on the coffee maker. 'Shall we go through while this does? Max, can you go and check for signs of washing; don't worry about the neck, as we have a guest. No need to expose Henry to the screaming.'

'I don't always scream,' Maxwell pointed out, reasonably, as he went out. 'Sometimes it is more a . . .' and he ran up the stairs two at a time, to his and Hall's amazement, '. . . hoodling sort of roar.' He burst into Nolan's room to gales of slightly hysterical laughter from within.

Hall and Jacquie went on into the sitting room and sat side by side on the sofa. Maxwell's chair awaited the great man's entrance, which he effected with a tray of coffee.

'Henry, Sweetness; sugar on the tray, milk in the . . .' he looked down at the tray, left the room, came back in with the jug, '. . . jug.' He sat down, and crossed his legs. 'So, Henry, how can I help you?'

'I don't think I have specific questions, to ask you just like that,' Hall said. 'It's more a mulling things over, really. Jacquie knows how I hate coincidences . . .'

'To the extent of not believing in them at all, I should say,' Jacquie said.

Hall nodded his agreement. 'Yes,' he said. 'That. But this case seems full of them. Everyone seems linked to everyone else. It isn't possible that the only night in the history of this police force when two people are murdered within a couple of hours of each other should involve two women who seem to have links with each other . . . but, there it is. Can't be ignored.'

'Which would you prefer?' Maxwell asked. 'That there is a link, or that it is just coincidence?'

'They can't both be victims of one killer,' Hall said. 'We have narrowed down the times of death and it wouldn't be possible, just logistically.'

'*Strangers on a Train*,' Maxwell remarked.

'Don't start the Hitchcock nonsense with me,' Hall said. 'This is real life, not a film.'

'True,' Maxwell agreed. 'But I bet there isn't anyone alive who hasn't thought how brilliant it would be if someone would kill their wife, mother, boss . . . no offence intended, to either of you,' he added, hurriedly.

'What about the children?' Hall asked. 'Are they friends, at all?'

'Hmm.' Maxwell had to think of ways to describe Dee MacBride without resorting to hyperbole. 'Tommy Morton is a nice child, I think, but hampered rather by being not very attractive and also being a bit . . . cowed. This makes him stroppy with his peers, because they are the only ones he can lash out at. The girls completely faze him, and when we come to Dee MacBride that's fair enough. She fazes most people. She's stroppy, too, but with everyone. She wants to hit out at men, due to her father's behaviour, I would imagine, but raging hormones are making her see that they have their uses. We need Sylv for this, really.'

'That was pretty good,' Hall said, impressed.

'What about the younger one,' Jacquie asked. 'She seems to have rather been forgotten.'

'And she is,' Maxwell said. 'Speak to any member of staff at Leighford about her and they are hard pressed to remember her name. Dee takes all the attention. Paula is the prettier one, but she plasters makeup all over her face, almost like a mask.'

Jacquie tutted. 'Are you sure that's not just your inner old git talking there, Max?' She turned to Henry. 'He hates too much makeup,' she explained.

'I hate makeup full stop on a girl her age,' Maxwell argued. 'She'll never have such nice skin again; why cover it up?'

The two police persons looked at him as if they had never seen him before.

'Well, they won't.' He looked at them. 'What? I've spent the last ten lifetimes, if memory serves, in the company of adolescent girls and, occasional spot notwithstanding, they are all better off with no makeup. How did we get here, anyway?'

'Paula MacBride,' Hall prompted.

'Yes. Sorry. Paula is the brighter of the two as well, I would say her mother's child, if you believe in the favourites theory.'

'So . . . you don't think she could have killed her mother.' Hall sounded disappointed.

'What?' Jacquie was staggered. 'Where did *that* come from?'

Hall shrugged. 'Desperation?' he suggested.

'I should think so, too. I don't think it could have been done by a child at all.'

'Any particular reason why not?' Maxwell was not one to underestimate what a child could do; his millennia at the chalk face had taught him that if nothing else.

'Physical, mainly. The fingernails were cleaned after death, Jim Astley has confirmed; there were tears under the nails following quite a rough job, but no healing or inflammation, suggesting it was after she died. There are absolutely no signs on the balcony that this happened up there; and, believe me, we have done a fine toothcomb search. So . . .'

'. . . it had to be done elsewhere and she was then carried to the balcony,' Maxwell finished her sentence. 'Unless . . .'

'Unless?' Hall didn't mind how bonkers the ideas were. They were bound to be better than nothing.

'Ignore me. I was wondering if she could have been . . . thrown?'

'Don't be ridiculous, Max,' Jacquie said. 'Anyway, we know she came from the balcony. There are scuffs up there which would account for it.'

'In that case,' Maxwell said, swigging the last of his coffee and getting up in search of glasses and the Southern Comfort bottle, 'I got nothing!'

Henry Hall shook his head at the proffered bottle and got up with a sigh. 'Well, thank you very much for the dinner,' he said. 'I'll see you tomorrow, Jacquie.' He leaned forward and shook Maxwell's hand. 'Max. Thanks for your . . . input.'

'I'll get your coat for you, guv,' Jacquie said. 'Sorry if we didn't have the answer for you.'

'No, no,' Hall said. 'It's been . . .' and Maxwell didn't hear the rest, as he went off down the stairs.

Maxwell was back in his chair, nursing a glass when Jacquie came back. A gin and tonic was sparkling on the table by her normal seat at the end of the sofa. She raised it to him and drank.

'So,' Maxwell said, thoughtfully. 'The coincidence is just that the kids go to Leighford High, is it?'

'No,' Jacquie said. 'Of course not. There are other . . . links.'

'I thought there must be,' he said. 'If the kids going to Leighford is all there is, then most crimes will be linked. What are the other coincidences? And why didn't Henry mention them?'

'Cold feet? You know how he hates to tell you anything.'

'What are they?' Maxwell was nothing if not persistent.

'We have reason to believe . . .' she began.

Maxwell raised an eyebrow and took a miniscule sip of his drink.

'There seems to be a link between Mrs MacBride and Thomas Morton. We don't quite know what it is, yet. He had left a short message on her answerphone which he won't discuss. When he heard she was dead, he was very upset. But then again, he was told by Rick Shopley, so that might be why. He isn't exactly Mr Compassion.'

'But he must have said something. Not just that he was upset.'

'He said it was confidential.'

Maxwell's eyebrows shot up. 'What an odd thing to say. Now she's dead, it all seems . . .'

'A bit by the way, exactly.' Jacquie had been mulling it over all afternoon. 'And on top of that, Mrs MacBride also had what almost amounts to a threatening call, earlier in the evening than Morton's. It was from what I learned to call in LA a 'burner', a mobile phone with no registered owner and no way of being tracked. If it is still being used, we can't find where or by whom.'

Maxwell watched TV. More specifically, he watched *CSI*. 'But can't you . . .' he waved his arms in the air, 'something to do with towers, isn't it?'

Jacquie smiled. She knew what towers were in his mind; the topless towers of Ilium at the very least. 'No. We can't.'

'Oh.' He looked hopefully at her over the rim of his glass. 'Voice recognition?'

'Tell me whose voice it is, we'll recognise it,' she said, letting him down gently. 'Until then . . . no.'

'What about Mrs Morton? Did she have an answerphone?'

'Not so you'd notice. She did have a nice little sideline, though.'

'Oh, really. Don't tell me — she was Mrs MacBride's cleaner.'

'Nope.'

'Hairdresser?'

'Wrong again.'

'Ah!' he sat up, spilling his drink. '*Manicurist!*'

'Nice thought. But no. She was by way of being what Henry delightfully calls "a talented amateur".'

'A what?'

Jacquie waited for the penny to drop.

'Oh!' Maxwell cast his mind back to see if he could remember what the woman looked like, but came up blank. 'Oh, I *see*. That does explain a lot. But, surely, not with Tommy in the house?'

'No. This was strictly a daytime business opportunity,' Jacquie told him.

'Did the husband tell you that?'

'No. I went to see Hetty. You remember, Henry's sister.'

'Of course. Who lives next door. Wait a minute! Is her name really Henrietta?'

'Now, wouldn't you like to know?'

'Oh, come on. Tell me,' he wheedled. 'I'll tell you what. If you tell me Hetty's name, I'll tell you who your murderer is.'

'Good deal,' she said, lying back on the sofa and closing her eyes, 'you first.'

'But . . .'

She opened one eye. 'When you can show me yours, I'll show you mine. But until then, no dice.'

* * *

'Why the scarf, Count, I don't hear you ask?' Maxwell's right eye loomed huge through the magnifying glass. 'Well, it must have been a *little* embarrassing for Sergeant Williams, not to mention painful, but he had a boil on the end of his nose and he rode the Charge with a scarf over it. Can't look unsightly in the face of the enemy. That was in Army Regulations.'

The cat yawned. What *was* the old duffer whittering on about now? This was their special place, Man and Cat, the attic at 38 Columbine which Maxwell called the War office. Jacquie only ventured up here twice a year, to pick up the Christmas decorations in December and to put them away again in January. Nolan *was* allowed, but he understood from a very early age that Dad's soldiers were out of bounds.

They sat, all 403 of them, perfectly painted, perfectly plastic in their 54mm finery, as they would have looked that chill October morning back in 1854. They'd had no breakfast and the damned Ruskies were already on the move. They were Lord Cardigan's Light Brigade and Sergeant Richard Williams, he of the boil, was about to take his place on the flanks of the 17th Lancers, a boy looking for glory.

Metternich knew better than to touch the Brigade, too. He was content to bask in the warm lamp glow, to sniff the glue and the paint and to try to work out why a man of Maxwell's vast brain should ruin his eyesight by fiddling with bits so small and so pointless. Metternich was used to handling little bits too, but at least they had a purpose; and they tasted just delicious. In his case, the fiddly bits had once belonged to a field mouse, but the distinction was immaterial.

There was a companionable silence for a while, broken from time to time when the Count forgot himself enough to purr and when Maxwell stifled an oath when he dropped something small, plastic and essential onto a pile of other small plastic bits. Metternich found himself growing tense as the silence lengthened. Normally, the mad old bugger had started asking him things by now. He did his best to answer, he really did, but it sometimes seemed to him that the old fool wasn't really quite firing on all cylinders. He certainly didn't take all of his comments on board, that was for sure.

Maxwell put down his magnifying glass and Sergeant Williams' arm. Metternich looked up expectantly, tongue still out from having a darned good forage amongst what remained of his personal bits. Thank goodness for that; here it comes.

'What would be confidential, Count, do you think?' he mused. 'If they were having a thing, that would be personal, but not confidential, wouldn't it? And don't get me wrong, I wouldn't blame them if they were; his wife it appears was no better than should be by all accounts and her husband is known from one end of the town to the other as a total arse, pardon my French. But . . . confidential? What a strange word to use . . .'

The cat carefully cleaned between his toes, his leg stuck out at an improbable angle. Other than that, he kept his counsel.

'Doctors, solicitors, priests — I know about all those, though I have to say I find it a bit pointless when a person is dead. But that's by the way. Thomas Morton, a very nice man though he may be, is nevertheless not any of the above. He schedules buses. And I know what you're going to say, Count. That the inner workings of the Leighford bus timetable is as confidential and impossible to access as any legal document; to some it may appear as Holy Writ. But I still don't see how that can be relevant.'

He fixed the black and white monster with a baleful eye.

'Have you put on a little weight, Count?' He gestured vaguely to his own midriff. 'Around the middle?'

The cat bridled and curled up. His middle was his own affair — well, possibly his and Mrs B's.

'Where else do people get to know each other?' Maxwell continued. 'Weightwatchers?' He gave the Count another steely glare but it got him nowhere. 'Hardly that. I never knew the late Mrs MacBride except as a dim background to her husband on the occasions he trotted her out, but she was certainly average, if not slim. And Thomas Morton is about three stone wringing wet. So, no. Hospital appointments of some kind? Unlikely, because unless it is something like the fracture clinic, where everyone is busy writing on each other's plaster casts, everyone is quite buttoned up in waiting rooms. Doctor, ditto. Dentist . . . what's confidential about the dentist?'

The cat yawned extravagantly, showing his perfect teeth, needle sharp and glinting in the lamplight.

'No need to show off. What else is there?' Maxwell tapped his paintbrush against his chin, remembering, for once, to use the dry end. Suddenly, his eyes lit up and he swivelled in his chair, bending down so he was nose to nose with the cat. 'I've got it!' he said. 'AA. Gambling anonymous. One of those things! I must tell the Mem!' And, pausing only to switch off the lamp, he dashed down the stairs, leaving the cat to his beauty sleep and, like Abou Ben Adhem, deep dreams of peace. Hell would freeze over before Sergeant Williams could get himself along to the regimental surgeon.

* * *

Jacquie wasn't asleep anyway, but she pointed out to Maxwell that his impersonation of a herd of stampeding rhino would have woken her if she had been.

'Sorry,' he said, 'sorry for the rhino thing. It's just that . . .'

'Don't tell me,' she said, turning on her side in anticipation of a long explanation, 'Metternich has cracked the case?'

Maxwell smiled fondly. 'He *is* good, isn't he?' he said. 'But in this case, no; it's all me. We talked it through, the Count and me, and I came up with . . . counselling! I bet they both go to counselling. I know I would, if I lived half the lives they did.'

Jacquie looked thoughtful. 'You may be right,' she said.

'Am right,' he muttered, getting into bed and switching off the light. He often thought better in the dark.

'But isn't counselling usually quite solitary?' Jacquie asked. 'I haven't ever had counselling, although sometimes I wonder why not — the job,' she hastily added, 'just because of the job. But I have been to a few offices and I think they all have an in and an out, so patients don't meet. So . . .'

'Hmm, point taken.' He was lying on his back now, looking for answers on the ceiling in the gentle glow of the nightlight from the landing. 'But I'm sure I'm right . . . we just need to fill in the gaps in the argument. Couldn't you just ask Thomas Morton if he has counselling?'

'He'll just say confidential again.'

'Yes, you're right. You need to be more specific. If he thinks you know, he may come clean.'

'Yes, but I have to be right first time. I can't just throw all the different counselling options at him until he puts up his hands and calls it a fair cop!'

He threw her a kiss. 'A fairer cop never drew breath, heart,' he said. 'Let's think this through. Perhaps they didn't go to individual counselling. Perhaps they went to some kind of group. Battered spouses, something like that?'

'That would easily apply to Thomas Morton, but not to Denise MacBride. There was no record of any abuse and although they weren't exactly love's young dream, they seemed to be civil, in the main. Just a bit gripey, you know, how married couples are sometimes.' Jacquie thought it was safe to share one little snippet, though. 'Even before they married, Denise MacBride did have a history of suicidal ideation.'

'Speak English, boy,' Maxwell drawled. It was an immaculate Foghorn Leghorn; Mel Blanc himself could have done no better.

'Sorry, but you know what I mean. She had made a few very half-hearted attempts, spoke of suicide, or perhaps threatened is more the word from time to time, though was much better later, according to her mother. She was in a difficult relationship, all the usual teenage stuff. Her GP had changed her tablets and they seemed to suit her.'

'Tablets. So, drugs, possibly?'

'I think not. She was on some pretty hard core antidepressants, but nothing like that. And I doubt Thomas Morton would be able to get away with so much as an aspirin without his wife putting a stop to it. No one in that house got to enjoy themselves but her.'

'Drink?'

'Same thing. She couldn't drink because of the tablets, he just couldn't drink.'

'Hmm. But you don't have to actually be drinking still to go to AA, do you? You hear of people who haven't had a drink for decades who still go to AA.'

'Fair point. But I still say no.'

'Gambling?'

'Again, I don't see how they would have the opportunity. He didn't ever have any money of his own, for one thing. And she . . . well, the picture I have is of a haunted, sad woman but not one with a big secret.'

Maxwell was so quiet for so long, his wife thought he was asleep and turned over herself to join him.

'Ah!' he suddenly said and she jumped a mile.

'For God's sake, Max! Do you have to do that? I was just dropping off, there.'

'Sorry. I just thought. What about those meetings they have for the *families* of people with addictions?'

Jacquie was interested. That sounded more likely. 'What, you mean like alcohol, gambling, that kind of thing? I don't think Geoff MacBride or Louise Morton have that kind of addiction.'

'No, maybe not,' Maxwell agreed. 'But they do — in the case of Mrs Morton, did — have an addiction, don't you think?'

'Yes,' Jacquie said, slowly as it dawned on her. 'Sex.'

'Bingo!' Maxwell said. 'Try him with that. I bet that will get him talking.'

'You do know you're a genius, of course,' Jacquie remarked.

'Tchah! I'd be a fine genius if I didn't,' Zero Mostel said from the other pillow. 'I knew the Count was onto something.'

'Yes, he's a genius too,' she agreed.

And the next time sleep beckoned, they just fell right in.

CHAPTER TWELVE

Rick Shopley was none too happy at having Thomas Morton ripped from his grasp. He felt he was getting somewhere at last, if it was only by dint of wearing him down, layer by layer, as eventually water will do to a rock. So when DI Carpenter-Maxwell swanned in, bright and breezy, all mumsy, no doubt, and said she would like to ask him a few questions, he was annoyed, but also interested to see how it would go. Not well, he didn't expect. The man was like a clam.

She sat down opposite the accused and folded her hands neatly in front of her. She had brought him a cup of tea, and herself a cup of coffee. Nothing for Shopley, the sergeant noticed sourly. How like a bloody woman to know that the evil, murdering bastard liked tea and not coffee.

'Thomas,' she said, gently. 'Do you remember me? We met when you first came in?'

Morton nodded.

'Good. I understand that my colleague has asked you how you know Mrs Denise MacBride and you don't feel able to share.'

'It's private,' he said, mumbling into his cup. It was so nice to have a proper cup of tea, not the horrible, scummy coffee which that horrible, scummy policeman brought him, time after time.

'I know you don't want to make us think less of her,' Jacquie probed gently.

'She can't help it if someone murdered her,' he said, almost finding the strength to snap at her. 'She's the *victim* here, you know. Not the murderer.'

'We know that, Thomas,' Jacquie said. 'But I think I know why you don't want to share your thoughts with us.'

Shopley snorted. Namby pamby crap!

Jacquie turned in her chair, her mouth smiling, her eyes not so much. 'Sergeant,' she said, in the voice which made even Metternich run and hide, 'I wonder if you could step outside for a moment. If you would then go and tap on DCI Hall's door, say I sent you. He'll know why.'

Shopley drew a breath to start his bluster.

'If you could do that now, sergeant, that would be marvellous.' Jacquie had absorbed some of Maxwell's best tried and tested methods, the smile, the dead eyes and the reasonable tone being the top combination for any occasion.

Shopley tried to stare her down, but couldn't. With a muttered oath, he left the room, not forgetting to slam the door.

Jacquie turned back to Morton, who had finished his tea and sat forward, his hands folded in unconscious postural echo. 'I think I know where you met, Thomas. I have the address here. Would you like me to say it out loud, or would you rather read it first, see if I'm right?'

'Is this recorder on?' he asked.

'Did Sergeant Shopley switch it on this morning, telling you he was doing so?'

Morton's days and nights were beginning to blur, but he thought so. He nodded.

'Would you like me to switch it off for a while? I can, if you want.'

He shook his head. He was rationing his words, as though he only had a few left to see him through for the rest of his life. Which would be much better from now on, whatever the outcome of all this. His life, Tommy's life; they would both be better without Louise. He pulled the piece of paper towards him with just the tip of his forefinger, spinning it round to face the right way up as he did so. He peered at it, his hand moving automatically to his pocket to reach for his glasses, but he didn't need them. Jacquie had written the words very carefully in large block capitals and he could make no mistake. His lips moved silently and he went pale, then he looked up to meet her eyes.

'How . . . how did you know?'

'It was . . .' how could she say it was something her husband and the cat had come up with? 'It was a hunch. Based on what we know of the people concerned.'

'We were both really ashamed,' he whispered. 'If you tell someone you are married to a sex addict, they just make rude gestures, and make off-colour comments. I couldn't really talk to anyone at work; they're nice enough blokes, but a few of them remember Louise and . . . well, I just couldn't talk to them. Denise didn't have any friends, not really. Her mum is a nice lady, but she didn't really understand. She didn't like Geoff MacBride,' he paused and a little smile played over his mouth. 'I don't know anyone who does, not really. But she didn't know what Denise was talking about. We used to have a little laugh about it. She used to talk about "urges" and "demands" and how Denise's dad had been "very good like that; no bother". But, that's not what it's about. Not really . . .'

'Did your wife and Denise ever meet?'

Morton was shocked. 'Oh, no, I would never have let that happen. Denise was a lovely woman, DI Carpenter-Maxwell . . . is that like *Mr* Maxwell, up at the school?'

She nodded.

'Tommy likes him.' He suddenly looked stricken. 'How is Tommy? He doesn't have anybody now, except me.'

'He's in a nice foster home,' Jacquie told him. 'Just him, with a really lovely couple. Older people. We thought he would be more comfortable with no other children, being an only one.' Only child Jacquie Carpenter-Maxwell, mother of one, knew how that went.

'That's kind of you,' the man said. 'He'll really appreciate that. Some quiet. That's all either of us ever wanted, you know. Some quiet.'

Jacquie knew it was important to get things back on track. 'So, they never met, Denise and Louise?'

'They might have bumped into each other, I suppose. Around town. But they didn't *know* each other. Not to speak to.'

'It's just that, you can see how we're placed, Mr Morton,' Jacquie said. 'Two women, both dead. And you seem to be the missing link.'

She waited patiently while he assimilated the appalling suggestion she seemed to be making.

'*I* didn't kill them, Mrs Maxwell,' he said. She didn't get called that, not here in the nick, but somehow, it sounded right. 'I didn't love Louise, I admit. I never had, I see it now. I won't tell you what my dad told me what I was when I married her, but he was right. I was just carried away with the thrill of the sex and everything. I didn't come from that kind of family. And the baby . . . I thought he was mine. She let me think that for just long enough for him to become the love of my life, then she told me he wasn't. She was that kind of woman, you see, Mrs Maxwell. Get your heart and then squeeze the life out of it, right in front of your eyes. But I didn't kill her. Nor did Tommy.'

'What about Denise?' Jacquie had to ask the question, though it felt like kicking a puppy. 'Did you kill *her*?'

His eyes went wide and he began to hyperventilate. Before she could react, he was on the floor, back arching, barking with the effort of getting some air into his lungs. She banged the emergency button on the wall and then was on her knees beside him.

'Come on, Thomas,' she said, quietly. 'Come on, just breathe now. Don't panic. Breathe. You're having a panic attack, but you can come out of this on your own. Just let your muscles go slack. That's it.' She found she was holding her own breath and had to work hard to let it out. It wouldn't do for the first aider to find them both flapping around on the floor like goldfish without a bowl. 'Come on.' She put a hand on his chest, not to help him breathe, but to let him know she was there. Where the hell was the bloody first responder?

The door crashed back and suddenly the room was full of people and equipment. She looked over her shoulder.

'We don't need the crash cart,' she said. 'Just someone to help me get him into a better position. And then if someone could call the duty doc — we should have him checked over, just in case. Thanks.' She turned her attention to the man on the floor, who was starting to relax. 'Thomas, Alice here and I are going to sit you up against the wall and then I'll stay with you until the doctor comes.'

'Didn't. Kill. Denise.'

'No, I'm sure you didn't,' she soothed, 'but we'll leave that for now, shall we?'

The civilian first aider crouched down on the other side and together she and Jacquie lifted Thomas Morton into a sitting position, slightly bent forward.

'I'll stay with him if you like, Detective Inspector,' Alice offered. This beat typing out reports by a good margin.

'Is that all right, Thomas?' Jacquie asked. 'Is it all right if Alice stays with you for a bit? The doctor will be here shortly. Just rest if you can.'

He put his head forward and nodded slightly, but enough. Alice sat down beside him, also with her back against the wall and began to speak quietly to him, about her cat, her dog, her car which was giving her trouble these cold mornings. Normal life. That was what Thomas Morton needed. Something he hadn't had for fourteen years. Something he might never have again.

* * *

Henry Hall was sitting calmly, as was his wont, behind his desk when Jacquie poked her head around the door. He gestured for her to come in.

'Sorry for the Shopley thing, guv,' she said, sitting in his visitor's chair. 'I couldn't be doing with him, with his snorting and grunting at every turn.'

'Don't worry about it,' Hall said, carefully placing the top on his pen and stowing it in his inside pocket. Henry Hall was possibly the last person in the world who always used a fountain pen; even Maxwell, tired of being permanently ink-spattered, had embraced the biro decades before. 'I needed to speak to him anyway, so you saved me a job. I've had a few concerns shared with me by colleagues.'

Jacquie quickly translated this in her head. So, his mates had finally decided to dob him in, had they? About time. The man put the I in Political Incorrectness. As well as the O in oik. 'Well, that's good. I knew you would just give him five minutes of the usual warning if he said I had sent him.'

'How did you get on with Morton?' Hall said, moving on. 'And thank you again for dinner last night, by the way. Max is some cook.'

'He's had the practice,' she smiled. 'And it was a pleasure. Sorry we couldn't progress things much, but I think we've made a bit of a breakthrough this morning. Except . . .'

Hall raised an eyebrow.

'He's had a bit of a panic attack. Alice — the first aider, you know?'

He nodded.

'Alice is with him, waiting for the doc. He's okay; I think it was all a bit much, really. I guessed, you see.'

'Did you?' Henry Hall wasn't stupid. He knew when he left 38 Columbine the night before that he had set Maxwell's synapses firing. It was a little like lighting the blue touch paper and retiring to a safe place.

'We, perhaps I should say. Max. Anyway, I put it to him that he knew Denise MacBride from an encounter group for the families of addicts, and it was right on the money.'

'Addicts?' Hall was puzzled. As far as he could remember, there was no drug problem in this case.

'Sex, guv, not to put too fine a point on it. Both MacBride and Louise Morton were, to a degree, sex addicts. Well, MacBride still is, I suppose, unless losing his wife this way has made him regroup. But I somehow don't think so. I'm not sure he qualifies, either. He just . . . chases women. I'm not sure that he is that indiscriminate, either. But Denise saw him as such, so she just wanted support. As for Louise Morton . . . well, she made a living out of it, I suppose, but the picture I'm getting is someone who was a bit rapacious, to say the least of it. So she might have got the diagnosis, had she asked for one. I don't think she saw it as too much of a problem.'

Hall, remembering Hetty and the hoover permanently on in the hall, agreed.

'But Thomas and Denise obviously became fond of each other. That's as far as I've got so far. He collapsed at around that point.'

Hall sat back and folded his arms. 'It's taken away that coincidental element, though, hasn't it?' he said, as happily as he ever was. 'Did Morton kill Mrs MacBride, though? Or his own wife? I know he could only have done one.'

'Yes. And it also removes the Strangers on a Train idea. He might get someone to kill his wife for him, but not if he had to kill Denise MacBride.'

'Yes, I do see that.' Hall leaned forward again and reached for his pen. He had forms to fill out, after all. 'I'll let you get on, then. Are you going to see Morton again, after the quack has been, I mean?'

'No. I'll let him rest for a while. He looked exhausted, apart from anything else. I think Shopley has been giving him a hard time.'

'I've told him he's off the case,' Hall said, 'so don't worry on that score. If he gives you any bother, let me know. He's on a written warning next and I wouldn't be sorry to give it.'

She stood up, dismissed, in the usual Hall way. 'I'm popping over to see the forensics boys,' she said. 'They've been playing with the answerphone recordings.'

'Good luck with that.' Hall didn't really hold with dickering about with recorded material. In his view, a few wobbly lines proved little, but it kept the boffins happy. 'Are they looking for anything specific?'

'I think mainly they're trying to pin down where the calls were made from. Background noise, that kind of thing.'

'Oh, you mean like a station, a party or something.' Hall, though he would have denied it hotly, also watched *CSI*.

'Something,' she agreed and left, closing the door quietly as she did so. A lesson for Shopley, should he be lingering near.

* * *

Maxwell walked that morning through a school so silent and demoralised, it felt frankly dystopian. He was still mulling over why anyone would ever want to remake *Omega Man* — again — when he flung open the door to his office. No milling crowds of white-faced zombies, so good news thus far. There was a note on his desk, though, written in Mrs B's immediately recognizable block capitals. It was like being shouted at, but he knew she meant well. The first time she had left him a note in her ordinary writing, he had assumed it was a kidnap demand, when all she really wanted was more J-cloths.

'MR M!' it bellowed. 'MY SISTER'S GRANDSON HAS LOOKED INTO ALL THIS GOOGLE STUFF AND THE BLEEDING WOMAN NOT BEING ON IT. HE SAYS THIS MIGHT BE BIG. HE WANTS TO WRITE A BLOG ON IT, BUT I SAID HOLD UP TILL I'VE SPOKE TO YOU. I'M AT YOURS THIS MORNING AS YOU KNOW. RING ME THERE BUT RING ONCE, RING OFF, RING AGAIN OR I WON'T ANSWER. YOURS MRS B.'

He found he had been holding his breath, as he so often did when being spoken to by the real live woman, and let it out in a rush. He knew in principle what a blog was, of course, but how adept Mrs B's sister's grandson would be at constructing one, that was another matter. How could he gently mention apostrophes and the use thereof. Semi-colons. It was a possible minefield. And what did they mean by 'big'? Leighford big? England big? *World* big? He needed time, so he folded the note into his pocket and began to think about starting the day.

He hadn't heard the door. That was the excuse he gave later when people asked why he had screamed like that. In perfect silence, Thingee One had come into his office and was just standing there, a tear-sodden lump of misery. After the first shock, he immediately leapt into ministering mode and soon had her sitting on his softest chair, a mug of coffee on the table in front of her. Helen Maitland had been the first person to respond to his scream — which he later renamed 'yell' — and as soon as she saw the situation, she took up her most frequently called upon role, that of bouncer and explainer outside Maxwell's door. Even she could only hazard a guess but, perhaps unsurprisingly in the circumstances, she was right on the money.

Maxwell handed the girl a wodge of tissues. This clearly was not the time when just one would do. She blew her nose extensively and then dropped them neatly in the bin and held out her hand for more.

'Feeling a bit better?' Maxwell asked. It was becoming a habit, having an office full of weeping women.

She nodded and opened her mouth to speak, but just collapsed in sobs again. Maxwell decided to leave her to make up her own mind when it would be possible for her to utter and he sat back, trying to look, at one and the same time completely engaged with her pain, but also completely disinterested, so she didn't feel overwhelmed. It was a difficult trick and he still wasn't sure it was quite perfected when she gave a final sniff that rattled the windows and she spoke.

'I've had the sack.'

Maxwell blinked. 'Pardon?'

'I've just had the sack. Mrs Braymarr just came into the office and sacked me.'

'Oh, she is here today, then?'

'Yes,' Thingee said. 'Aren't we lucky?'

'But you must have had some kind of warning, surely?'

'She told us all yesterday that we would have to apply for our own jobs. She said that there would be two less jobs in the office from next week, that we weren't meeting targets, whatever that means. How can you have a target for answering the phone?' Her voice rose to an outraged squeak. 'I mean, you can only answer it when it rings, can't you?'

'True. So . . .' whatever Maxwell thought of Fiona Braymarr, he still needed the facts to be straight. 'So, you *did* apply for your own job, did you?'

''Course I did,' she said. 'I need my job. I would have said I like working here, but it wouldn't be true, not since *she* came. She set us all against one another, like . . .' she went off at a tangent. 'Do you watch David Attenborough at all?'

'If I must,' Maxwell answered. He remembered him from his Komodo Dragon days; CGI dinosaurs just didn't really do it for him.

'Well, we've got them all recorded. It's handy when there's nothing else on. The other day, we watched that one, can't remember the series, but it was the one where these eagle babies are in the nest and if there isn't enough food, the biggest one pushes the others out when the parents aren't watching. And the adults don't seem to notice. Well, that's us, isn't it, Mr Maxwell? We're like those eagle babies. We're all pushing each other out of the nest and no one on the outside seems to be noticing anything. As far as the world is concerned, Leighford High School is just going to be called Leighford Academy and that's the only change. But it *isn't* the only change. She's broken our school, Mr Maxwell. It isn't right.'

He handed her another wodge of tissues. It seemed about the only gesture left right now. She blew her nose and got her story back on track.

'So, we all applied. I thought I had done well. I did all the stuff they say to do on the internet. Transferable skills, value added. All that. And . . .' her face screwed up and she readied the tissues, but was all right in the end. 'And, do you know what she said, Mr Maxwell?'

He shook his head, dutifully.

'She said . . . she *said* that I hadn't done it myself. That someone else had written it for me and so she was going to let me go. She didn't give me a chance to speak, Mr Maxwell. And I *did* do it myself. I *did*.'

Maxwell held out an arm and she burrowed beneath it, the tears back with a vengeance. She didn't know how many hundreds had tucked under that arm, back in the days when it was allowed. She only knew she felt better there. He patted her and leaned his cheek against the top of her head. It could have been Nolan, Jacquie, even, heaven forfend, Mrs Troubridge. His arm had no favourites and he let the girl sob herself quiet. But his time wasn't being wasted. He was using it well, to plot the downfall of Fiona Braymarr.

* * *

Jacquie never minded a change of scene and the forensics lab would do as well as anywhere else. She always got a warm welcome from Angus, who had carried a torch for her for years. He was married now, with a baby on the way but that didn't matter; dreams don't die easily and Jacquie Carpenter (he didn't really want to face the Maxwell part) had been in his too long to disappear overnight. His wife had tidied him up, to Jacquie's delight; he no longer had that aura of recent joints and not-so-recent underpant change and so she was grateful to the unnamed girl smiling out of the photo blutacked to his computer screen.

'So, Angus,' she said, pulling over a chair and cosying up beside him at his desk. 'What have you got for me?'

'We've had a bit of fun with this, DI Carpenter . . .' he let the pause go on just a tad too long '. . . Maxwell,' he said. 'At first, to be honest, I thought that idiot on the sound console — calls himself an expert, but, I dunno . . . an NVQ in music, it's not enough, is it?'

Jacquie shook her head. It was as good as anything else, as far as she could tell, but who knew?

'He sent a report through, it was so convoluted I had to have him in to explain it. So he did and now I can explain it to you.' Angus didn't tell her that he would no more allow the sound expert near her than fly, what with his shiny hair and good teeth; no way in hell was he getting up close and personal with Jacquie Carpenter . . . Maxwell, not while Angus had seniority, at any rate.

Jacquie knew better than to ask to go to the horse's mouth, so kept quiet. 'I had a word with Henry Hall,' she said, to change the subject from the shortcomings of the sound expert. 'He would appreciate it being kept simple, so if you extract what he calls the wobbly lines I think he is more likely to read it.'

'Will do.' Anything for DI Jacquie Carpenter . . . Maxwell! Angus hutched himself nearer and bent over his keyboard. 'So, what we have here . . .' he pointed to the top row of wobbly lines, '. . . is the message from the unknown person. By the way, we couldn't get any kind of handle on that phone. I think he must have ditched it.'

'I thought he would have,' she said. 'You can get a phone for a fiver, after all. Why would you hang on to it after it had done the job?'

'Exactly,' he said. He personally got the heebie jeebies when he was near any phone which wasn't the very latest on the market, but he could see how some people could manage with a phone that cost a fiver. He would imagine that the old git that DI Carpenter . . . Maxwell was married to probably had one of those old ones with a separate car battery and a stand on his shoulder for the brick-like handset.

Jacquie could read this man like a book. 'A Blackberry,' she said, a propos of apparently nothing. 'My husband has a Blackberry.'

Angus blushed and went back to his keys. 'So,' he said, 'I can remove the voice element,' he pressed a key and the wobbly lines changed shape, 'and what remains is the background noise. We can remove elements of that as well, but I'll leave that for now. I'll just minimise that into the corner of the screen and we'll go to the next call. Oh, I'm assuming you don't want the last one, the one from that Morton guy done? You've got him for the wife, haven't you?'

'Rumours of his arrest are a little premature,' Jacquie said, 'but we're making progress with him, I suppose you could say. He's unwell at the moment, under the care of a doctor.'

'Oh.' Angus tossed his head, dismissively. 'Playing the bonkers card, is he? Good plan. Anyway, here we are on the call from MacBride. Again, we'll remove the voice . . .' he touched a key, '. . . resize the window . . .' he was almost speaking to himself, '. . . and — voila!' He leaned back and did a big reveal, hand extended, his face transformed by a grin. 'What do we have?'

Jacquie could have said 'wobbly lines' but knew that was not the right thing. She peered at the screen and then sat up, blinking. 'Angus? Are they the same?'

He was as proud as if she had produced a rabbit out of a hat. 'Top marks!' he said. 'They *are* the same. Well, there are a few small discrepancies, but nothing to worry you, not really. The two calls, basically, came from the same place.'

'Well, blow me down!' Jacquie looked at the screens, frozen in mid-wobble. 'The Ellisdon.'

'Wow! That's *good*. We couldn't tell where it was. We were working on that . . .'

'No, no,' Jacquie laughed. 'I would love to take the credit, but I can't. We know that MacBride phoned from there. It's in his statement.'

'You know that for a fact, do you?' Angus asked, archly.

'Well . . . I assume it's been checked, yes. I will tell you that he fudged the facts a bit, but I think he did stay there, yes. We just need to know who with.'

'Ooooh,' Angus smelt a scandal, if it was possible for there to be a worst scandal than a man's wife being thrown off a balcony at his place of business. 'Do tell.'

'It's complicated, Angus,' she said. 'I'm sure like the rest of the county you know all about Geoff MacBride and his wandering . . . his wandering. So, we assume he was up to his old tricks this time. It's only a matter of time before we find out exactly what went on, where and with whom.'

'Any doubts as to his proclivities?' Angus said, sitting back, arms folded.

Jacquie opened her eyes wide. 'Geoff MacBride? Proclivities? Angus, he almost wears a badge — "Heterosexual male, not fussy. Stroke here". I don't think he's ever met the owner of two X chromosomes he didn't at least take a quick punt at.'

'Well, I only ask because we did analyse the voices in the background and we don't think there are any women there.'

'Perhaps he likes the silent type. Perhaps he doesn't meet her in the bar . . .'

'Hmm. Okay.' Angus was disappointed. He wanted to be the man to out Geoff MacBride.

'Is that it? It's great to tie down the location of that first call, Angus, but I must . . .'

'Hang on,' he said. 'I think you'll want to see this.' He tapped a few more keys and two more windows appeared, one above the other, full of the usual wobblies. 'What do you think of that?'

She looked and looked. As far as she could see, it was a couple of matching patterns again, but whether they were the *same* patterns was impossible for her to tell. 'Sorry.' She shook her head. 'Two more lots the same.' She looked again. 'Sameish.'

'Pre*cisely*!' Angus tapped the desk in a mad mini-drumroll. 'It isn't exactly the same because the words are different. But . . .' he looked around at her, wanting to see her expression, 'it's the same voice.'

'The same as what?' She was still none the wiser.

'Look at the file name,' he said, pointing.

'One says "anonMcBtp",' she said. 'Oh, right, anonymous call, MacBride tape. And the other . . .' she looked at him. 'Husband?'

'Right.' Again, a drumroll, followed by a brief moment of air guitar. 'Which means . . . ?'

'Angus,' she said, putting her hand on his arm and making him go quite lightheaded. 'Angus, what does it mean? Just the facts.'

He sighed. Not the reaction he had been hoping for at all. 'It *means*,' he said, 'it *means* that the man who made the anonymous call was not only calling from the Ellisdon — if that turns out to be accurate — but he was still in the bar when the husband rang. If they weren't actually together, he was certainly in earshot. As you can see,' and he pointed again to the screen.

'Is that in the report?' Jacquie asked, bending down to pick up her bag, her keys already in her hand. 'No wobbly lines.'

'Maybe just a few. I can print out a version without.'

'Don't worry. DCI Hall is just going to have to manage. Angus, you and your sound expert are my favourite men. I can't believe you've found all this from those recordings. You're geniuses, both of you!' And she grabbed up the report and was gone.

Angus sat back. *He* was a genius, fair enough. But the other guy? NVQ Music! He didn't think so.

CHAPTER THIRTEEN

Thomas Morton felt better, sitting up in the bed in the small sick bay at Leighford nick. There was something about being in bed in his clothes — some of his clothes, anyway; he had taken off his trousers, but hung onto everything else — which took him back to childhood, when his mum had tucked him up when he came back from school with tummyache or a bloody nose. He got both, often together, most weeks. He felt . . . cared for, that was it. He knew, deep down, that everyone was just going through the motions. That secretary or whatever she was who had stayed with him; the doctor who had given him a very brief once-over; that nice DI, who was married to Mr Maxwell up at the school — none of them *really* cared, but he had learned over the last fourteen years or so to take caring where he found it. He snuggled down, feeling rather sorry for himself. He wasn't going to cry, but he felt like letting the tears go. He couldn't really see how he had ended up like this. His job was probably gone. Did you get an insurance payout when your wife was murdered, even if you didn't do it? If you didn't, then he would lose the house. He would lose Tommy. He would lose . . . everything. He hadn't meant to cry. But the tears were running down his cheeks, just the same.

* * *

Afternoon Thingee, aka Thingee Two tapped on Maxwell's door. Unlike her morning equivalent, she had made the director's cut and lived to lose calls when forwarding another day.

'Yes?' Maxwell had a free afternoon, teaching-wise, on Thursdays, ostensibly to catch up on paperwork and generally regroup, but it hadn't been going very well so far. Morning Thingee had just been the shape of things to come. He had had so many of his Own coming to see him, full of news of fresh disasters, that he hardly knew how to begin. The rumour mill was working overtime and so far he had heard that the Music Department had been axed, that Art would no longer be on the syllabus, that there was going to be whole body search of each student before they were allowed onto the premises each morning and any girl in a short skirt — or a boy, for that matter; gender issues were very high on Fiona Braymarr's hit list — would not only be turned away but would not be allowed to return and would have all currently held exam certificates revoked. Some of the rumours were so bizarre that Maxwell simply dismissed them with a wave of his hand. But, on the other hand, anyone who could sack Sylvia Matthews was probably capable of anything.

Thingee popped her head around the door.

'Thingee, old thing, come in.' Maxwell's heart fell. Not another sackee, surely?

'Mr Maxwell, can I have a word?'

'Of course. Can I just ask, though — is there a queue of any kind out there?'

Thingee looked over her shoulder. She had been at Leighford for long enough now to recognise most of the student body and looked back in to report. 'Just Elena,' she said. 'Year Eleven, I think.'

'Oh, that's not a queue. That's just Elena trying to bunk off a lesson of some description. She's been a bit bereft since Nursie . . . I mean, Mrs Matthews left. Come on in, Thingee and tell me your woes.'

Thingee did come in and sat down, but the woes weren't hers. 'Mr Maxwell, this will sound a bit funny, probably, but this isn't anything to do with school.'

Maxwell closed his eyes and tipped his face to the ceiling as though to a healing sun. 'Thank you, God,' he said, then, looking at the girl, 'you don't know how pleased I am to hear you say that. I'm sure you can imagine what it's been like this week. Everyone . . . well, I don't need to draw you a picture. How can I help you?'

She set her lips in a tight line, clamped her hands between her knees and rocked tensely. 'I don't know how to begin. You'll be really annoyed, Mr Maxwell.'

'Perhaps not. Try me.'

She drew in a deep breath and relaxed, leaning back and clasping her hands in her lap. He was impressed. She was clearly a people watcher to be able to adapt her posture like that. Either that, or a fan of *Lie To Me*. Either way, it worked, because she started in on her story without any more shilly-shally. 'My brother is in a bit of trouble, Mr Maxwell. We've been so worried and my mum suggested I have a word with you. Because of . . . well, because and also because of you being married to a policeman. A policewoman, sorry. And my brother really likes her. And my nephew, he really likes you and . . .'

'Hold on, Thingee. Who are these people?' Maxwell had a good idea already, but wanted confirmation.

'Oh, sorry, Mr Maxwell. I forgot you don't know my name. I'm Sam. Samantha . . .'

'Morton.' Maxwell could have kicked himself. 'Of course I know your name. But Thingee is easier, don't you think?'

She smiled. 'We've never been really sure,' she said.

'Not always a hundred percent up to date,' he smiled. He had good reason to remember her predecessor, Charlotte, now happily recepping at a nail bar, and all the better for it. 'I usually have the gist, though. Now, Sam . . .'

The girl leaned forward. 'Thingee, please,' she said. 'I'll feel funny, otherwise.'

'Now, Thingee, then. Your brother is Thomas Morton and your nephew is Tommy.'

'Yes.'

'I'm sure you could have had some time off . . . actually, belay that. Of course you couldn't have had time off. What was I thinking? But you haven't said. Is your mum looking after Tommy?'

'No,' Thingee Two said. 'She feels bad about that, but Louise . . . my sister-in-law, you know . . . well, she made things so difficult between Mum and Thomas that we don't really know Tommy very well. It's a shame, because Mum is a lovely gran. My sister — she's between me and Thomas — she's got two lovely little girls and Mum has them when she's at work. But she's only seen Thomas a handful of times, so . . .' she shrugged.

'He's with a lovely couple, or so I understand,' Maxwell told her. He didn't need to tell her where he had plucked that nugget of information. 'Older. Quiet. I think that's what he needs, probably.'

'No shouting. Yes, I do see that. But the reason I'm here, Mr Maxwell, is for Thomas. He had a bit of a turn at the ni . . . sorry, police station, this morning. Your wife was with him. She was very kind.'

'Of course she was.' He knew she couldn't be otherwise.

'But he's feeling very down. They rang me from the . . .'

'Call it the nick, Thingee,' Maxwell urged. 'I always do.'

'Well, they rang me to say he had had this turn and then they rang me again to say he was very low, crying and that. They've got my number because, well, if anything had ever happened in the street or at work or anything to Thomas, it would have been a fat lot of good ringing Louise, wouldn't it?'

'Really?' Maxwell did his best to look dumb.

Thingee gave him a penetrating look. As she had heard it, his wife told him everything and then he went and solved the crime. That was how it had always been told, from one generation of Old Leighford Highena to the next. 'Mr Maxwell,' she said, 'I know you know all about Louise. Or, at least, enough about her to know she wasn't exactly nice to Thomas. Or Tommy. But it wasn't just that.'

'She kept herself busy, I gather,' he said, diplomatically.

'Yes, indeed.' Thingee was grateful for the euphemism. She wasn't looking forward to explaining Louise's extracurricular activities.

'So Thomas *did* know about her, then?' This might clear up something it would probably hard to get out of the man himself.

'You'd think so, wouldn't you? I think he knew she had . . . outside interests, as you might say. I'm not sure he knew the extent. I mean, one day, I was driving past with my boyfriend and I saw a man coming out of her house and another one literally going in on his heels. She didn't really hide it.'

'Interesting. Did you notice anything about them? Did you know them?'

'One did look familiar at the time. I said as much to Darren . . . that's my boyfriend, Darren. Anyway, it was hours after and I suddenly remembered. It was that touchy feely bloke, the one who comes to all the meetings. Anyway, him.'

Maxwell stored that piece of information away and tried not to react too much. 'And the other?'

'No. I didn't know him.'

'Car?' Maxwell knew nothing about makes of car except the one his wife drove, and only then so he didn't make embarrassing mistakes when shopping, such as standing patiently beside the wrong vehicle as she and Nolan drove past giggling. But he knew it could be a helpful tool for the police.

'No. I didn't see him in a car. He was old, though.' She looked at Maxwell and reconsidered. 'Older. Balding. Big chap, a bit stooping, but he had a spring in his step, I'll give him that. He was wearing very bright clothes, for a bloke his age. He seemed to be on foot. It was funny, though, because he crossed in front of us and then, when I glanced back, he was crossing back over again. That was odd, wasn't it?'

'I'm not really that up on the behaviour of men who have just . . . been visiting someone, Thingee. But it does sound a bit strange, I agree.' Another piece of information, on the basis of no bit too small? He stored that away too.

'So, anyway, Mr Maxwell, I can't stay much longer because if Mrs Braymarr tries to ring in and I'm not there . . .'

'Oh, she's off out again, is she?'

'Yes. Apparently, Thursday afternoons, she is at the Academy Hub, wherever that might be, feeding back.'

'Sounds lovely. Who's in charge?'

'Mr Diamond is in. He isn't taking calls, though.'

'No. I can understand that. So, you want to speak to me about Thomas, is it? Or Tommy?'

'Thomas. I worry about him. Although we're the ends of the family, you know, eldest and youngest, we were always closest when I was little. I've missed him. I'd like him back, if you can manage it, Mr Maxwell. So, can you go and see him? Let him see that we all believe in him. I know he didn't kill Louise, although he had every reason. So . . . please, Mr Maxwell. Can you?'

She didn't indulge in the storm of weeping that Thingee One, Morning Thingee had done. But the welling eyes were one pair of welling eyes too many for Maxwell that Thursday afternoon and he stood up.

'Let me get my coat, Thingee. I'll see what I can do.'

* * *

The desk sergeant looked up and his heart fell. He wished he could press his button, but it had been moved out of reach by maintenance; he really missed his button.

'Mr Maxwell,' he said, with the usual false bonhomie. 'Can I help you? Come to see the wife?' That was a little near the edge of acceptable, but he was still cross about his button. He suspected that DI Carpenter-Maxwell had had more than a small hand in its removal.

'I would like to see my wife, in the first instance,' Maxwell said. 'But in fact, I'm here to visit Mr Thomas Morton.'

'This isn't a hospital, Mr Maxwell,' the desk sergeant pointed out. 'There aren't visiting hours, you know. You can't just pop in with grapes and a copy of *Hello*.' He still bore a grudge about when he had been in for his boil. He had had just one visitor, who had eaten the grapes and had clearly read the *Hello* from cover to cover; they had even started the crossword, making a total hash of fourteen down.

'I'm aware of that,' Maxwell said, with a polite smile. 'That's why I would like to see my wife first. But I am here at the request of a family member who is concerned about his welfare.'

The desk sergeant thought for a moment. It was all too easy these days to end up as a headline in the *Daily Mail* if you weren't careful. 'Man, thirty-three, dies in police custody'. He picked up the phone and snarled into it. 'Your husband's here, ma'am.' He waited while she answered, looking at Maxwell with hostile eyes. 'He says he's here to see Morton, ma'am. Says one of the family sent him.' He looked at Maxwell again and his lip all but curled. 'Will do.'

'Shall I go on up?' Maxwell suggested.

'That's what the lady said,' the sergeant said, and opened the doors without another word.

* * *

Fiona Braymarr was feeling unusually stressed that Thursday. The Academy meeting was usually simple; she had never had any problems controlling them before but for some reason, the hold she had over them felt very tenuous. Everyone sat in their usual seats; the sleeping ones were sleeping as per; even the doughnuts were laid out in exactly the expected formation, but there was something in the air. At exactly three o'clock the chairman cleared his throat and sat forward to welcome everyone. So far, so normal. But the tingling in her spine and the slight butterflies in her stomach warned her that this may be a bit more of a challenge than an everyday Thursday update. She blamed Maxwell. She had taken to doing that, ever since she had met him. The man had 'Nemesis' written right though him, like a stick of rock.

'Thank you for coming, everyone,' the chairman said. For God's sake, why have a real man at all? Why not just have a recording. 'Before we begin, I would like to say a very special thank you to you, Geoff, for coming to this meeting, when you have had so sad a bereavement.'

Small murmurs of assent from round the table were countered by a mutter of acceptance from Geoff MacBride. And that was all Denise MacBride was worth, that spring afternoon.

'I have had some communications this week,' the chairman continued, 'some through the post, some as emails. Of course, whenever we start the process of academization,' Fiona Braymarr was pretty sure that wasn't a word, but it would do as well as any other, 'we have letters. No one ever seems to want change these days. But, Mrs Braymarr, I have to say never as many as this. And so vituperative. You really seem to have rattled some cages this time.' The chairman had called her Fiona once. Just once. He had never ventured to do so again.

'Cages needed rattling, David,' she said crisply. 'When schools are failing, one must prune where necessary, root and branch.'

One of the sleepers roused himself and sat forward so he could look her in the eye. 'Failing, Fiona?' he asked. He was too old to care about her frosty looks. And he only sat on boards like this to get him out of the house so if he was kicked out of this one, he would simply find another. Or take up golf. Bowls. Curling. It was all one to him. 'Define failing, if you would.'

She took a deep breath. Who was this old duffer? He'd never spoken before, as far as she could remember. 'Perhaps I oversimplified,' she said, sharing a dazzling smile around the table. 'By failing, I simply meant a system descending into chaos. Systems need attention to keep them healthy and the schools in Leighford were not getting the attention they needed. They were not improving, they were simply coasting. In my experience, coasting means going downhill.'

The old man at the end of the table smiled at her. Was it just her imagination, or was the smile condescending and not altogether friendly? 'Fiona,' he said, 'have you ever heard of the phrase "If it ain't broke, don't fix it"?'

'Of course I have,' she snapped. 'But why wait until something is broken? Why not just prevent the breakage if you can?'

The old man sat back again and closed his eyes. 'Like bubble wrap,' he remarked to his coffee cup. 'Couldn't you have just wrapped the schools in cling film for a while and watched what happened? These mass sackings have raised a lot of dust.'

Fiona Braymarr was equal to any challenge, especially from old gits like this. 'Mass sackings is an oversimplification,' she said, 'All I did . . .'

A phone rang further down the table and every head turned. Phones were turned off in Thursday meetings, by Fiona Braymarr's order. Some hands went surreptitiously to pockets but the culprit was soon clear. It was Geoff MacBride. He looked at the number and pressed a button. 'Sorry,' he mouthed.

'All I did,' she said, 'after a very long look at the bottom line of all the institutions under consideration, was remove any staff who, in the final analysis, were giving back less than they were being paid. It was that simple.'

The old man at the end of the table spoke again. 'But, the High School nurse, Fiona? Draconian, perhaps.'

'There are perfectly good first-aiders in house,' she said, not looking at him.

The chairman tapped the table gently. 'I think we should move on,' he said. 'I will have a chat with you afterwards, Mrs Braymarr, if that would be convenient, but for now . . .'

Again, the phone ringing and this time, Geoff MacBride jumped up and went out of the room, already speaking in urgent tones into the handset.

'Point of order, Mr Chairman,' Fiona Braymarr said. 'Phones are to be switched off in meetings, or so I understood.'

A few heads round the table nodded. Others turned to give their neighbours significant looks. Perhaps there was trouble in Paradise.

'That is the rule,' the chairman said, 'but Geoff did ask if he could be excused that rule on this occasion, because of his . . . situation. Police, that kind of thing. I could hardly refuse, in the circumstances. Do you know how things are progressing?'

She drew back her head and looked severely at him. 'Why should *I* know?' she asked, archly. 'You and he seem to have discussed it. Did he not tell *you* anything?'

The chairman looked abashed. 'No . . . I . . .' He shuffled papers desperately until the mood passed. 'As I was saying, if we could go to any other business? Does anyone have anything to raise from last time?'

And so the meeting continued, as meetings will. The doughnuts were eaten, the coffee was drunk, sleeping was done and by the end, all that was left were some crumbs and a rather sour atmosphere. The chairman, intent on stuffing his briefcase with his paperwork, didn't see Fiona Braymarr leave and although he needed to speak to her, he wasn't sorry to have missed her. If he had had a motto emblazoned anywhere, it would have been something along the lines of 'sufficient unto the day is the evil thereof'. And he knew that Fiona Braymarr probably represented enough evil for a month of Sundays.

Geoff MacBride was out in the car park, leaning against his latest toy, a bright red Lexus with his usual personalised plates. Fiona Braymarr stalked over to him, her knees stiff with tension. He turned to her but didn't change his position, except to drop and then grind out a cigarette.

'Smoking, Geoff?' she said, icily.

'Wouldn't you?'

She flicked the Lexus with a fingernail. 'Not very . . . loyal, is it? To the Brand, I mean.'

'I don't always drive what I sell,' he said. 'Anyway, how can I help you?'

'By telling me what the hell was going on in there. With the phone. You know I don't allow . . .'

'*You* don't allow? What has that to do with the price of fish? I know that lily-livered chairman is terrified of you, but the rest of us aren't. You're a bloody teacher, Fiona. That's all. A teacher who's jumped up way above her pay grade to think she's God. I've been thinking a lot since yesterday . . .'

'Come along, now,' she sneered. 'You only ever think with your . . .'

He leaned over and grabbed her wrist, twisting it painfully. 'Don't say it. I'm tired of it. It's over, Fiona.'

'It? I'm not sure there was an "it", was there?' Despite herself, she was feeling quite emotional. She hadn't shed a tear for many a long year and she wasn't going to shed one now for a car salesman with ambitions. But the meeting hadn't gone well; the old git who usually slept his way through Thursday afternoons had got to her. And an unusual number of complaints! That was Maxwell, she just knew it. He went back to the Dark Ages and for some reason, people liked him. They listened to what he had to say. She wouldn't put it past him to . . .

'So,' Geoff MacBride interrupted her thoughts. 'That's it, Fiona. I'm putting in my resignation to the board today. In fact, I'm putting in resignations to *all* the boards and committees I sit on today. I'm getting the girls back from my old bat of a mother-in-law and I'm going to rebuild some bridges. It isn't too late.'

She leaned in very close, so he could smell the coffee on her breath. 'Oh, yes, Geoff,' she said. 'It's always too late.' She poked him painfully in the chest with a razor-sharp extended nail. 'New woman, is it?'

'Pardon?' He knew she could be hard, but he was becoming aware of just how much. He and Denise hadn't exactly been love's young dream, but most people at least paid lip service to the fact his wife had been murdered only days before.

'On the phone. New woman?'

'As a matter of fact, no. An old one, if you must know. The cops are checking up on the husbands of anyone who I . . . to tell you the truth, I don't know how they have compiled the list, but as far as I can tell, they are pretty much on the money. Rumour travels fast in a town like this.'

'Husbands?' She licked her lips. She felt panic rising in her throat, and it wasn't a feeling she liked.

'It's embarrassing, actually. And I think it will get worse before it gets better. I don't know why they're doing it, but they are contacting all the husbands of anyone I have ever been . . . with . . . and getting them to give a voice sample.' He shrugged. 'Clutching at straws, but there will be a lot of wives having to do a lot of explaining before this is over.'

'And you have no idea why?' Her voice sounded odd in her own ears, tight and high.

'None. I'm going over there now, as a matter of fact. I think they could have at least let me know, then I could have warned them. You know, to have their stories straight.'

She had her mojo back after the initial shock and managed to sound suitably dismissive. 'Oh, yes,' she sneered. 'The police are going to forewarn everyone. That's really their style. Just how stupid *are* you, Geoff? Don't answer that.' She looked him up and down. 'Well, if this is goodbye, then, what can I say? I'll miss you? Please don't leave me?'

He shrugged. He hadn't meant to tell her like this, in a carpark, in the growing dusk and chill of a mad March afternoon. He had seen himself getting at least one more night out of it, a night where he would give it his all and leave her begging for more. But things didn't always turn out the way you plan. 'This was always just what it was, Fiona. But let's stay civil, if we can. I will miss you, as it happens. You're not the nicest woman in the world, or even the most attractive, if I'm brutally honest. But,' and he softened his voice, 'we did have some good times, didn't we?'

She didn't speak for a moment, then nodded. 'Oh, yes, Geoff, some good times.' Then, with a turn of speed that would make a mongoose gasp, she lashed out and raked his cheek with her perfect nails. 'Good times.'

He clapped his hand to his face. This was going to look just marvellous in the cop shop. They already had him down for a philandering bastard. This would just put the tin lid on it. 'You bitch!'

She turned her back and walked back to her car, opening it with the remote as she went. She slid into the driver's seat and, out of sight of everyone, put her head down on the steering wheel, fighting the dry scream of panic that was sitting, waiting, at the back of her throat.

* * *

In the shadow between an SUV and an overhanging hedge, he watched with a wry smile on his face. At least he hadn't made a mistake; she *was* seeing that weasel-faced car salesman. Still, it looked as though she had given him his comeuppance well and truly. She was a fragile little thing and so gullible; men just took advantage of her left and right. If he didn't look out for her, who would? She looked distressed, poor soul. He toyed with going to her that night, to her room, to fondle her, to stroke her hair, to tell her everything would be all right, that he would look after her, just like in the old days. But no. Leave it for now. When she had finished making that crappy school somewhere worthwhile, as only she could; then he would reveal himself to her, show her how he had been guarding her, watching her back. She would love him then. She would have to love him then.

* * *

'Heart.' Maxwell air kissed his wife as he walked along the landing. 'Sorry to descend again, usual reassurances etcetera, etcetera. Turns out Thingee Two is Thomas Morton's sister.'

'Did you know?'

'I didn't, as it happens. The family are not Highenas and it just never cropped up.'

'So . . . ?'

'So, she tells me he's had a turn and is now rather low. She thinks I might be able to cheer him up.'

'That's as maybe,' she agreed. Maxwell, in full-on jester mode, could cheer up anyone with a pulse. 'However, I can see you have something to tell me.'

'You can *see* that?' He was horrified — was he really that easy to read? He would have to work on his poker face.

She raised an eyebrow. 'I admit you can sometimes keep things to yourself, but as a rule, my love, I can read you like a book. And, before you ask, so can Nolan and the cat.'

A door opened behind Jacquie and Henry Hall popped his head out. 'Hello, Max,' he said. 'You look as though you have news.'

Jacquie said nothing, merely smiled and spread her hands. 'And Henry,' she said.

'It isn't much.' Maxwell was a little on his dignity. 'I just had a chat with Thomas Morton's sister and she just had a few oddments to add. She had seen one of Louise Morton's punters going in and although she was stuck for a name, she described him well enough for me to know who it was.'

Hall opened the door to his office. 'Shall we just step in here?' he suggested.

'You won't need to take notes,' Maxwell said. 'It's not an easy name to forget. It was Geoff MacBride.'

'Well, well, well . . .' Hall made a note of it nevertheless. 'He's never struck me as a man who needs to pay for it.'

'Perhaps it was a freebie,' Jacquie suggested.

'Possibly,' Hall mused. 'Did she just see him?'

'No, there was someone else,' Maxwell said, not sitting down because his main aim was to go to see Thomas Morton. He leaned on the back of a chair. 'She didn't know him at all. An older man — well, bless her, she said "old" but then adjusted it, in deference to my own advanced years. Old*er*, a bit stooped, wearing bright clothes. I don't know what constitutes bright to Thingee Two, but I assume not the tweed she expects of old gits of a certain vintage. It could mean anything from a pair of chinos up.'

Hall had stopped making notes. 'Is that it?' he said.

'Umm . . . yes. I thought I'd just tell you policepersons.' Maxwell hadn't expected back flips, but the bum's rush seemed a little harsh.

'Thank you,' Hall said. 'I just need Jacquie now, if that's all right. Put your head round the next door along and someone will escort you to the sick bay.'

Jacquie looked at her boss, as surprised as Maxwell was but just opened the door to let him out.

'See you at home, then,' he said.

She nodded and closed the door behind him. Then, she turned to Hall. She wasn't usually blunt with the man, but they went back a long, long way. 'For God's sake, Henry,' she said. 'What was that all about?'

* * *

Alice, the first aider, escorted Maxwell to the sick bay, a pleasant room on the corner of the building, unlike a school san only because there was a lock on the door and the wall into the corridor was reinforced glass above waist height. The bed was crisply made with a blue, candlewick cover and the pillows almost crackled with freshness. It was a room which had an air of disuse about it, whilst being almost aggressively clean. Alice tapped in the code and opened the door.

'Mr Morton?' she said, gently. 'Are you up to a visitor?'

The man was lying in the bed, curled over on his side in the foetal position, with his face to the wall. 'Who is it?' he muttered.

'It's Mr Maxwell,' the girl said.

'Mr Maxwell from up at the school?' His voice sounded just a touch brighter.

'Yes, that's right.' Alice, Highena of just a few years before, though never one of Maxwell's Own, was able to confirm without checking.

'All right, then.' The voice was still quiet, but he rolled over and sat up, pale against the pillows.

'Hello, Mr Morton,' Maxwell said. 'May I call you Thomas? Sam sends her love.'

'Sam?' The man's eyes filled with tears again. 'Sam?'

'Well, she works up at the school,' Maxwell said. 'She asked me to pop in.'

'Louise didn't like Sam. Or my mum and dad. Or Jaime; that's my other sister. Tom, Jim and Sam, they used to call us, when we were kids.'

'I suppose families . . .' Maxwell left a gap, for Morton to fill.

'Louise just didn't like to see me with people who loved me, Mr Maxwell,' Morton said. 'She told me as much. She didn't really keep much back, Louise didn't. She'd tell Tommy how he was fat, ugly. When he needed glasses, she called him four-eyes. He was only six, Mr Maxwell. He didn't understand.'

'I'm going to say something a bit tasteless, Thomas,' Maxwell said. 'I think probably the world may be a better place without Louise.' He looked hard at the man in the bed. 'What do you think?'

'*My* world is,' he agreed. 'Tommy's world. But, and I know this is hard to fathom, there were people who loved her. Well, liked her, at least. She had friends.' He gave a little chuckle. 'Men, of course, but women as well. And if some of the men were more obsessed than in love, well, it's the other side of the coin, Mr Maxwell, sometimes, isn't it?'

'Do you know about the men, then, Thomas?' he asked.

He shrugged. 'They've asked me that. I don't know what the question means. I can't tell anyone what I don't know; they used to ask that at school, I remember. "Ask if there's anything you don't know". How do you do that? I know about Mike, from the office. He always carried a bit of a torch and I think they went out for lunch, from time to time, still. I know the bloke from next door used to come around, do little odd jobs for her, things she didn't think I would do properly. Umm . . . there may have been some more. She used to have girls' nights out, once or twice a week, but she never brought her friends home.' He looked into Maxwell's eyes and spoke in matter-of-fact tones. 'She was ashamed of me, you see, Mr Maxwell. I'm not good looking, or hunky or anything. She only married me because Tommy was on the way and she knew I'd say yes. But she didn't want me to meet her friends.'

Maxwell forbore to follow that with, 'So the answer's no, then.' He felt sorry for this man, but thought the time had come for him to stop being so apologetic and to start thinking about the future for him and his boy because, no matter who the boy's biological father was, it was clear that he and Thomas Morton were closer than most relatives bound by blood. 'It's nice she had someone, I suppose,' he said. It was the best he could do in the circumstances.

'I know what you're thinking,' Morton said, suddenly. 'You think I did it. But I didn't, you know. I didn't.'

Maxwell patted his arm. 'You know, Thomas,' he said, in the same tone he would use to his boy. 'I don't think you did.'

* * *

Maxwell took the pretty way back to the foyer, past Henry Hall's and his wife's offices but both doors were firmly closed. He even went so far as to raise his fist, primed to knock, but then thought better of it and went down the stairs, thinking. He pressed the button inside the double doors to the exit and cannoned straight into someone coming the other way. Both men smiled, nodded, clapped each other on the shoulder and sidled past, like all men do who collide accidentally with another. It was only when the other man had disappeared into the gloom of the interview corridor that Maxwell realised who it was. It was Geoff MacBride, sporting a scratch down his cheek of which Metternich would be proud. Either he had been with Morton longer than he thought, or Leighford Police moved at the speed of light. He couldn't help a glance at his watch; he did still have to get Nolan, after all. But no, he wasn't late. Speed of light it must be.

CHAPTER FOURTEEN

Thursday night was fish and chips night Chez Maxwell and Jacquie came home, as always, with a gently steaming carrier bag, to find, as always, a bathed and beatific Nolan and a similarly bathed but slightly less beatific Maxwell waiting patiently for the goodies. For some reason, Metternich wasn't keen on fried fish — Maxwell said it was because he was watching his waistline — so it was just the three of them. Mrs Whatmough's school was of the oldest possible kind imaginable, so it was unsurprising that the talk was mainly of Lent; in Mrs Whatmough's book, there was no such thing as a free chocolate egg, so privations were very much on the menu. Even Shrove Tuesday was a needless frippery in her book; sometimes she was lucky and it fell in half term, but this year she had grudgingly allowed it to happen on her watch. But every pancake had come at a price; a promise to give up something until Easter. After some discussion, Nolan had settled on pickled onions, so the meal that Thursday was a pickle free zone. The mushy peas, however, flowed like water and there would be repercussions later, if Maxwell knew his child.

When the last crumbly, greasy nubbin of batter had been chased out of the crunkles of the paper, when the last chip had been forced into the last odd corner of everyone's laden stomachs, when the last Scrabble tile had triumphantly been placed — a rather flukey 'xu' from Maxwell — the evening began in earnest.

'Tell me again, before we start talking about the inevitable,' Jacquie said, 'what a xu is.'

'It is one hundredth of a dong, since you ask,' Maxwell replied, 'and no smut, please, we're British.' He was taking out the coffee cups and replacing them with glasses of their alcoholic drink of choice.

'Of course. I always get it mixed up with zho.'

'A yak and a small coin; I can see how easily that can happen.' He raised his glass, as Scrabble victors will, with a smug smile on his face. 'Cheers.'

'Cheers.' She sipped her drink and sighed appreciatively. 'Sorry about Henry this afternoon, Max,' she said.

'What *was* that about?' He hadn't planned to ask, so it was good she had started here.

'I don't know. He'll tell me, I suppose, when he's good and ready, but as for now, he's gone all Horrible Henry on me. But I suppose the real reason that you have poured me the strongest g and t in the history of the world, is that you want to know why Geoff MacBride was in the nick today.'

'Ooh, you little mind reader, you,' he said. 'You could give Derren Brown a run for his money any day of the week.'

'Indeed,' she said. 'And also, of course, he told me he'd bumped into you on the way in.'

'Yes, that would also help,' he said. 'You'll never be a real rival to Derren if you tell me all your secrets, though. Did you haul him in?'

'Because of Morton's sister's story? No. We might have done, eventually, but no. He came in of his own accord. And steaming mad, as a matter of fact.'

'Really? Why was that? I should have thought he has had an easy ride thus far. When you compare it with Thomas Morton, that is. Both have wives who have been murdered and yet only one as far as I can tell is banged up at the nick. Or has that changed now?'

'No. Or perhaps I should say, yes. Morton has gone home now. Back to his mother's actually; we weren't happy about his being on his own and she was delighted to have her boy back. At the moment, there is nothing to really pin it down to him, except motive and of course there's masses of that. There is also more DNA than you can shake a stick at in that house, mostly upstairs as you can imagine. It may never be sorted, this one.'

Maxwell snorted. Never be sorted? Not when he was on the case. 'And MacBride. Explain his steamage.'

'Well, I told you about the threatening call to Mrs MacBride.'

'Yes.'

'We have a bit more on that now; I'll tell you that in a minute. But before the sound boffins came up with this new wrinkle, we thought it must be from one of the many cuckolded husbands that dear old Geoff has left in his wake. Due to the content, of course.'

'Right. So . . . I think I know where this is leading. You've been on to said husbands and shit has hit the fan.'

'In a nutshell, yes. We couldn't get to them all, of course, because even I-like-to-spread-it-around MacBride keeps some of his ladies under his hat. But we contacted a fair few. Well over a dozen, actually and of course lots of the women could supply other names. I think you may be one of a small minority of men in Leighford who won't be receiving a call.'

'Well, that's nice to know,' he smiled.

'And so, as might be expected, shit has indeed hit the fan. One of the women rang MacBride and gave him an earful. Well, I say one of the women — actually, she is the latest to be thrown over, so was madder than many. I suppose with some, time has been a healer, they've told the husbands and it's all blown over, that kind of thing. But it's still very raw for this one; she's only just been replaced, as you might say. So she's really gunning for him. As is her old man, I need hardly say.'

'But nothing from the current squeeze?'

'Not as yet. He is either taking a breather . . .'

Maxwell snorted.

'. . . or this one is a bit special, and he's keeping her more under wraps. I think we'll be watching this space. With his wife dead, she might be moving up a notch. But it is now more complicated.'

Maxwell gave an excited wriggle. He liked complicated. 'How so?'

'The sound guys have extracted various sections from the answerphone and have worked out that the anonymous call came from the Ellisdon bar.'

'Where MacBride was.'

'Correct. But also, the same voice was in the background when he was calling.'

'That must have been awkward, if it was Mr Number One Squeeze.'

'Yes. That's why we don't think it was, because MacBride's voice shows no very overt strain in the recording and surely, if the husband of the woman he had stashed upstairs . . .'

'Really?' Maxwell raised his eyebrows.

'Well . . . don't you think so? We're looking into that as we speak, but it's hard to work out when you can still book a hotel room anonymously, if you lie and use cash. Or a company credit card.'

'Yes, I suppose so. That makes his alibi a bit rocky though, surely.'

'It was always rocky. Anyway, that's why he came in. But it was handy because I could then hit him with his visits to Louise Morton.'

'I wish I could have been a fly on *that* wall,' Maxwell said, wistfully.

'You could have heard a pin drop. He went as white as a sheet. I thought he was going to keel over, for a minute. Two in one day would have been a bit much.'

'You're so hard, that's your trouble, you scary woman policeman.'

'I'm working on that,' she grinned. 'But he was back with the old bluster before too long. He was indeed in the habit of going to see Louise Morton, he said. They had known each other for years. In fact, he was surprised that we hadn't discovered that she had briefly worked for him before going to work for the bus company. Before she married Thomas Morton. Before Tommy was born.' She sipped her drink and looked at him, while the penny slowly dropped.

'He's Tommy's father?' Maxwell was incredulous.

'Yep. He didn't then go on to explain whether he was therefore getting freebies or he was there to catch up on family stories of how his lad was faring. But that's the situation as it stands now. Thomas Morton and Denise MacBride were friends without benefits, but I think he was genuinely fond of her. And Geoff MacBride has been knocking off Thomas Morton's wife, since before the Flood. So, Mr Clever. You like complicated. This complicated enough for you? Hmm?'

Before he could answer, the phone by his elbow rang.

'Ahoy, ahoy.' Maxwell always got a bit nautical when he had been eating fish. 'Oh, bugger.' He clapped his hand to his forehead.

Jacquie gave him an old-fashioned look. Cold callers were annoying of course, but Maxwell was usually rather more civil. She could hear the phone squawking, but couldn't tell who it was.

'I meant to . . . it just slipped my mind. And I'm sure you can imagine what it's like right now.'

Quack.

'And dusty, too, of course.'

Ah, Jacquie realised; Mrs B.

'I do understand; blogging can be big business these days. Well, why not tell him to go ahead. Hang on . . .' he moved the phone further from his mouth and spoke to his wife. 'Mrs B's sister's grandson has been looking into Fiona

Braymarr's Googlelessness and wants to write a blog about his findings. Problem?'

'That's legal, Max. Not law enforcement.'

He flapped a hand. 'Yes, yes, I know. But . . . is it unreasonable to bring that kind of thing to the attention of the cyber public in general? Is it libel, in other words?'

'I should think as long as he raises it as a hypothetical problem, it should be fine. He mustn't say anything that implies Mrs Braymarr has done anything wrong, for example. He should keep it to a kind of "how odd that this very hard-working head teacher is not visible on Google" and then go on to discuss how that can happen. Then, I should think he'll be all right.'

Maxwell spoke into the phone again. 'Did you get that?'

Quack.

'Sorry not to have . . . Much the same. See you soon, bye.'

'Mrs B's great nephew is a blogger?'

'Apparently so. She dabbles herself, too, so she tells me. I haven't looked her up yet, but her online persona is Moppet.'

Jacquie laughed. 'Clever. She is such a dark horse; I love that woman, even if she is the worst cleaner in the world.'

'Well, she moves the dust around, I suppose. Doesn't do to let it linger in one place.'

'And the Count adores her. As does Mrs Troubridge, come to that. They just sit and drink tea when she comes and does.'

'Have you seen Mrs Troubridge lately?' Maxwell suddenly felt guilty; he hadn't clapped eyes on the old trout since he had scared her witless with some ill-advised first footing at New Year.

'She's well. I saw her the other day; she doesn't want to chance going out until all risk of frost is past, apparently.'

'What is she?' he asked. 'A dahlia tuber?' He had happened upon the last few minutes of *Gardeners' World* earlier in the week and considered himself a bit of an expert. And the opening lines of Walter Scott's *Ivanhoe* trickled into his memory — 'In that pleasant district of merry England that is watered by the Monty Don.'

'Afraid of falling. She is getting a little bit frail, Max. A broken hip isn't a great idea at her age.'

'True. As long as she's all right. Where were we?'

'Mrs B's great nephew . . .'

'Yes. He is a computer expert — he actually does it for a living, rather than keeping it up his sleeve and surprising people, unlike his great aunt.'

Jacquie laughed. 'I still think that's amazing.'

'But useful,' Maxwell pointed out. 'You have no idea how often she has saved my bacon at school. Well, anyway, he was on the case of the missing Google profile of Fiona Braymarr and became quite intrigued. The blog, as I understand it, isn't so much about her as about how one becomes invisible on the internet.' He held up a hand. 'Don't ask me! I was told, but it wasn't English as I know it. Suffice to say, it is very unusual.'

'I should say it is. I would think someone as high profile as her would go on for pages.'

'Well,' Maxwell said, thoughtfully. 'She has no reflection, so why would she have a Google profile?'

'Fair enough. Ask Mrs B to let me have the link — it will be interesting reading.'

Maxwell's face went into technology mode, an expression specifically designed to look as though he knew what was going on, but clearly showed he would not be joining in the chat.

Jacquie smiled. She knew the thread had been broken. 'Shall we chill out to something on TV? Not crime, if you can find anything else.'

After some fruitless scrolling through the channels, her husband came up empty. 'Do you have a book on the go?'

She foraged down the sofa cushions and held it up.

'Me too. That's fine, then. Top up?'

'Please. Max . . . ?'

'Yup.' He was already deep in yet another Kennedy conspiracy theory; and all he knew for certain was that George

Butler didn't do it. Dallas policeman and local KKK leader, yes. But a gunman on the grassy knoll? Never.

'Do you know why Henry lost it today?'

'He's a funny age,' he muttered.

'Be sensible. It isn't like him, not really.'

Maxwell put down his book. 'No, it isn't. Yes, I think I do know why he lost it.'

'Why?'

'It's only a gut feeling. Think it over. Get back to me.' And he was back in Dallas, thinking Mannlicher-Carcano.

Jacquie held the book on her lap, but didn't read a word. Her mind was going over and over the last few days and what she had learned. It couldn't be the boffins' discovery; nor the Morton/MacBride links; could it be . . . Hetty? Had she phoned again when she was out of the room and put him out of sorts? She felt a tingling up her spine as the thought occurred to her.

'The man crossing the road was Hetty's husband.'

'Oh, hello.' He closed his book and smiled up at her. 'Why do you think that, heart of my dreams?'

'Because . . . because he crossed over, then crossed back again. So if Hetty . . .'

'Whose real name is . . . ?'

'You won't get me that easily. So if she saw him approaching the house, it wouldn't be from next door.'

'Good. And?'

'And he was wearing bright clothes. Like a golfer.'

'Ah ha. *And* Thomas Morton thinks he is a really kind man, helping out around the house with jobs Louise thought Thomas was too rubbish to undertake. He told me that this afternoon.'

'Hetty also said that Colin often is out in the evening at golf club do's. She doesn't like that kind of thing, so doesn't go. I wonder if he has ever taken a partner . . .' She swung her legs off the sofa and felt for her slippers. 'Does the golf club have a phone number, do you think?'

'Must do. They hire themselves out for functions, don't they? We had Whatsherface's retirement there last year. You remember. Textiles woman. She'd been there for years, apparently, but I didn't even know she existed. Shame on me, I know, but there it is. Stitch, stitch, stitch.'

'I remember. I'll give them a call.' She reached into her bag for her phone and tapped the screen, scrolling through until she found what she was looking for. It still fazed Maxwell when she did that and then spoke into it in the normal way. He was getting better with computers. He almost had phones licked. It was when they met in the middle that his brain started to sizzle.

It took a while before she was speaking to the golf club secretary and he did sound as though he had been sampling his stock rather freely. But she kept him to the subject at hand and even managed to make him understand that the conversation must remain confidential. He did call her 'little lady' once or twice, but on balance she thought he had got the message.

'Well?' Maxwell was agog.

She took a deep breath and looked at him with a sly smile playing round her lips. Then, she took pity on him. 'Colin Hampshire, who is, by all accounts, a bit of a sly dog, has, from time to time, appeared at golfing functions with a bit of a cracker — and I quote — on his arm. Everyone likes Hetty and she is a helluva baker — and I can vouch for that — so they all keep schtum. And anyway, what with old Col not being much of an oil-painting and as boring as all get out, they all assumed he paid the woman. There have certainly been rumours that she supplemented her fee out on the eighteenth hole with other members, if the weather was clement.'

'Well.' It was all Maxwell could manage at short notice. 'And Henry obviously realised that at once. How could Colin . . . sorry, what was the surname?'

'Hampshire.'

'How could Colin Hampshire think he would get away with it?'

'He did, though, didn't he?' she pointed out, reasonably. 'If Louise hadn't got herself killed, there would have been no reason for this conversation or any of the others which have led us here to take place.'

'That's true enough. Well, old Col, eh?' Maxwell raised an eyebrow. 'Are you going to tell Henry you've worked it out? Put him out of his misery?'

'In the morning. I'll let him stew for a while.'

Maxwell picked up his book again and was soon miles away. Damn George Mohrenschildt! What a dark horse. Jacquie had often tried to attract his attention at times like these and failed, so she thought she would try an experiment.

'Hetty's name is Ethel,' she whispered, so quietly she hardly heard it herself.

He showed no sign of having heard and just carried on turning pages, occasionally referring to the end of the book, following an endnote. She was rather disappointed. She had thought that he couldn't resist reacting and she was sure he had heard. But nothing.

* * *

Later that night, with the lights off and the only sound that of distant traffic on the flyover, Maxwell turned his head and murmured, 'Poor woman.'

And they lay there in the darkness, grinning.

* * *

Everything comes to he who waits and it was, finally, Friday. Maxwell bowled along on White Surrey feeling that things might be looking up. True, his school was going to hell in a handcart, but once the murders were solved, he could tick those boxes and concentrate on how to rid himself of Fiona Braymarr. He wished he could work out how; a Pied

Piper approach was an attractive thought. Entice her with sweet music down to the Esplanade and, when she had reached a reasonable rate of knots in her dance, just step aside and watch her sink. But he had a horrible feeling that she would be the one rat, stout as Julius Caesar, who would make it to the other side. The fact that that would mean she would end up in France was small comfort. No — there had to be a better way. He coasted down the road to the school, touching the brakes lightly as he went. Surrey had reached the age now when applying the brakes at anything less than death-grip pressure made no difference to the speed, but the squealing noise at least gave Mavis due notice. He wouldn't have minded, in principle, clipping one edge of her hi-vis, but suspected that it might involve a lot of explaining, so he took steps to avoid it on a daily basis. He looked up, expecting the normal sight of her standing like an ox in the furrow, lollipop aloft but there was nothing. A gaggle of Breakfast-clubbers were ambling up the entrance driveway, but of Mavis, there was no sign. He could hardly wait to get inside to check.

He tapped on the reception desk with a hastily-removed cycle clip and after a surprisingly long interval, the pale dogsbody appeared, peering as always through her hair. Fighting down the urge to grab it and pull it back into a ponytail, Maxwell addressed the girl he knew was in there somewhere. This was no time to pretend he didn't know her name.

'Jodie,' he said. 'Where is everyone?'

'There's only two of us left in here now, Mr Maxwell? Apparently, it's all we need? And the cleaners? They've gone as well?'

Maxwell had forgotten her adherence to the moronic interrogative but let that pass this once. 'But what about Mavis?' It really *was* a question, but he also hoped it made her feel more comfortable. He had never exchanged this many words with her before.

'The lollipop lady? Oh, no, she hasn't been sacked — she was run over?'

Maxwell's jaw dropped. He was not a cruel man, so meant what he said next. 'Is she all right?'

'Broken arm? Or leg? One of those?'

'Where did it happen?' He was trying hard not to use only questions, but it was an easy habit into which to drop.

'In her drive? Her husband did it?' There was a pause. 'By accident.'

Even Jodie didn't put a question on that remark — the poor man was apparently distraught.

Maxwell let the smile out now — as long as she wasn't dead, or anything worse, it was all right to grin. Poetic justice at its best. 'We're collecting, I suppose,' he said, rummaging in his pocket.

'No.' Jodie kept her voice level, for emphasis. 'It's not allowed.'

'Ah.' He patted her hand. 'Keep smiling, Jodie,' he said, although how anyone would be able to tell was a mystery. 'Thanks for the information.' And he went up the stairs with an added bounce. The universe was giving itself a shake and things were beginning to look up.

The raised voices were audible from about halfway up the flight and he took the rest two at a time. He triangulated the sound and found to his surprise it was coming from Helen Maitland's room. He crashed in through the door like Liberty Valance and the shouting stopped as if a switch had been flipped.

Zachary Budd had once been voted — at the Year Eleven Prom, in fact — the boy least likely to say anything. He wasn't morose or a martyr to nerves. Neither did he have more syndromes than China. He was just very quiet. So it was all the more surprising that it was *his* voice that Maxwell had heard and *his* face that stared, grim and determined, across the desk from Helen Maitland.

'Zach,' Maxwell said softly, adopting the family doctor approach, 'what seems to be the trouble?'

The boy subsided. Whatever rage had been building inside him for the past sixteen years went under wraps again at the sight and sound of Mad Max. He sat back down in the chair that Helen had offered him. 'I'm worried about my future,' he said.

Maxwell blinked. Surely, the boy was *far* too young to remember Dustin Hoffman in *The Graduate*; he had had the same concerns and had resolved them, at least temporarily, by getting his leg over Anne Bancroft. For the most fleeting of moments, Maxwell imagined Helen Maitland in the role, then screamed inwardly and banished such thoughts for ever. 'Say on.' He sat on the edge of Helen's desk and knew from her expression that she had already heard all of this, much of it at a volume to burst eardrums.

'I've got AS Levels coming up, Mr Maxwell.'

Mr Maxwell knew that.

'We all have. Year 13 have got A2s.'

So far, so obvious.

'But who's going to teach us?' Zach asked. 'We've already had two teachers for French and three for Business. Mr Johnson sort of let the cat out of the bag that he wouldn't be here next term. Continuity — haven't you always said how important that is?'

Maxwell had. The stability of a home, the sureness of a relationship, the continuity of a school — these were the things that led to success. And of the three, the greatest was the last.

'Are you a delegate, Zach?' Maxwell asked. If the Sixth Form Council *had* sent him, he was an unlikely choice.

'No, sir,' the boy said. 'But it's all they talk about. In the Common Room, it's all *any* of us talk about. Can't anything be done, sir? This Academy stuff. It's like they're taking the heart out of Leighford High. And that can't be right, can it?'

Maxwell smiled. He wanted to hug the boy, but he knew the implications of that. 'Unfortunately,' he sighed, 'we're all of us between a rock and a nutcase — unprofessional of me though it is to say it.' He looked at Zach's crestfallen face and the concern written on Helen Maitland's. She had already said much the same thing, but in a rather more delicate way.

Suddenly, Maxwell stood up. 'How are you on Westerns, Zach?' he asked.

'Okay,' the lad shrugged. 'My dad's got quite a few DVDs.'

'The Magnificent Seven?'

'One of his all-time favourites,' Zach smiled.

'Right. When you get home today, fast forward to the point where horrible old Eli Wallach has kicked the seven out of the village. And James Coburn, the hardest of them all, says, "Nobody hands me my guns and says 'Run'." Well, Zach,' he closed to the boy, 'that's pretty much what I'm saying now. Coburn goes back, doesn't he, with the others and they kick seven kinds of shit out of the baddies. Well, you watch this space.'

The boy got up and, although it was completely out of character, shook Maxwell's hand. He smiled at Helen Maitland and was gone.

'Can I load your guns for you, Max?' she chuckled.

'You can, Helen,' he said. 'You can. I just hope it doesn't dawn on young Zach too soon that James Coburn dies in the attempt.'

* * *

Jacquie and Henry Hall went back a long way. Although she was far from being the oldest member of the team at Leighford nick, she was pretty sure that she was one of the longest-serving and this gave her rights above and beyond her rank. She and Henry counted themselves as friends. They visited each other's houses; remembered birthdays; knew, by and large, where the bodies were buried. But, even so, asking a man if he was aware that his brother-in-law was seeing the amateur prostitute next door and, worse, was parading her in public in front of people who knew his wife; that was going to be tricky. So, she armed herself with coffee and a slab of what purported to be flapjack on the canteen's pricelist before she tapped on his door.

'Yes.'

Oh, oh. Terse. He was always terse, of course, but Jacquie's ear was fine-tuned as to degree. She stuck her head around the door nevertheless and proffered the cardboard tray of coffee.

'Oh, Jacquie.' He sounded a little more enthusiastic to see it was her, but not by much. 'Come in. I was just about to send you an email.'

'I've bought some flapjack,' she said. 'It's hard to tell it from the tray, but I know it's on there somewhere.'

'Did you want something specific?' he asked, popping the top off the coffee and stirring it. He hated froth but only the cappuccino was drinkable. 'Or are you simply psychic?'

This was banter in World of Henry, so she felt more comfortable. 'It depends,' she said, grasping the nettle. 'If you were about to send me an email about Colin, I'm psychic.'

He leaned back in the chair. 'Psychic it is, then,' he sighed. 'I'm sorry about yesterday. It knocked me for a bit of a loop, actually.'

'I should think so,' Jacquie said. 'I hardly know my brother-in-law, but it would knock me for a loop, too.'

'Then I went home and had a think about it,' he said, 'and to be honest, I don't think that kind of thing is quite up old Col's street. He's just . . . not that sort of man.'

'Guv . . . I'm afraid he *is* that sort of man. I made a call last night and I don't think you're going to like what I heard . . .'

CHAPTER FIFTEEN

Friday afternoon was a long time in coming but, as all things do in the end, it arrived. The weather had got itself in a tizzy, as it only can in March and gusts of wind from every quarter whipped around Leighford High School, rattling the bike sheds and scattering the fag ends in Smokers' Corner. Huge gobbets of rain hit the windows. In the grounds, the few daffodils that had survived the onslaught of two thousand feet were lying flat to the ground pointing north one minute, then were taken up as though by savage hands and hurled back to the ground again, this time pointing south. And all the while, out to sea, the sun sent silver shards through the clouds to pick out the wild, white horses in the Channel. Maxwell stood looking out of the window, leaning on the sill and seemingly lost in the crazy beauty of the day.

Below him, what should have been the fourth evening meeting of staff and Fiona Braymarr was getting under way. The new regime in this respect was not going well. On Tuesday there had been a desultory attendance, mostly made up of the brown-nosers and those so far out of touch with the mood of the moment that they went without realising the potential for pariahdom. On Wednesday, it was brown-nosers only, and several of those had thought things through and had come down with unspecified urgent medical appointments. Thursday was a James Diamond day, as Fiona Braymarr was busy feeding back. And so, Friday had come around.

It was surprisingly well-attended. Heads had been put together and the consensus was that, with axes falling hither and yon, it was better to face the enemy. The science people had the biggest axe to grind, having lost their support staff. They were closely followed by the Business and CDT Departments, whose computers had been amusing themselves all week by crashing, one by one. It was like watching a line of virtual dominoes topple, but less exhilarating. They had the Head Geek from Year Ten in the frame — he was known for being more attitude than aptitude but God, could that kid hack a computer! It was like poetry in motion. Maxwell had him tipped for MI6 if he ever grew up and didn't make a fortune out of WikiGeeks first. Then came the sundry Humanities — rumour had it that She was going to amalgamate them all into one small sub-department, on the basis that they were the soft option. The Maths Department had just come along for the ride.

The room buzzed like a wasps' nest poked by a stick. Sensitive souls could almost smell the brimstone in the air. Usually, the room was set out for meetings by the caretaking staff or, failing them, the cleaning contingent. But in the absence of both, the staff had dragged chairs out into rough rows and it gave the place a rather ad hoc air. There was no desk at the front for the SMT to hide behind, and no chairs for them either. From the back, someone pinged a rubber band and a paper pellet hit the far wall. The faculty had suddenly become the Sons of Anarchy.

The sole surviving member of the Religious Studies team looked around anxiously. She had studied Charles Mackay's book on the madness of crowds when she was doing her Masters and she had found another fan in Maxwell. He had said to her after the first meeting — only five days ago; it seemed impossible — '"Men, it has been well said, think in herds; it will be seen that they go mad in herds, while they only recover their senses slowly, and one by one."' She had taken it to be a warning to avoid the meetings and now she wished she had taken heed. She noticed that he was noticeable by his absence. She bent down to pick up her bag prior to sidling out, but she had left it too late. The doors swung back and Fiona Braymarr was among them, flanked by Janet Taylor, looking green around the gills as always and a very slow-moving James Diamond. It didn't take a genius to see he was back on the tablets.

Silence didn't fall over the meeting as it had earlier in the term. It was more that the mutterings turned inwards. From a wasps' nest on high alert, the sound was more of a prey animal crawling as quietly as it could back to its burrow at the arrival of the predator, there to regroup and plan the killer's downfall. Diamond looked out over his staff and saw what they had become. They were at bay, although they all still sat around as usual. They were still wearing their sober teachers' clothes, yet it looked like camouflage. And the scents of Marc Jacobs and Issey Miyake could not mask the pheromones of distrust and anger. Through the fog of his medication, he thought he might enjoy today.

* * *

Maxwell stood, unusually undecided, watching the weather as it gathered itself together to deliver something special. He knew there were warnings out all along the coast, of high winds which might cause structural damage; of high seas and rivers which could result in flash floods. Fortunately, Columbine was at risk of neither, tucked as it was on a slope, in the lee of a hill and reassuringly high enough above sea level. But the weekend was going to be a challenge to many, that was clear. He suddenly decided and turned to leave, to bend his unwilling feet to join the meeting below him in the staff room. The school had that feel about it; not empty, and yet missing the scurrying feet, like the rats in the wainscoting of an old house. He took one step and the phone rang. It was probably nothing. He took another step. But wasn't today Nolan's first go at judo? Visions of A&E swam in his head and he snatched up the receiver.

'Maxwell.'

'Mr M.' Mrs B sounded more flustered than was her wont. 'I thought I'd miss you. Ain't you at the meeting? It's about now, ain't it? She'll have you for that; she's a cow, that one.'

'It is. You're in luck. No, I'm not. Indeed it is; I was just leaving to go there. She won't if I have anything to do with it and finally, yes. She is.' Maxwell missed Mrs B — having a conversation with her was a good workout for his brain; if he could keep up, he knew that senility was not upon him just yet. 'How can I help you?'

'It's my sister's grandson, our Jacob.'

'Need help with the punctuation, does he?' Maxwell didn't mean to sound flippant, but now he had decided to attend the meeting, he didn't want to miss a minute.

'No.' Mrs B sounded unusually terse. 'He's been questioned by the police.'

'Pardon?' Maxwell was suddenly all attention. 'Whatever for?' His first thoughts were that the lad had been hacking into somewhere. His second thoughts were that he hoped it was nothing military. Or his bank.

'I just had a call from his missus. It wasn't Mrs M's lot, she said. Well, she didn't say that exactly, she said . . .'

'Yes, I get the idea. So, what were they?'

'I couldn't quite tell from what she was saying. She's hysterical. She opened the door to them and they just came in and took him. They had one of them banger things, for knocking down the door.'

Maxwell had always secretly longed for one of those, but could see that being the wrong side of a door being given the full treatment would not be much fun.

'They didn't use it,' she went on, 'because our Ellie opened the door, but they would've.'

'But, what did they *want*?' Surely the wife, no matter how shocked, would have an idea as to that?

'She didn't get the details. But she said she heard them say to him, as they took him out, that it was in connection with his searches and subsequent blog on the subject of Fiona Braymarr.'

'What?' It made no sense. Who *was* this woman? She was a dire people manager, that was clear. But being rather brusque and not too hot at HR didn't usually make a person someone of interest to . . . whom? Special Branch? MI5? The Stasi? KGB? Maxwell's imagination ran riot. 'Mrs B. Don't worry. I'll ring Mrs Maxwell and see if she can find out what's going on.'

'I've already done that, Mr M, no offence,' Mrs B said. 'I thought it was best to go to the horse's mouth. But she's out.'

'I'll track her down,' he promised. 'Where are you?'

'I'm at my sister's place. Everybody's here. I'll text you the number, shall I?'

'Ooh, if you like, Mrs B. I'm sure I'll be able to find it somewhere.'

'Don't come that with me, Mr M, if you don't mind the cheek. I know you can understand texts.'

'Got me, Mrs B,' he chuckled. 'Text me the number, then, and I'll let you know how I get on.'

'Don't forget.' The woman wouldn't let his previous oversight be forgotten in a hurry, he knew that.

'I won't. I'll get on it now. Sooner I'm gone, sooner I'm back.'

'Right oh. I'll leave it to you, then.' Maxwell heard raised voices in the background. He was sure he heard someone say 'old git' and other phrases he wasn't so sure about. 'What was that?'

'Nothing. Nothing, Mr M. I'll let you get on.' And the phone abruptly went down.

He broke the connection, dialled 9 and then Jacquie's direct line. After what seemed like hundreds of rings, it went to voicemail. He rang off and dialled again, this time to the front desk at the nick. The desk sergeant was unhelpful, much to his own delight. Everyone was out and he didn't know when they'd be back. Was there a message?

Now, what to do? The meeting must have well and truly started by now and Maxwell should by rights be at it, but he had promised Mrs B and so he had to run with this hare now, not go down and join the hounds. Or perhaps a pack of hares; it was hard to say. He rang back to the direct line and left a message; it was hard to be succinct, but in the end he just needed her to call him back. He would stay in his office, he told her, until five. Then, he would be on his mobile. Nolan was judoing and then going out for pizza with the Plockers. He remembered to say he loved her.

He sat behind his desk, not a normal place for him. It was covered in neat piles of marking but nothing ever got done there; he looked upon it as just a rather wide shelf. But he needed room now to see if he could make some sense of it all. He needed to make a plan, a flow chart, anything that would clarify all the bits and pieces going through his head. He pushed one pile carefully to one side and began to write.

Several pages later, he admitted defeat. Anything he came up with just looked like a demented spider's web and there were so many brackets, question marks and heavy underlining it looked like nothing else on earth. If he had had to make some kind of comparison, it would have been with Guy Fawkes' signature *after* the torture. Pacing achieved nothing, but eventually he gave in to that basic human need and did indeed pace back and forth, every now and again giving the phone a threatening look. Despite them, it refused to ring.

* * *

Jacquie had had some tricky conversations in her time, but the new number one slot now belonged to the one in which she had convinced Henry Hall that his brother-in-law was having a relationship with a prostitute, albeit a neighbour and probably at the cheaper and more amateur end of the spectrum; mate's rates sounded a little flippant, so she didn't use the phrase. On all levels, it was a horrible thought. Not only was he spending money on a woman when he had a perfectly pleasant one of his own, but he was parading said woman in front of friends, people who might bump into his wife in Tesco or while she was walking Killer on the beach. She had never met Colin Hampshire, and yet she really wanted to punch him.

Henry was quiet for a long time and Jacquie was on the point of tiptoeing out of the room when he spoke. 'We'll have to go round there. Interview the bastard.'

It wasn't like him to use any language other than the strictly correct, so this was Henry showing his feelings. 'Shall I check who's available, guv?'

'Available? What for?'

'Available to go and interview Mr Hampshire. I assumed you didn't want to do it yourself.'

'Of course I want to do it myself!' he said. 'I don't want Hetty to have to put up with strangers in the house, asking her husband about the tart next door and what he did and how often.' He stood up and reached for his coat, hung tidily on a hanger behind his chair.

'I don't think we need that kind of detail,' she said, hurriedly. 'Just whether he saw anyone else. Umm . . . where he was on Monday night. Hetty says golf club do, but we don't know that for sure. There was no need to check it out.'

'So,' Hall said, sharply. 'He went on his own to that one, did he?'

Jacquie looked thoughtful. 'That's a good point, guv. We'd have to check how often he took Louise Morton. I don't think it's every time.'

'Just the gala events, probably,' Hall said. 'You know, the sort where you push the boat out a bit. Black tie. Champagne. Prostitute.'

'Guv.' Jacquie had to make one last attempt. 'I really think that perhaps we should send someone else. Someone less . . . connected.' He looked at her mulishly. When Henry Hall put his foot down, it usually stayed put. 'Why don't I go?' It wasn't a great idea, but she needed to put some space between Hall and Colin Hampshire. She wanted this family to survive this thing; two had already been torn into pieces and that was bad enough. Another one would certainly be one too many.

'Don't worry,' he said, opening the door for her. 'You're coming anyway. Fetch your coat.'

As she was shrugging it on and shoving the scarf into the pocket in case the weather turned once more, the phone rang. She was almost allergic to leaving a phone ringing but as she took a step towards it, Hall's voice concentrated her mind.

'Leave that! I need to go now.'

Jacquie thought of what Maxwell would say if he heard that. His two bêtes noires were currently 'need to' and 'reach out'. What, he would have said, is wrong with 'want' and 'ask'? But picking Henry up on his grammar was possibly not really the best plan right now. Leaving the phone ringing, she scurried after him along the corridor and down the stairs.

In the car park, with the wind whistling around the corner of the building, on a straight course from Siberia, he threw her his keys. 'You drive. I'm too angry to drive.' No one looking at his face would have known it, but she took the keys anyway and set off towards the outskirts of Leighford, to interview Colin Hampshire.

In the car, Hall was silent, sitting in the passenger seat, his chin sunk onto his chest. He was usually a critical passenger and although it was good to be able to drive through moderate traffic without his constant admonitions, it did give the journey something of the flavour of the tumbril. When they drew up outside Hetty's house, he didn't move, even to unbuckle his seatbelt. Jacquie sat silently by his side; this had to be his call. His timing.

Hetty was at the window, peering out, trying to identify the two callers outside. Recognition was beginning to dawn on her face when Hall suddenly sprang back to life.

'Let's do it,' he said to Jacquie. 'I want you to ask the questions. Is that all right?'

She could only agree, but felt that this was going to be a tightrope act if ever there was one. Going over Niagara Falls blindfolded would be a walk in the park by comparison. She nodded and got out of the car, but Hall was at the door first.

Killer was doing his stuff already and Hetty opened the door, a beaming smile on her face. She lifted her cheek to be kissed and her brother planted a peck there, muttering into her ear that this was official.

'Oh, dear,' she twittered. 'Hello, Jacquie.' She fluttered her fingers at her and gestured her inside. 'Let me just shut Killer in the kitchen. Shall we go into the lounge? Colin's in there watching the golf.'

'Is that Henry?' someone called from the room. 'I'm watching the Puerto Rican Open. Come on in while I watch Saunders take this putt . . .'

Jacquie and Hall waited patiently in the doorway.

'Oh!' Hampshire threw his hands in the air. 'Beautiful.' He pointed the remote at the screen and the television went dark. 'Don't worry,' he said. 'I'm recording it, anyway.' He turned in his seat and smiled at Jacquie. 'Come on in. I imagine old Hetty'll be in with coffee and cake in a minute. She usually is.'

The two policepersons sat opposite the man and Jacquie gave him a quick glance. She imagined that Hall was seeing him with new eyes as well. As described so well by Sam Morton, he was older, balding, stooped and wearing, in deference to the Puerto Rican Open, light golfing clothes. The effect ended at the feet, which were encased in tartan slippers, complete with gnawed pompoms, doubtless courtesy of Killer. It was hard to see him as a ruthless roué, it was true. But this was probably the secret of his success in keeping his liaisons to himself. Who would look at him and suspect a thing?

'Actually, Colin,' Hall began, 'I think we'd rather have this conversation without Hetty present, if that's all right with you.'

Colin Hampshire had not been a policeman all those years for nothing. Also, despite his rather cavalier flaunting of Louise Morton, he was not quite as heartless as that had made him seem. He had worried, in a small, hidden corner at the back of his mind, that Hetty would find out, ever since he had started his little visits and it would almost be a relief to have it out in the open. It would cause a few ructions, he didn't doubt. But good old Hetty, she had a big heart and she wasn't interested in that kind of thing these days anyway. And what with the varicose veins and the sagging tits — she wouldn't blame a red-blooded man for looking elsewhere. Not good old Hetty. So he smiled at Hall and said, 'I think I know what this is about, Henry. I don't mind Hetty being here. We always share everything, you know that.'

Hall and Jacquie looked at him in amazement. Neither could imagine how they would feel if their own very significant others confessed as Colin Hampshire was about to confess, to an affair with the next-door neighbour. For money. In public. But he seemed quite unconcerned and so they waited until, as predicted, Hetty joined them, carrying a laden tray.

Jacquie glanced at Hall. He was as white as a sheet and looked sick. She had agreed to do the questioning, and so began. Hetty was pouring coffee and slicing lemon drizzle. Her husband was lounging in what was clearly always his chair, the best spot in the room with an unimpeded view of a television the size of a window. In the bookcase, row upon row of golfing books; on the mantelpiece, row upon row of golfing trophies. This was his house, his room; he was confident that he would always rule supreme and his arrogance suddenly flicked a switch in Jacquie and she let fly.

'We're here, Mr Hampshire . . .' she began.

'Oh, Colin, please,' he said, leaning forward to pick up the first slice of cake and the first cup. She noticed that his teeth were grey and uneven, that the scalp beneath the plastered comb-over was flaky and dry. She felt a twinge of sympathy for Louise Morton; the things we do for love are one thing, the things we do for money quite another.

'I think I would rather be a little more formal at the moment, Mr Hampshire, if you don't mind.' Jacquie caught Hetty's reaction out of the corner of her eye and felt sorry, but this had to be got through as quickly as possible. 'I am here to ask you about your relationship with Mrs Louise Morton, who, as you know, was found dead at her home on Monday night.'

Hetty put out her hand and Hall took it gently between both of his own.

The man leaned back in his chair, his paunch filling the front of his pink, diamond-patterned sweater. 'She was just a neighbour,' he countered. Suddenly, telling all in front of Hetty didn't seem such a good idea.

'We have several eyewitnesses who say otherwise,' Jacquie persisted.

'Who?' the ex-policeman blustered. 'They're lying!'

'I can't name them of course,' Jacquie said. 'I'm sure with your police experience you know that. But they are reliable and we are convinced that their information is accurate. You have been seen on numerous occasions at formal events with Mrs Morton and also you have been seen once leaving her house.'

Hampshire opened and closed his mouth several times, but no words emerged. Finally, he spoke, but to his wife. 'You never wanted to come, Het, did you, eh? You didn't really like those formal things, did you? Didn't have a dress, or the shoes.'

His wife licked her lips and her voice when it came sounded from very far away. '*You* told *me* I didn't like the formal things, Colin,' she said. 'You said they were boring, that the food was awful and the speeches worse. When I found a dress I liked, do you remember, that green one? You told me it made me look like mutton dressed as lamb. You told me that I had bingo-wings and saggy tits.' She turned a stricken face to her brother. 'I'm sorry, Henry. I never wanted you to hear all this.' Her voice sank to a whisper. '*I* never wanted to hear all this.' She cleared her throat and spoke again to her husband. 'You were cruel to me, Colin. You said at my age it was best to just get on with what I do best. Baking. Looking after the kids. Walking the dog. But you, *you* weren't old, dear me, no! You could step out, if you wanted. You could take tarts to the golf club, go round next door, *next door*, Colin. When I had to turn the hoover on to drown her and her clients out, it was *you*!'

'Het! Het, old thing. It wasn't like that. I was . . . fixing washers, light bulbs, that kind of thing. And I didn't mean to upset you, about the dinners and such. I just thought . . .'

'Thought? *Thought*? You've never thought a moment in your whole life, you pig! When is my birthday?'

Hall knew, but clearly Hampshire had no clue.

'It was last week. I put the cards up. The cards from the children, from Henry, from *Henry's* children, for God's sake. And you didn't even notice.' She turned to Hall. 'I can't believe I've been so blind, Henry. I'll have to tell the children, but not today. Can I come and stay with you and Margaret?'

'Of course,' Hall said, patting her hand again. 'Pop upstairs and get some bits together. Are you thinking of bringing Killer?'

'No, I bloody well am not,' she said, drawing herself up. 'Yappy little thing. And what a stupid name. No, *he* can have it. Take it for walks and pick up its smelly crap. No, I'm just bringing a few bits. And my solicitor's contact details.' She swept from the room and, little and dumpy as she was, she made a darned good exit.

The three remaining sat listening to her footsteps receding up the stairs. Hampshire was the first to speak.

'She doesn't mean it,' he said, with a dismissive wave of his hand. 'She won't go. I notice you didn't check with the wife,' he said to Hall. 'See if it's all right for her to come back with you. You know she won't go.'

Jacquie waited for a moment to see if he would break down, would realise that his life was, to all intents and purposes, over. But no; the man's hubris seemed to be boundless. 'We will be taking a formal statement later, Mr Hampshire, if you could call into the station at your earliest convenience, but for now, could you shed any light on Mrs Morton's other clients?'

'I wasn't a client!' For the first time, he looked uncomfortable. 'I was just being a good neighbour.'

Hall leaned forward. 'Colin,' he said, quietly. 'Perhaps this isn't the time to say this, but I've never liked you. You've never treated Hetty right, not from the start. But it looks as if that is all over now, so now that's out of the way, I can give you a bit of advice. You're not the only policeman in this room and by a good margin you're certainly not the *best* policeman in this room. So don't give me any more crap. You were a client of Louise Morton's. Like all the others, you paid for what she dished out. I can't say I condone it for any of them, but for you, I haven't enough words to show my contempt. You treated my sister as less than nothing and now we want the truth out of you. And don't think I will hesitate to give your name to the prosecution when all this comes to trial. Believe me, you're going to be up front and centre. So now, Colin, would you like to listen to my colleague here and answer what she asks you.' He turned to Jacquie and nodded politely. 'I beg your pardon, Detective Inspector Carpenter-Maxwell. I interrupted. Please, go on.'

Jacquie raised her pen and Hampshire shrugged. 'All right. I did pay Louise for sex. And I wasn't the only one. I never saw anyone else, though. She didn't . . . there was usually only one or two a day booked in.'

'Booked in?' Jacquie was interested. 'Did she keep a book, then? A physical book?'

'It sounds a bit of a cliché,' the ex-copper said, 'but she had a little book in her bag. She used to tick me off when I paid.' He spread his hands. 'I didn't mean to do it. I went round there one day, after I'd retired, to see if she needed any jobs doing.'

'So, you help out in the street in general, do you?' Jacquie asked, with a straight face.

'What does that mean?' Hampshire's aggression was growing.

'You help other people in the street. Like, the person on the other side of you here, the person across the road?'

'No,' he admitted. 'I just helped Louise with a few jobs. Well, that husband of hers is rubbish, isn't he?'

Jacquie and Hall showed no response and their silence forced him to carry on.

'So, one day, she said that she ought to repay me, for the little jobs I'd done, you know. So . . .'

'I don't think we need details,' Hall said. He had heard his sister come back down the stairs and knew she was standing, listening, in the hall. She needed to hear it, but not every last bump and grind. Hampshire was, naturally, unaware that his wife was in earshot and was, as Maxwell could have told them, as eager to share as any teenager after their first time.

Hampshire's face fell. He had longed to tell someone about it for so long. All that shouting, screaming, compliments; it all counted for nothing if no one else knew. But, he knew a brick wall when he met it, and settled for a shortened version. 'So, a long story short, she thought I was bloody marvellous.' He would get that in, if nothing else. 'So, the next day, I went back. I thought she would want some more, you know. She seemed to enjoy it so much . . .' As he relived the humiliating second visit, his face fell and he skimped the detail. 'There was someone else there. The doors were locked. I could hear . . . well, anyway, I went back later, had it out with her and then she told me. If I wanted to . . . do it again, it would cost. So,' he shrugged, 'that's what I did.'

'And the social events?'

'I paid for those too. I wasn't thinking. I didn't think how Hetty would feel.'

'No. Clearly not,' Jacquie said, closing her notebook. 'Oh, by the way, Mr Hampshire. Where were you on Monday night?'

'A farewell do at the golf club.'

'And yet you didn't take Mrs Morton.'

He looked shocked. 'God, no,' he said. 'I only took her to formal do's. No need spending money just for a farewell do.'

'Thank you. Please come down to the station to give a formal statement as soon as possible,' Hall said. Then, to the man's face and with a world of meaning. 'Goodbye.'

* * *

The drive back to the station was not the easiest one that Jacquie had ever endured. The silence in the car was like treacle, Louise Morton and her elderly inamorato the rutting elephants in the room. She was glad to deliver the woman to the ministrations of her sister-in-law and get back to the haven of her office. Her voicemail light was blinking, her mobile had missed calls to further order, but for now, she just needed a quiet think and to check on Henry. The calls could wait.

CHAPTER SIXTEEN

The staff room was empty now, but it retained the sour atmosphere which had characterised the meeting. Fiona Braymarr had been nettled by the feedback session the day before. Complaints? She'd give them complaints. And that lily-livered idiot MacBride. He seemed to think it was in his power to ditch her when he wanted to; as if it was his choice. She had persuaded herself that the reason she had spent the night alone was because she wanted to — she would have lain down on hot coals rather than admit to anyone how long she had spent at the window, watching. But not just for MacBride. She was also watching for the lurking dread that never quite left her, the dread that she knew was back on her trail. There had been searches, internet searches. There had been calls. He was near. She could almost smell him and if she therefore gave the staff of Leighford High School short shrift, it wasn't just because they had rediscovered the power of the pack — it was because Fiona Braymarr, almost unbelievably, was scared shitless.

* * *

In his office, which had once been Bernard Ryan's office, whose office now was a desk in the corner of Janet Taylor's office, James Diamond sat down and reached in his pocket for his Afternoon Pill. His GP had been quite adamant that they would do no good unless he kept to a strict timetable and so he had invested in a little vibrating pill-keeper and he kept it in his breast pocket at all times. The pill was only small, it needed no water or effort to swallow, but it took the edge off and at the moment, James Diamond needed the edge taking off. But this afternoon, he could have done without his little pill. Because, this afternoon, he had seen Fiona Braymarr's carapace crack. Just a tiny bit. Soon, he thought, as he let his head roll back onto the back of his chair, which had once been Bernard Ryan's chair, soon, he would have his school back . . .

* * *

In his office, which had always been his office, since Adam had been in the Militia, Maxwell had stopped pacing. He had moved the phone nearer to his elbow and had been reduced to marking some Year Eight books; it wasn't improving his temper to read how King John had *signed the* Magna Carta for the umpteenth time, but it was saving him from going mad. He lifted the receiver on average about every thirty seconds. Sometimes, he even dialled 9 for an outside line — but then, he put the phone down. If he had left a message for his wife and she hadn't replied to it, it was for a reason. Another call wouldn't help. He turned to another exercise book and his eyes popped. As if to restore his faith in human nature, this delightful child had written that King John had sealed Magna Carta. Joy! Sadly on the next page the information imparted was that Diamond was a wanker. Still, you can't have everything and he gave both sentences a big red tick of approval.

* * *

It had been no good. After he had watched the previous afternoon, it had nagged at him. The look of fear and distress on her face had haunted him and he hadn't slept. If it wasn't the car salesman who was scaring her, who was it? Somebody at that bloody school, that was it, for sure. She took on too much; she put on a front that only he knew was false. She had to go in strong, to weed out the bad seed. That was something he had taught her. He had had to do it sometimes with . . . well, the police who had torn her from him had called it something he was uncomfortable with. He called it love. Tough love. And that was what she used when she helped to save these morons. Tough love.

He shrank into the hedge as they walked past, the gaggle of teachers, walking to their cars. It was wet under the lee of the budding hawthorn, but if he had been standing in the middle of the path waving a flag, they would never have noticed him. They were all too wrapped up in their own little worlds. He didn't listen to their stupid prattle as they walked past. But one name did stand out as they went. Maxwell. Maxwell would sort her out. Maxwell would see the bitch got her just desserts. Maxwell would get her out, just you see.

He pulled his cap down low over his eyes and stared at the school building. Perhaps it was time he had a word with Mr Maxwell.

* * *

Fiona Braymarr was not a woman who stayed down for long. In her office, which had once been James Diamond's office, she sat behind her immaculately clear desk and tapped impatiently on the surface with a perfect fingernail. It was clearly impossible to sack the entire rabble that made up the remaining staff. She had a stack of resignation letters in a file on a shelf behind her and so by the time September arrived, there wouldn't be many of them left, anyway. She had found in her previous appointments that this happened. When the going got tough, it wasn't the tough who got going, but the whinging, weak ones who couldn't take the heat. She would leave — as leave she would, in just a few terms' time — a school that was stronger and more ready to take on the challenges ahead. If most of the staff were new; if some of them, recruited from the internet, barely spoke the language; if the infrastructure was a tottering shadow of its former self, Fiona Braymarr didn't care. She had moved on and changed her name so often, she had made it her business not to care; like a snake that sheds its skin, so she could grow a little and move on. And perhaps, one day, she could leave the dread with the sloughed shreds of her life and she could be normal. Until then, though, she had been balked of her prey and was casting around for something to maul. Who could it be today? Her eyes lit up and, in the face of sense and experience, she made up her mind.

Maxwell.

* * *

Maxwell looked at the clock and saw to his surprise and slight consternation that it was gone five. This would certainly complicate the issue. With the message he had left in mind, Jacquie wouldn't be trying to get him at school any more. And with his mobile safely on the mantelpiece at home, it was not a lot of use ringing him on that, as she would know perfectly well. The weather wasn't getting any more pleasant either, so, one way and another, he might as well get, literally, on his bike. He put his coat on and looked around for his scarf. He knew he had had it that morning, but it seemed to have become separated from the rest of his going-home togs. He knelt on the seat of his chair and bent over the back — it wasn't unknown for it to get itself down between there and the wall. It wasn't there; so, scarfless, he straightened up and shoved himself upright, turning as he did so.

He wasn't quite sure why this should be, but people seemed to be making a bit of a thing about creeping up on him these days. First Thingee One and now Fiona Braymarr, standing in the doorway, looking not unlike Tilda Swinton in *Constantine*, but not so angelic. He decided to be curt, but civil. At this kind of time on a Friday, he was entitled to be about his own business.

'Mrs Braymarr,' he said, with a nod. 'I can't stay, I'm afraid. Late already. May we reschedule for Monday?'

She closed the door behind her and he felt the temperature drop. Who says Hell is hot? 'No, we can't. I noticed you were not at the mandatory meeting today.'

All right. If this was to be the showdown, so be it. Maxwell shifted his metaphorical six-shooters a fraction of an inch, he flexed his trigger finger and adjusted his stance. He really *was* the man who shot Liberty Valance. And Fiona Braymarr ought to have known that. He was ready. 'I'm not sure you have noticed that in fact I have attended *none* of the mandatory meetings this week,' he said, evenly.

'I was informed you were needed elsewhere on Tuesday,' she said. 'I am not an unreasonable woman, I hope.'

We all hoped that, he thought, and where did that get us?

'But today's meeting was . . . difficult. I have done this job for quite a while, Mr Maxwell. I *do* know what I am doing. The staff here seem to think otherwise.'

'I think we would all feel better if we could find out how well your previous victims . . . sorry, that slipped out . . . your previous *projects* were faring now. But as you may be aware, you are not on Google.'

She shrugged. 'I've never looked, actually.' She smiled, an unexpectedly sweet one. 'Do *you* Google yourself, Mr Maxwell?'

'Touché. I can't say that I do. But you — you're the Google generation, Mrs Braymarr. I would have thought it was meat and drink to you. How do you get work, apart from anything else? Do you apply?'

'No,' she said. 'Of course not. I am part of a team of . . . I hesitate to call us Superheads, that is just a term the press uses, but we are rather special, if I say so myself. We troubleshoot. We fix.'

'You ruin.'

'I think that's taking it rather far. I can't just go into a school and leave it as it is. What would be the point?'

Maxwell frowned at her. She seemed to be an intelligent woman, but why was so little she said sense? This was going to be a long haul and meanwhile, no one knew where he was and he hadn't helped Mrs B's sister's grandson a jot. He shrugged off his coat and walked round the row of chairs to take his seat at one end. It was, after all, only a few short weeks ago since he had semi-crushed a headmaster and with no nursing help on the premises these days, it paid to be cautious. He patted the back of the next seat but one. 'Let's sit, Mrs Braymarr, shall we? I have a feeling this may be the last conversation we have except in the presence of my union representative, so we may as well be comfy.'

She stood, irresolute. 'I don't want to make this too chummy, Mr Maxwell . . .'

'Believe me, Mrs Braymarr. Chummy is not on the cards. I just think we could have a nicer and more productive exit interview, if this is what this proves to be, without me getting cramp in one leg. Come on. Sit.' He patted the chair again.

Slowly, like a cobra trying to outwit a mongoose, she circled the chairs, approaching it from the far end. She sat, gingerly, checking the seat cushion briefly before she did so. Perhaps she too expected to find a prone James Diamond lying there. With just under half an hour to go before the sun went down, it wasn't exactly bright over by the window, and with the lashing rain it changed from moment to moment, but it was better than standing facing each other under the unforgiving glare of a fluorescent tube. He leaned back a little; she clearly liked her space and if he were to be asked, he didn't want to be too close to her, either.

'So,' he said. 'Who goes first?'

'It depends what we want to find out, Mr Maxwell, don't you think?'

He nodded slowly. This woman was not pleasant, but she wasn't stupid. She was trying to diagnose the sickness of the school by taking his temperature; he could only hope she intended to stick the thermometer in his mouth, not up his bum. 'I want to find out how much more damage you intend to do, Mrs Braymarr. It's as simple as that.'

'It isn't damage, as I see it, Mr Maxwell.' Was it a trick of the light or did she look suddenly vulnerable. 'I look at schools before I go in, you know. I don't just lay about me at random. There is a bottom line financially and I must meet my targets.'

'But these are *people*,' Maxwell said. 'Not just numbers. If you came and just waited a term or so; get to know us.'

She leaned forward and then hutched a seat nearer. 'Mr Maxwell,' she said. 'I'm not made of stone. If I got to know you all, I wouldn't do my job as well. I would get to like some of you. I would get to *dislike* some of you. And then I wouldn't make the proper choices.'

He hutched one seat further away. He couldn't remember now whether he was on the last seat or the one before last; fortunately for his dignity, it proved to be the one before last. 'In most people's opinion, Mrs Braymarr, you made the improper choice when you decided to come to Leighford High School.'

She had expected this interview to be easier than this. Although she had already discovered that Maxwell was like a terrier at a rathole when he was on the case, she had still expected that she could persuade him that she was one of the good guys after all. She needed to ramp it up a notch. 'I can see your point, Max,' she said. She slid the nickname in as smooth as silk. 'I may have perhaps been a little draconian, but this school was not going to be a paying proposition, without pruning staff. And without Leighford High, none of the other schools in the town would have been offered Academy status.'

He shrugged.

'To their detriment, I feel. So, I *had* to make this work. For the good of the children.'

At last! She had actually said it and he could let rip. In full Helen Lovejoy mode, he tore his hair and wailed 'Won't somebody think of the children?'

It made her jump. She hadn't seen Mad Max in all his glory before and his Helen Lovejoy was something of a tour de force. 'What?'

'I assume you don't watch *The Simpsons*.' It was a statement, not a question.

'What?'

'Thought not. Anyhoo, it matters not that you have no idea what I am talking about. The point is, the children are the last ones you care about. Earlier today, I managed to calm down, with extreme difficulty, the quietest and nicest boy in this school, who was distraught about not only his own but his peers' chances of getting any exam results worthy of the name.'

'No, that's not fair! I am dedicated to improving results.'

'You doubtless are,' he said. 'But forcing people to leave because they simply can't stand it here any longer isn't the best way to do it, in my very humble opinion. I have put up with a lot in the past week, Mrs Braymarr, although I confess it seems far longer. I have seen my oldest and dearest friend lose the job she loved. A woman who was the glue which kept this school together, kicked out without so much as a by your leave.'

'Ah, yes,' she sneered. Men and women stuff; she understood that all right. 'I did hear that you and Mrs Marriott . . .'

'Matthews. Please do her the courtesy of remembering her name.'

'Matthews, yes, that you and Mrs Matthews had a bit of a . . . *thing* . . . going on. Does your wife mind? Her husband? I'm surprised, to tell you the truth.' She was using one of her other weapons now, the twin barrelled gun of rumour and innuendo. It had scored more hits than any other. 'What with your wife being that much younger and her husband . . . you'd think you would be more careful.'

Maxwell was used to gibes like this. He and Jacquie didn't really notice the age gap. In fact, they didn't really notice that Nolan was a child; as far as they were concerned, he was just an unusually short human being. But it all seemed to matter to other people. But he didn't like Sylvia being dragged into it, just the same. 'Sylvia and I love each other, yes. And if you have no one you love with whom you don't want to leap into bed, I am truly sorry for you, Mrs Braymarr. I really, really am.'

The compassion in his voice knocked her for six. No one had cared about Fiona Braymarr in a long, long time and she found it hard to cope with. And all the worse for being true. Looking back, it was years since she had felt anything but passing lust for anyone. She hadn't even *liked* Geoff MacBride, with his ironed Calvin Klein underpants and his nasty cheap knock-off not-quite-Paco Rabanne aftershave. There had been one or two where she had come close; but she had had to sack one and the other had gone back to his wife, so she had had no choice. She found she quite literally couldn't speak. If she had done so, she knew she would end up in tears. And, like falling in love, she hadn't done that for years.

It was almost too dark to see now, but he could tell he had struck a chord. 'I don't want to pry, Mrs Braymarr,' he said, getting a sudden gut feeling and deciding to go for it, 'but have you moved to Leighford? From wherever you come from, I mean.'

She shook her head.

'Are you in a hotel, then?' he asked, all innocence. Various cogs were clicking into place in his head and he thought that while she seemed to be winded, he could serve the sucker punch. 'I would imagine a person like you, on a top salary, used to nice things, wouldn't exactly slum it, so . . .' he put a finger to his lips, as if thinking, '. . . I would assume you would be somewhere nice and classy. Somewhere like the Grand in Brighton, if you don't mind a drive. Or the Ellisdon, if you prefer to be closer at hand.'

She cleared her throat. She could speak now, as long as he didn't do that kindness thing again. 'The Ellisdon, yes. That's right. The Academy board very kindly made arrangements for me.'

Well, that tied in; Jacquie has said that it was impossible to go beyond the company credit card. 'Comfy, is it?' His smile in the darkness was like something lurking in a swamp.

'Very.' This conversation was a little tangential, but it gave her time to think.

'Mr MacBride like it, does he?'

She was silent for a moment. How could he know? He couldn't know; he was just fishing. 'Who?'

'Now I know you're fibbing, Mrs Braymarr. You must know Geoff MacBride. He's our Chair of Governors for one thing. But you know him better than that, don't you? He was in your room, doubtless discussing staffing levels and similar, when his wife died. Or was horribly murdered, depending on how graphic one wishes to be.'

Fiona Braymarr had not got where she was by not thinking on her feet. She weighed her options quickly and decided on her course of action. 'I have clearly underestimated you, Max.' He hadn't taken her up on her implied offer to be more friendly, but she could persevere. 'But how did you know that he was at the Ellisdon on that night? Wifie been talking out of turn, has she?'

Ooh, but she was cunning. Happily, Maxwell didn't care. He knew a woman on the ropes when he saw one and decided that she would be in no position to damage Jacquie once he had finished with her. 'We did chat about it, yes. Actually, as Tommy Morton's appropriate adult and as the two cases are interlinked, she told me nothing I wasn't entitled to know.' As he said the words, they sounded like a load of old tosh even to him, but they would serve. 'So, I am right, then?'

She shrugged. 'So what if you are? I did have a small liaison with him, but it's over now.'

'Ah.' Another cog snicked into place. 'That explains the scratches.'

'I didn't know you had met Geoff since . . .'

'Not so much met, more bumped into.' He looked at her as well as he could in the dark. 'Do you want the light on, Mrs Braymarr? It's as black as Dick's hatband in here.'

'You do like to play the simple old soul, don't you, Mr Maxwell? But I do have the measure of you, you know. You are actually very clever.'

This puzzled Maxwell. He had no idea that she should have presumed otherwise.

'It's no good trying to use this against me, Max.' She reverted to the faux friendship which had been falling so flat. 'I'm divorced and his wife's dead. So no harm, no foul.'

'No.' He had to agree she was right, there. 'Unless one of you killed his wife, of course. Or both of you, working together. Or Louise Morton, mother of his son and also his bit on the side every second Wednesday or whenever his turn happened to come around.'

'Why would I want to kill anyone, Max?' she asked. 'I have what I want. A new challenge every term or so. Top class accommodation. A salary you classroom scum can only dream about. My choice from any of the men I come across in the course of my work — I rather had my eye on Bernard Ryan in fact, though he seems to be unwell much of the time.'

Maxwell smiled. 'I don't think Bernard is really your type,' he said, keeping his voice level. 'Anyway, I think his husband is more the kind to make a fuss than the wives you usually usurp.'

'Husband? Really? I must speak to my researchers. They seem to have missed that one.'

'Clearly. But killing isn't always just a matter of stone cold reason, is it? Rarely is, in fact, if you think about it. I'm just thinking about this particular scenario. MacBride threatens to leave you. You follow him home. You decide to speak to his wife. It turns ugly.'

She stood up. 'Can you hear yourself?' she said. 'You haven't known me long, but you must know I would never behave like that. I was annoyed when MacBride threw me over. But I had something else on my mind at the time, something else to . . . well, I won't lie to you, Max. I had had a shock. I was not myself.'

'A shock? Anything I should know?'

'No. Just something personal. I do *have* a personal life, you know. Feelings. Things like that. I'm not the devil incarnate. Nor am I War, or Death, or Pestilence or whatever you compared me with on Monday morning.'

'I'm impressed.'

'I'm glad. So you should be. Which was it, just for the record?'

'War.'

'Hmm. That's good.' She grinned and even in the gloom, he saw her teeth flash. 'We could have been friends, Max. Do you know that?' She was suddenly on her knees on the seat next to him, leaning over and forcing him back. 'More than friends, perhaps.'

Before he could stop her, she had her mouth clamped on his and he couldn't move. She had her knee on his lap and was holding his arm down firmly on the back of the seat. Her other hand was rummaging at the front of his trousers. Her other hand was wound in his hair, tilting his head back. He hadn't been subject to such a determined attack since . . . Her *other* hand? Something was wrong, but which hand was someone else's?

'It's all right, my precious,' he heard a voice croon above his head. In his mouth, he felt her whimper. 'I saw his evil wiles from the start. He forced himself on you. You don't need to worry. I got here in time to witness what you had to do.'

The hand in his hair tugged hard and her mouth left his. A torch shone in his face and blinded him. She still had hold of his arm, but had stopped her rummaging. He could tell that she was crouching down, as far away from his attacker as she could get. But she still had hold of his arm. 'I'm sorry, Max,' she said. 'I'm so sorry.'

'Don't apologise to him, my darling,' the voice said. 'He's scum. Rapist scum.'

'May I speak?' Maxwell said.

The torch swung and smacked him around the head. 'No,' the voice hissed. 'No, you may not. You may *not* speak in the presence of my wife, you scum.' The torch swung again. 'Scum!' It swung back for a third time and this time, Fiona Braymarr took the blow on her arm.

Maxwell's head was tugged back even further across the back of the seat and he heard his spine grind. It occurred to him that at his age, he probably shouldn't be able to adopt this position.

'Now look what you made me do!' The voice was whining now, passing the blame. 'I've hurt my darling's arm. Sweetheart, are you all right? Tell your Alan, tell me.'

'No,' she said. 'No, darling. I think you may have broken it.' The torch swung and she hurriedly continued. 'No, sweetheart. Don't hit him again. He's old. You won't need to do much to finish him off. But don't you want to talk to him, first? Don't you want to find out how much he wanted me? You know you like that.'

Maxwell didn't like Fiona Braymarr. Never had. Never would. But at that moment, as her hand squeezed his arm encouragingly, he could have kissed her all over again.

The torch lowered slowly. 'He *did* want you, didn't he?'

'Yes.' Fiona Braymarr's voice had taken on a singsong sound, consoling and almost hypnotic. 'Yes, he did. I had to do it, didn't I, Alan? Thank goodness you came along and saved me.'

The pressure on the back of Maxwell's head eased a little. The torch flashed onto Fiona Braymarr, moving up and down, slowly.

'He didn't hurt you, baby, did he?' the voice crooned.

''No,' she said, still holding Maxwell's arm, as if to ground herself in some kind of normality. 'He didn't hurt me. Alan?'

'Yes, my lovely darling?'

'I like him, Alan. I don't want you to hurt him.'

'You *like* him?' The pressure grew on the back of Maxwell's head and his neck gave another protesting click. He raised his hand in protest and couldn't help a small cry of pain.

'No. No, Alan. Not that much. I like him as much as . . . well, I like him as much as George. Do you remember George? You let him, go, remember?'

Maxwell was not comforted much by the way this conversation was going. And he still couldn't see who had hold of his hair.

There was a silence from behind him, then a grunt of assent. 'George. Yes, I remember him. Harmless, you said he was.'

'And so is this one,' she said. 'That kiss was just for a joke, wasn't it, Mr Maxwell?'

Instinctively, Maxwell tried to nod, but the grip on his hair stopped him. 'Yes. Mrs Braymarr was teaching me how easy it is to kiss . . . umm, to kiss in the dark. I've been having trouble. Technique, you know.'

'Is this true, Moyra?'

'Moyra?'

'I'm sorry, Mr Maxwell,' she said. 'I have been flying under false colours. My real name is Moyra Dunbar. This is Alan Dunbar, in case you were wondering. My husband. My ex-husband, to be exact.'

'Charmed, I'm sure,' Maxwell said. He reached round with his right hand but Alan Dunbar wasn't that easy to fool.

'She calls me ex,' he said. 'But I don't accept that. A marriage is forever. I look after her. I promised. Till death us do part.'

'Alan takes things very literally,' she said. Then, remembering she must placate the man, 'bless him.'

'She's too trusting, you see, Mr Maxwell,' he said. 'She goes off with anyone who asks her. She's got herself into some scrapes. She even changes her name, so they can't find her afterwards. But I can always find her. I always can track her down. To protect her.'

'Yes,' she sighed. 'That's right.'

In the silence that fell for a moment, as all three contemplated the position, two voices sounded from the ground floor. It was impossible to hear the words, but Maxwell knew it was the two remaining office staff, locking up for the night.

Once they turned that key, the whole place would be alarmed and anyone trying to get in would set off bells and whistles in the police station and the fire station. Sirens would be the order of the day as they all rushed to the scene. Maxwell was not famed for listening to notices in meetings, so he didn't know whether that also applied should anyone try to get out. But he would be giving it a go, first chance he got. The voices receded and then, far off in the car park, two engines fired up and disappeared into the silence.

'So,' said Alan Dunbar brightly. 'We're locked in, now. That's cosy. Mr Maxwell. I'm going to get Moyra here to tie you to the chair. And then we can chat in a bit more comfort, can't we?'

'That would be nice.' Once, as a small boy, Maxwell had seen, on the outskirts of Dreamland on a family holiday to Margate, a supposedly headless woman. It had scared him sleepless for days but when he calmed down, he wondered where they had got the body from and what had happened to the head. He was beginning to think he knew the answer. He didn't know you could get cramp in your scalp, but apparently, it was possible.

'Do you have any string, Mr Maxwell?' she asked.

'In my desk drawer,' he said. Also in his desk drawer were some scissors which at a pinch would make a goodish weapon. But did she want to stab this man, this ex-husband? Was blood-by-marriage thicker than water or would she save Maxwell, should it come to the point? He would give her the tools for the job, if nothing else.

'Tie him tightly, now,' the madman said. 'No tricks.'

'No tricks, darling,' she said. She walked round to the desk by going past the man and Maxwell heard her drop some featherlight kisses on his ear. 'No tricks.'

'Don't try that kind of nonsense,' Dunbar said. 'You know I don't like you demeaning yourself like that.'

'No,' she sighed. 'I'm not likely to forget.'

She came back with the string and tied Maxwell's ankles efficiently to the legs of the chair. Dunbar gave her the torch and, still holding Maxwell by the hair so he had to bend forward painfully, he checked the knots.

'Good work,' he said. 'Now his hands. Over the back.'

She went round behind the chairs and did as he told her.

'Now, that's better,' he said. 'We can all just sit properly now and talk things through like sensible adults.' He pulled Maxwell's chair round from behind the desk and motioned his ex-wife to sit at the far end of the row of chairs, as far from Maxwell's malign influence as possible.

'Do we have anything to talk about?' Maxwell asked. 'I mean, I have a lot to ask Fiona . . .'

'Moyra!' Dunbar corrected him.

'Moyra, then. But I think I would be asking questions to which I already know the answer. Such as "Why did you change your name?" has the obvious answer; to hide from you, you madman. The question "Why do you go to bed with any man with a pulse?" has pretty much the same reply; because my ex-husband is a *madman* who doesn't like touching me there. Am I getting close?'

Dunbar leapt to his feet. 'I'm going to kill him, Moyra. He is impugning you. He is demeaning our love. He . . .'

'Do you know,' Maxwell said reasonably. 'I don't think we hear the word "impugning" enough in general conversation these days, do you, Moyra? It sounds to me as if Alan here is trotting out some platitudes he has been using either out loud or to himself for some time now. What do you think?'

As Fiona Braymarr, she had not liked Peter Maxwell much. As Moyra Dunbar, she needed him as she had never needed anyone before. She was sure that this time, Alan was here to kill her, to end their misery. This folie a deux that she had begun when she was too young to know any better, before she knew he was as mad as any man could be and still walk around undetected. She knew how to handle Dunbar. She had to hope that Maxwell would be able to tell and not descend into heroics which would get them both killed.

'Alan looks after me, Mr Maxwell,' she said, in the little singsong voice. 'He always has, always will.'

'Yes,' he said, sitting back down. 'Ever since we met, I've looked after Moyra. She was still at school, you know, when we met. She went to university in the town, so we weren't parted. She could have gone anywhere she wanted. Oxford. Cambridge. They both offered her a place. But she wanted to stay with me. Didn't you, Moyra?'

'That's right.' She took over the tale. The way Alan told it, it sounded almost normal and that would never do. 'Alan looked after me *so* well that in the end, I worried that it would be too much for him and I ran away.'

'She's so kind like that,' Dunbar said. 'Always thinking of others. But I found her, didn't I, sweetheart?'

'That's right. And Alan got into a few scrapes on my behalf, didn't you, my love?'

'Someone called the police,' he said, lowering his voice. 'If I ever find out who did that . . . ?'

'And, in the end, they separated us,' she said, quickly. 'For our own good.'

'Yes.' In the backwash from the torchlight, Maxwell could see him nodding his head. 'The thing was, Mr Maxwell, I had lost someone before Moyra. And although I didn't love her like I love Moyra, I realise now, I did suffer, when she left me. So I didn't ever want that to happen again. And if I didn't watch over my Moyra . . .' his voice broke, 'she might leave me.'

'I won't leave you, Alan,' Moyra said, her voice so defeated that it was hard to recognise Fiona Braymarr any more.

'Denise left me,' he said, in flat tones.

'Denise?' Maxwell could feel the hairs stand up on the back of his neck. 'Denise MacBride?'

'MacBride? That was her name, when that animal had married her, yes. But that wasn't her name, not really. Her name was . . .'

'Denise MacBride?' Moyra was on her feet with Fiona in the ascendant. 'You knew Denise MacBride?'

'Of course. I thought you knew. I thought that was why you . . . allowed that animal to defile you. To teach her a lesson.'

She was speechless with rage and shock and Maxwell knew it was vital to shut her up for just a few moments, so he could get as many details from the man while the going was good. 'But she didn't know she had had a lesson taught to her, did she, Alan? You had to tell her.'

'That's *right*. I did. I went to see her and she recognised me. She . . . well, she said some things she shouldn't have said. She called me names, names she had called me when she left me. About . . .' he dropped his voice, 'about not *doing* it. She was the same as all the others. Always wanting to *do* things. It's not right. Not when you love someone, is it, Moyra?'

Maxwell felt rather than saw her shake her head.

'She took us into the garage. We got into an argument and she flew at me. It was all her fault. She flew at me.'

'So . . .'

'So, nothing. I threw her off the balcony. I'd never killed a woman before. It was almost too easy.' His voice had become dreamy, faraway. 'She fell, over and over and over, then CRASH!' Maxwell and the woman both jumped. 'Onto the bonnet of the animal's shiny new car and crash again as her head hit the glass.' He looked up at his ex-wife; Maxwell saw the glaucous gleam of his eyes in the faint light. 'It was an accident, Moyra,' he said. 'She flew at me.'

'An accident,' Maxwell said, drily. 'And yet, you went down and cleaned her nails afterwards.'

He chuckled. 'Yes. Into a paper bag so nothing was left behind. I can't be arrested. I have to look after Moyra.'

'And what about Louise Morton? What did she do to you?'

'Who's she?' His puzzlement seemed genuine. 'But now, Mr Maxwell, I am bored with talking. I think I'll just . . . have I slit anyone's throat, Moyra?'

She spoke through a sob. 'Yes,' she said. 'David's.'

'Oh. Yes. David. You really liked him, didn't you?'

Her voice was just a whisper now. 'Yes.'

'I think I'll strangle this one,' he said, as though discussing what wine to choose with dinner. 'Could you pass over the rest of that string?'

She got up and took up the ball of string from the table behind her and walked round the front of the chairs to where he stood, his hand out. As she passed, Maxwell saw a glint of metal in her hand, but before he could react, she had lunged, plunging the scissors deep into Alan Dunbar's chest. He went down like a poleaxed steer and Maxwell flung himself out of the way, overturning two chairs as he did so. He heard but thankfully didn't see Dunbar's final moments and finally, the light was switched on and Moyra, now completely Fiona Braymarr again, spoke from above his head.

'I hope you will be a friendly witness, Max, when this comes to trial.'

'Don't worry,' Maxwell said, still prone beneath his chairs. 'You've done me a real service tonight.'

'I saved your life!' she said, affronted.

'Yes. But I've also found my scarf.'

* * *

'So,' Maxwell said, as he came to the end of his story in the interview room at Leighford Nick, 'I thought you would come barging in with that banger thing they use on the telly. To rescue me, you know.'

'But *why* would you think that?' Jacquie had to ask. 'I didn't know where you were.'

'I told you I would be at school. Mrs B knew I was at the school.'

'Until five, Max. I rang her when I saw the number on your mobile — why do you leave it on the mantelpiece always, by the way? A fat lot of good it would do you there. It was almost seven by the time you called to report what had happened. I admit I was beginning to worry, but it's not as if you're too young to be out on your own. I just assumed . . . well, I don't know what I assumed, but I didn't think you were being held captive in your office by a mad person. It's not reasonable to expect me to guess that, now, is it?'

Maxwell was miffed. 'Well, you'll know next time, perhaps,' he said, sniffily.

'I'll make a note of it,' she said, and did.

'What's going to happen to Fiona? Moyra, I suppose I should say.'

'Well, she did kill a man, but for the best of reasons. She has been in hiding for years, with the help of the police. She was a witness against Dunbar when he seriously injured a man she was seeing and he was sent for treatment at a mental institution. He appeared to be cured . . .'

'What? He was clearly barking!'

'I'm not sure that's a diagnosis, Max,' Jacquie said gently. He had had a hard evening, one way and another and she wasn't going to be too strict as far as nomenclature went. 'As far as we have found out from records we can find, he has been stalking her ever since she left him and before that, he watched her every move. He had been jilted more or less at the altar — he's older than her, not that that's anything to go by, of course — by a woman who we have discovered was later Denise MacBride. He was always a bit unbalanced, with very strong views about the sanctity of a woman and other rather unusual ideas, to put it mildly. MacBride's mother-in-law was a little blunter even than you, Max. She had thought her daughter had had a lucky escape. She had stopped worrying about Dunbar and then she had seen him in the street. She told her mother, who thought she was imagining it. The poor woman is distraught, as you can imagine. But, let's get you home. Nole is with Mrs Troubridge and I had to make him promise not to use any judo holds on her.'

He got up and hobbled round the table. His ankles felt rather bent and he was sure he had a bald patch on the back of his head. 'Argh!' He had had a sudden thought. 'Have you explained to Mrs B?'

'I spoke to her while you were getting checked over for broken bones and your usual repercussions. Apparently, her great nephew or whatever he is, has been released. No charges. It was all a bit of a storm in a teacup, but he's writing a blog about it.'

Maxwell was a little bent out of shape and temporarily shorter of hair than usual, but of all the people who had gone through that day, he was probably not in the worst shape. Colin Hampshire, to take just one example, had already ended up in A&E having cut his thumb on a half-open tin of corned beef. Jacquie couldn't help sharing that as they walked out to the car, with Maxwell filling in the gaps with Tony Hancock impersonations.

'And then,' he said, 'Patrick Cargill says to Tony Hancock, "Well, we can't all be Rob Roys, can we?"' He looked up and waved. 'There's Henry. Who's that with him?'

'Hetty,' Jacquie said, puzzled. 'I wonder why they're here?'

'Statement, perhaps?'

'Hmm, perhaps.'

Hetty and Henry drew level with the Maxwells and Henry nodded grimly. 'Max. Jacquie.'

'Oh, hello, Mr Maxwell,' Hetty said, brightly. 'Henry's told me *so* much about you I feel I know you already. How are you, you poor man? I understand you've had a bit of an evening of it, one way and another.'

'I have,' he smiled. What a nice woman.

'Why are you here, Hetty?' Jacquie asked. She had to stop the ice water that was trickling down her spine. The question needed to be asked.

'Oh, I'm just here to give a statement,' she said, happily. 'Well, more of a confession, really. Henry found that silly little book in my bag. You know, the one with all the names. My Colin went every other Thursday morning, apparently. A hundred pounds a time. Two hundred pounds a month, Mr Maxwell, on a prostitute. It's not as though we have much money, you see. And he couldn't even remember my birthday.' She looked at Jacquie and her eyes were bright with unshed tears. 'He forgot my birthday, Jacquie. It was last Thursday. I expect that was why it slipped his mind.' She squeezed Henry's hand. 'So I went round there with some cake, on the Monday. And I stabbed her.'

Jacquie and Maxwell stood still and silent, swept with the waves of sadness coming from the brother and sister in front of them.

'It was my birthday, you see,' she said. 'My birthday, and I had to switch the hoover on, to drown it out. Then, I made a mistake. I switched it off too soon and I heard her. I heard her call out. "Colin!" she said. And some more I won't trouble you with.' She dipped her head, her cheeks hot with blushes and tears. Then, she wiped her hand down her face as though to wipe away the last forty years and turned to her baby brother with a smile. 'Come on, Henry. No lagging, now. Race you to the door, shall I?' and she leaned on his arm and, hand in hand, with wandering steps and slow, through the car park made their solitary way.

The Maxwells watched them go. 'How will Henry cope with this?' Maxwell asked.

'Like Henry,' Jacquie said. It was all she could hope for.

CHAPTER SEVENTEEN

That Monday morning, Leighford High School was buzzing. The news had been unspecific but everyone knew the score. 'Woman, thirty-seven, arrested in fatal school stabbing.' It mattered little to them that Fiona Braymarr had in fact been thirty-eight; it was enough that she was arrested and out of their hair. They had all missed the item about woman, sixty-two; what was she to them?

Legs Diamond opened the meeting at eight thirty prompt with a gleam in his eye. He was unusually upbeat and perky; no one need know it was due to early withdrawal symptoms from the Morning Pills. He had the Easter holidays coming up soon and he would have them licked by the Summer Term. Everyone wanted to take Maxwell and carry him shoulder high around the grounds, but he wasn't there. Maxwell, Diamond explained, was taking a few days' leave for some rest and recuperation. Well deserved. And Morning Thingee led the applause.

* * *

A watery sun lit the pedestrian precinct in Leighford that Monday morning. It was quiet, as it always was on an early Monday. No one really needed provisions; Sunday leftovers would suffice until Tuesday. Even the truants usually managed to attend school on the first morning of the week and the giros weren't due yet. The man who owned the doughnut shop was winding down his blind, humming to himself. 'Oh, cinnamon, where you gonna run to?' He smiled to himself. He sang that every morning and yet it still made him smile. A life composed of fried dough and sugar; what was not to like? His attention was caught by two figures, converging very slowly towards each other across the empty precinct. One was an old lady, on one of those sticks that always puzzled him, with the three little legs at the bottom. She was making heavy weather of it and yet he had seen her not three days ago, making good progress across the square with three shopping bags and a dog on a lead. He hoped she hadn't taken ill. He took a step towards her to ask.

The other figure was the slowest skateboarder he had ever seen. He seemed to be using the board as a scooter without a handle, pushing along just a few inches each time and wobbling dangerously when his foot was off the floor. He couldn't make out any detail, except that he was wearing the obligatory jeans at half-mast and a baseball cap on backwards. His youngest said that Mr Maxwell, up at the school, called them IQ reducers and he reckoned he was probably about right.

The two were still on a collision course. It was akin to watching the *Titanic* and the iceberg and about as inevitable. Incredulous, the doughnut fryer looked on as the old lady, at the last minute and with the agility of a ninja, sidestepped and stuck her stick into the wheels of the skateboard. The boarder fell heavily, but rolled at the last minute and got the old girl around the ankle in a grip of iron.

As the doughnut guy slid to a halt alongside them, he heard the IQ reduced skateboarder growl, 'Okay, grandma. You're nicked.'

He didn't know it, but he had just become one of the only two people on earth who had heard Peter Maxwell say 'okay' and live to tell the tale.

THE END

THE JOFFE BOOKS STORY

We began in 2014 when Jasper agreed to publish his mum's much-rejected romance novel and it became a bestseller.

Since then we've grown into the largest independent publisher in the UK. We're extremely proud to publish some of the very best writers in the world, including Joy Ellis, Faith Martin, Caro Ramsay, Helen Forrester, Simon Brett and Robert Goddard. Everyone at Joffe Books loves reading and we never forget that it all begins with the magic of an author telling a story.

We are proud to publish talented first-time authors, as well as established writers whose books we love introducing to a new generation of readers.

We won Trade Publisher of the Year at the Independent Publishing Awards in 2023 and Best Publisher Award in 2024 at the People's Book Prize. We have been shortlisted for Independent Publisher of the Year at the British Book Awards for the last five years, and were shortlisted for the Diversity and Inclusivity Award at the 2022 Independent Publishing Awards. In 2023 we were shortlisted for Publisher of the Year at the RNA Industry Awards, and in 2024 we were shortlisted at the CWA Daggers for the Best Crime and Mystery Publisher.

We built this company with your help, and we love to hear from you, so please email us about absolutely anything bookish at feedback@joffebooks.com.

If you want to receive free books every Friday and hear about all our new releases, join our mailing list here: www.joffebooks.com/freebooks.

And when you tell your friends about us, just remember: it's pronounced Joffe as in coffee or toffee!

Printed in Dunstable, United Kingdom

77044566R00150